DEVIL
IS
FINE

ALSO BY JOHN VERCHER

After the Lights Go Out

Three-Fifths

DEVIL IS FINE

John Vercher

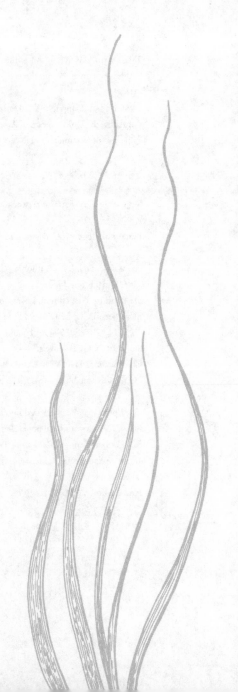

CELADON
BOOKS

NEW YORK

DEVIL IS FINE. Copyright © 2024 by John Vercher. All rights reserved. Printed in the United States of America. For information, address Celadon Books, a division of Macmillan Publishers, 120 Broadway, New York, NY 10271.

www.celadonbooks.com

Kelp art by DiViArt/Shutterstock

Library of Congress Cataloging-in-Publication Data

Names: Vercher, John, author.
Title: Devil is fine / John Vercher.
Description: First edition. | New York : Celadon Books, 2024.
Identifiers: LCCN 2023049327 | ISBN 9781250894489 (hardcover) |
    ISBN 9781250894496 (ebook)
Subjects: LCGFT: Novels.
Classification: LCC PS3622.E7336 D48 2024 | DDC 813/.6—dc23/eng/20231023
LC record available at https://lccn.loc.gov/2023049327

Our books may be purchased in bulk for promotional, educational, or business use. Please contact your local bookseller or the Macmillan Corporate and Premium Sales Department at 1-800-221-7945, extension 5442, or by email at MacmillanSpecialMarkets@macmillan.com.

First Edition: 2024

10 9 8 7 6 5 4 3 2 1

For Michelle's bathrobe—
I couldn't have done it without you.

To forget a wound and scratch it issues a special kind of pain—the pain of the wound and the pain of having to acknowledge it's no longer forgotten.

I never wanted to write about slavery or its legacy, but I cannot seem to escape the intergenerational reality.

—CHET'LA SEBREE, *FIELD STUDY*

ONE

The morning we buried you, a road flagger danced in the street.

The route from the church to the cemetery took our procession down that two-lane stretch of County Line Road, the one we'd both often complained seemed perpetually under one form of construction or another. The project that day required a bucket truck, crane extended to the top of a leaning transformer, the result of soft ground and high winds from the storm the night before. The truck, long and wide, made travel in the opposite lane impossible and it was our turn to wait.

My car was two behind your hearse, your mother in the car ahead of me, my mother and father in the vehicle behind. I found it odd the road crew had chosen to stop a hearse from making its way through. Maybe they didn't want to interrupt our caravan when they'd seen just how long it was, knowing they couldn't keep the other line of traffic waiting much longer without the inevitable horn honking. Or maybe they didn't care about funeral protocol. When I was a kid, my father had knocked my baseball cap off with a slap to the back of my head when I'd failed to remove my hat as a motorcade passed, its orange flags whipping. I didn't know how I was supposed to have known any better, but my stinging scalp told me I wouldn't forget any time soon.

I didn't see at first that the stop sign at the end of the flagger's pole was moving, but when I did, I couldn't look away. Leaning to the side, I could see around Vanessa's car—is it strange for me to call your mother Vanessa?—I saw the artist in his glory. His one-size-fits-all reflective orange vest draped over an oversized white T-shirt and dark baggy jeans, cuffs spilling over a pair of stained tan Timbs. Thin braids snaked from beneath his construction hat, playing curtain to the wireless earbuds pumping whatever song moved him to moving. He two-stepped back and forth, side to side, pivoting around the pole, lifting and dropping it to the asphalt, a cane in his one-man step show. I envied his obliviousness to the row of hazard lights blinking in front of him, finding fun in what I always thought had to be the most mundane of tasks. But there he was, enjoying himself, not giving a damn how boring I thought his job must have been.

I eyed the empty passenger seat. Your seat. You would have loved him, this dancing man, you would have said, "Homie is getting it *in*, huh?" Hearing your voice in my head, I stopped obsessing over your seat and stared ahead. Vanessa's—it is weird, isn't it?—*your mom's* compact car did little to shield the hearse from my view, but though I'd looked away from where you'd once sat, I couldn't take my eyes off where you now lay.

What if you awakened? What if all the prayers I'd thrown up asking for the miracle of your return were answered right then? You'd rouse to a satin-lined darkness. The vision was so vivid, eyes open or closed, I couldn't rid myself of it. I imagined your straining to find a swallow of air in that coffin. I hyperventilated. Pressure built in my chest. I whispered between gasps.

"Not now."

The first panic attack came after the accident. The first, at least, in several years. But now, what should have been a five-minute drive to the grocery store became an evening spent at urgent care. The first time, the nurse practitioner explained to me how a panic attack could feel just like a heart attack, like an elephant sitting on my chest. Was that a baby elephant or a full-grown one, I'd asked. What if it feels like, say, a pygmy hippopot-amus? Is that just indigestion? She wasn't amused. To be honest, neither was I. But why be austere about your mental health and the ramifications of not taking it seriously when you can dismiss it with a joke?

Cars in front of me, cars behind me, cars crawling by in the opposite lane, a steep drop-off where drainage ditches had been dug to channel runoff from heavy rains. I had nowhere to go when an attack came. And one *was* coming. Maybe it would be quick. Maybe the other line of cars was long, long enough to let the panic pass before it was our turn to go.

The dancer stopped. He pulled a walkie from his belt and spoke into it. Red became orange. "Stop" became "Slow." The hearse's brake lights extinguished, followed by your mother's. And I couldn't move. Arms straight, elbows locked, skin taut around my knuckles gripping the steer-ing wheel, I braced for a phantom impact, my back pinned to the seat. The patch of skin on the back of my thigh, just below the crease in my right buttock from where they'd taken the graft, itched. So did the pale scar tissue on my cheek. But I couldn't scratch either place. I couldn't sit up. I couldn't breathe. I was going to make everyone late.

I can't breathe.

I can't sit up.

We're going to be late.

Please don't. I know what you're doing, but it's not helping.

Then a tap on the windshield. The dancer. He made a rolling motion with his gloved hand. Afraid to let go of the steering wheel lest I fall down this hole and never recover, I pressed my lips together and shook my head. I waited for the annoyance, the muffled shout through the glass to get the hell on. Yet the exasperation I expected at my lack of cooperation never came. Instead, he spoke, loud enough I heard him through the window, but with an unanticipated calm, stretching and contracting his lips around each syllable.

"It's okay."

I slipped my hand off the steering wheel and accidentally locked the door, unused to the layout of the new car, before I pressed the window button long enough for a sliver of air, wet with a new mist forming, to pass through a small opening, then resumed my grip on the wheel. Ahead, the hearse along with your mother's car had pulled into the driveway of a real estate office located in a stone façade building. Your mom stood at the driver's side of the hearse, leaned over at the open window. My eyes darted to the side, catching the movement of the road worker stepping closer to my barely opened window.

"My guy. You good?"

I shook my head again.

"You need an ambulance?"

Another stiff shake.

"Panic attack, huh?" A curt nod. "Yeah. My sister gets them. She says it feels like she going to die when they hit her." He unclipped his walkie from his belt again. "Let your side through, Joe. We going to be a minute." Joe's voice squawked something in protest through the microphone, but the dancer wasn't having it. "Just let them through, man. Nobody on your side's going to complain." He lifted his chin at me. "Right? They the ones getting to move."

He turned his pole so the "Slow" side faced the other lane and cars crept along again. Though my head stayed facing the road in front of me, my eyes traveled from your mother at the side of the hearse to the passing drivers watching me, probably in wonder, though I convinced myself it was out of pity. Behind, my parents sat, seemingly unbothered, my mother's face a Parkinsonian mask, my father's equally expressionless, though not manifest of any malady save a surplus of staidness. None of these things I saw unlocked my hands or arms. Nor did my phone buzzing in the cradle clipped to the air vent. Your mother calling.

"Put your window all the way down, man," the dancer called out to me. "Get some air." I shook my head again. "Okay, it's cool. You tell me when you ready to move. I got you."

His kindness was a hand on my shoulder, squeezing, not urgent, but comforting. I released the wheel with my left hand, shook it out, let the window all the way down. He was right. The fresh air helped.

"Family?" he said over the passing cars. I cocked my head, and he tilted his toward the hearse. A looser nod this time.

"Son," I said.

He blew air out through puffed cheeks. "That's the wrong order, ain't it?" He squinted at the light gray sky, the sun working its way through the cloud cover. "Don't know why He does that."

My grip loosened and blood filled my fingers. Slack returned to my elbows. "Me, either. Can I . . . I just need another minute."

He waved me off. "Take your time, man. I don't hear any horns."

Though I'd sworn I'd heard impatient honks a moment before, he was right. Nothing but the sound of tires hissing on the wet asphalt. My phone buzzed again. I sat forward, freeing my back from the seat, and took the phone from its cradle.

"I'm coming." A deep breath. Hers and mine. "I'm sorry."

"Okay. It's okay."

I disconnected and replaced the phone, then released the hand brake. Before I took my foot off the brake, I dipped my head in thanks to the dancer. He returned the nod and spoke into his walkie. Before he spun his pole and signaled for us to move on, he took off his construction hat and held it at his side. We exchanged another nod and I drove to catch up to you.

A field of black flowers bloomed, umbrellas unfolding against the mist turned light rain pelting their petals. The absence of the church's walls and roof had done nothing to diminish the overwhelming gathering of classmates, family, and friends who'd come to see you one last time, huddled together, seated in plastic folding chairs sinking further into the wet ground a centimeter at a time.

I'll be frank, Mal, I was shocked. A kid who hadn't been an athlete, wasn't prom king, no chorus, no Key Club, who didn't belong to any specific clique, instead seemed to belong to them all. The jocks, the nerds, the academics, the artists, the geeks, the goths—they'd streamed in through the doors of the church until some had no choice but to stand behind the final row of pews. I'd seen less attendance at Christmas mass and wondered if they'd ever stop coming. I'd thought such throngs only feasible in films. Never had I suspected you'd known—touched—so many. There'd been so much about you I hadn't realized.

The ground squelched and gripped at my shoes, threatened to pull them off my feet as I walked to the front row of seats and took the empty one next to your mother. The rain, though light, came at an angle, driven by occasional gusts, remnants of an earlier squall. Beads of precipitation clung to her lace veil. She remained focused on your remains, her eyes flitting to me a single time in acknowledgment of my presence. I adjusted my umbrella to sit atop hers, a phalanx protecting us both. Her free hand rested on her knee. I slid mine underneath, palm up, and squeezed. She did not return the gesture. I watched our hands not hold each other for a moment, then watched her, hoping she was watching me, too. She wasn't. She minded your casket, rain rivulets cascading off the gunmetal-gray lid as tears down unfeeling cheeks.

Tears I'd yet to shed.

I wanted to cry for you. I knew I should. I thought certain those tears would come as the priest read the eulogy. He was as warm as he could be, but because he'd not known you—no matter how hard I'd tried to remedy that, and I know this isn't the time or place—there was no heart hoisting his words. No familiarity. Regret for a life lost, of course, but the loss was not personal. He knew me. He knew your mother, to some extent. He'd not known you other than to know you were our son. If no tears came then, they would come when you were lowered into the ground. Then, certainly, my body would find the faculties to mourn you.

You don't believe it, either?

The machine's mechanisms, once activated, caused the coffin a small but sharp lurch upward. Your mother let out a hushed gasp and pulled her hand away from mine, brought it to her chest, her fingers fluttering. Her tears flowed unfettered in that moment as the glistening curve of the casket disappeared below our line of sight. I kneaded her shoulder, but the act seemed to induce tension, not make it recede. There was no comfort to be found in my touch, so I took it away. How familiar that sensation.

Your burial site sat on the cemetery's hilltop, the incline too steep, the ground too wet for my mother's wheelchair to make the climb. Despite my entreaties to help them sit by our sides, my father refused. He stood next to my mother at the hill bottom, a large umbrella shielding them from the increasing rain. He returned my solitary wave with a near-imperceptible nod.

I never told you about the one and only time I'd seen my father cry, and how it scared me more than anything I can remember, then and since. He was as old as I am now, and I still have no idea why he was crying. But everything I'd known—everything I'd believed—about him, about his stoicism and strength, crumbled as easily as he did in my mother's arms as she lowered him to the floor. His body shook with big gulping sobs, childlike in their drama, but if their design was manipulative, I couldn't see it. My mother soothed him as she would have me in such a crisis, stroking the back of his head, whispering everything would be okay. I wanted to ask what was wrong, what could bring him to such a state, but fear choked the words in my throat and fixed my feet to the foyer floor. My mother opened her eyes and when she saw me, gestured for me to go to my room, freeing me from my paralysis. I was grateful. I fast-walked down the hallway, shut my door behind me, and sat on my bed, bewildered. His sobs carried down the hallway and my eyes stung. I wanted to join him in his misery, despite my ignorance of its origin. But seeing what crying did to him kept my tears at bay—that day, and the many days that followed.

The wheels of the casket hoist clicked their teeth together a final time and you were laid to rest. Returned to the dust from whence you came. Lowered so you could ascend.

Your mother wept. We stood.

I glanced over my shoulder, waiting for one hand to be placed on it while another was thrust forward in offering sincere and heartfelt condolences. But neither happened. All rose from their chairs and, hunched against a summer wind growing ever stronger, left us to our mourning, filing down the hill to where they'd parked. Some paused and offered condolences to your grandparents, then waited in their cars until we led them in ours to the repast at the apartment your mom and I had once shared. No longer a home since I'd left. Since she'd asked me to leave. No longer a home with you gone.

We stood short of the edge of the grave, not close enough to see down into it, as if not seeing made it not so. Her quiet tears fell in tandem with the rain.

"This was good," I said. "He would have been happy."

She scoffed and shook her head. "What kind of thing is that to say? Happy?"

"To see how many people he'd touched. I had no idea how many he knew."

She fixed her regard on the horizon. "You think he didn't know that when he was alive?"

"That's not what I meant."

"What *do* you mean? Do you even know?"

"I don't want to fight, Van."

"Then don't say such stupid things. Don't pretend anything you say like that matters to anyone but you."

"I only mean that if he could see—"

Now she turned to face me. "But he can't, can he? He's not sitting on some cloud, listening to all the nice things people have to say about him. I know that's what you think. What you believe."

"You used to, too."

She rolled her eyes, though her face didn't betray exasperation. She was exhausted. I was exhausting her.

"Yeah, well, not anymore." She cleared tears from her lids with her thumb. "He wouldn't have wanted any of this. But you insisted."

"Now, Van? We're going to do this now?"

"There's never a good time for you, is there?"

"Don't you think if I could take this back, I would? When are you going to stop acting like I did this on purpose? Why do I have to be the bad guy?"

"Because you are!"

No melodramatic hand to her mouth. No checking over her shoulders to see if anyone had heard her shout. She faced me, eyes electric with rage, forcing me to feel all her fury. You know the face. I'd seen her give it to you one time you'd mouthed off and wondered how you'd ever let yourself do so again. I was frightened for you then, just as I was afraid for myself now. Under her glare, I was a sculpture of ash. Insubstantial. Her next breath would send me scattering. Still, she stared. Her eyelids twitched, unblinking. Fearing I might collapse to dust, I glanced down. At this, she seemed satisfied and turned back to the rows of tombstones across the field. Her breath came in short bursts until she calmed herself with a long, deep one.

"All that time," she said, "you kept insisting he see God as his father. When the only father he wanted was you."

Is that what you wanted, Mal?

I opened my mouth but had nothing to say. "People are waiting," she said. "We should go." She walked past me and down the hill.

Stunned, I hadn't noticed I'd lowered my umbrella. Raindrops tapped me from my daze. I watched your mother walk away. Despite all she carried, despite all I'd given her to bear, she held her head high. Shoulders pulled back. At the bottom, she was met by aunties, uncles, and cousins, her parents long since passed. As she embraced them one by one, I saw them see past her to me, and though their faces maintained a loyal sternness I'd come to know all too well, I witnessed there a softness, too, one that would offer hugs if I came to collect them. I nodded my thanks. To a one, they nodded back.

I turned back to where you rested, took another step closer to your grave, and stared down.

I can't breathe.

I can't sit up.

We're going to be late.

Chest tightened. Fingers tingled. I retreated from the brink.

Not again, not so soon.

The scar on my cheek pulsed. Focusing on the sensation was a distraction that kept the attack at bay. One foot slowly in front of the other, the tension in my lungs receding, I followed your mother's path to our cars. My father waited for me, the umbrella only just shielding him and Mom, rivers of rain running down the sides, spattering her wheelchair armrests. When I reached them, he squeezed my arm, gave it a pat, then handed me his umbrella. I covered him and Mom as he wheeled her back to their car. We parted without a word. I returned to my car, drove to meet your mother, and followed her out of the cemetery, watching the long line of mourners fall in line behind us.

Back on the main road, I saw another hearse approaching, doubtless on its way to where we'd just left with our procession, presidential in its enormity. Behind him, hazards flashing, flags flailing, trailed two cars. Only two. I could not help but notice the negative space behind them.

As we drove past them, I thought of my father, fetal on the floor, cradled in my mother's arms.

And I cried harder than he had.

TWO

Days later, the letter arrived.

I'd almost missed it, sandwiched between circulars and catalogs, the envelope unremarkable in every way, almost tossed with the rest of the junk if I'd not seen the esquire designation before snapping my wrist toward the recycling bin. At my desk, I tore through the top of the envelope and read. The contents brought only confusion, no matter how many times I read it.

The matter of an inheritance from my mother's father, your great-grandfather, and could I call the office as soon as possible, make an appointment, as there were matters to discuss as your named next of kin.

The language was clear, the facts within succinctly stated. And yet it made no sense. I couldn't get your great-grandfather to give me the time of day, much less an inheritance. Was this his idea of a joke? Had he played the long game, planned a pernicious prank from the great beyond? Were it so, much as I loathed the man, the thought fostered a modicum of respect for the commitment. That notwithstanding, how many times I read the letter I'd lost track, scanning for some proof of error, an overlooked "no" or "not," anything to invalidate the information contained within. But my search provided no such negatives. Having determined it was too late in the day to act on the attorney's polite requests, I slid the letter into the outside pocket of my messenger bag and packed for my return to classes the next morning. I had decided I'd end my bereavement leave from the university two days early and phoned David, my department head, telling him I'd be coming back tomorrow.

I know that seems soon. You might feel you deserved more grieving than I'd given myself time for, and you'd be right. But as frequently as I'd cast myself the artist unburdened by the need for social interaction, your absence proved my fancies fraudulent. My apartment was empty. No clichés of loud or oppressive silence. The quiet was vacuous, a singularity, each room a compartment of sensory deprivation. The want of your voice—with or without the venom that had laced it as of late—created a void into which I was being pulled, stretched like so much taffy.

That lack is how I came to talk to you in this way. Yes, of course, I am in essence talking to myself. Perhaps that you can't answer me—or that your imagined answers are mine—is the only reason I'm comfortable admitting something so strange in the first place. There is odd comfort in this confessional. An unburdening. If you were here, I'm certain you'd tell me talking to myself was no different from talking to God. There was a time I'd have been sure of my response to that rebuke. I've now no certainty as to how I'd react.

Sleep never came easy for me, but even less so that night. I fidgeted in bed, anticipating my colleagues' crinkled chins and dour downturned mouths, their funeral faces offering sympathies, their Anything I Can Dos, as if there were anything they could do, their outstretched hands and arms, their teary eyes and I Can't Imagines. Feet slid back and forth until friction flamed the skin of my heels. Arms and legs made snow angels on the less-than-fitted sheet, searching for regions of cool. Pillow an omelet folded on itself, either not thick enough or too much so, comfort ever elusive. With each change of position, each turn of my head, I caught a flash of white in my periphery, the envelope holding the letter peeking from my bag's pocket, antagonizing me with its enigma, the One Ring calling to Frodo, and with that thought I remembered your Golem imitations, shirt off, shorts hiked up, an impossible curve in your spine as you leapt about the living room on all fours, gasping for your Precious. The recollection of your uncanny impression, the sound you made like a bubble was stuck in your throat, now placed one in mine. I threw back the covers, crossed the room, and pushed the envelope further into the bag until it was hidden from view, half expecting to see a flash of feline pupil, fire wreathed, or worse, to be stuck with that vision of you.

Only when the letter was out of view did I sleep.

I didn't call the attorney the next morning. *Too much to do, so much to prepare*, the mantra of my justification. Make sure the contents of my shoulder bag were just so. Tighten up the beard, iron the shirt, sharpen the crease in the slacks. Subtract all signs of sadness.

Then there was rehearsal, practice my Thank You, I'm Goods, As Well as Can Be Expecteds, I Will, Yes, I *Will* Be Sure to Call If I Need Anythings.

You see, Mal, there was simply no time to call the attorney.

Obviously.

Rationalization the mother of procrastination.

After class ended, I sat in my office, hypnotized by my monitor's screen saver, footsteps in the hallway breaking my trance, making me a prairie dog peering over the top of my ergonomically elevated laptop at the heel click of company coming, sinking into my chair as to whomever the shoes belonged breezed by my doorway. Conversations trailed off into echoes, then silence, students and staff lamenting or celebrating the minutiae of their lives, blissful in their unawareness or willful ignorance of the notion that those complaints were trifles. Those trivialities times to be treasured. I envied them. I hated them. I wanted them to sit with me. I wanted them to go away.

Office hours dragged on, due in no small part to the dearth of visitors, student or otherwise. It seemed no one on the faculty had put in the same rehearsal time I had for how they should approach me upon my return. Throughout the day, they trafficked in polite avoidances. Eye contact, sure, but brief, mouths tight lest something untoward and unintentionally thoughtless slip out, for who really knows what to say in these instances. I know I never did. Maybe ending my leave early hadn't given them enough time for proper preparation, but really, that was no excuse. Just lazy.

While I waited out the last fifteen minutes of my office obligations, I spun my chair toward the window behind me with a view onto the freshly mowed quad. I never told you that the years I'd put in at the college had earned you a tuition remission. If you'd wanted it. I hadn't told you because I'd convinced myself you would have taken the foot off the accelerator with your studies and coasted. Or would you have, I wondered. Would you ever have accepted something like that from me. Would you have sat with me on the manicured lawn below, shared lunch, talked to me about your classes, your day, your current crush. Would you have taken my class.

Would I have wanted you to.

Red flickered across the quad, the inconsistent illumination of the neon sign above the door to the Teachers' Lounge, the faculty-frequented watering hole situated aside the university employees' parking lot. For years, the *O* and *E* in "Lounge" had been burned out, apropos this loss of letters, as the owners had defied the smoking bans for as long as they'd been able, thus the ceilings, the walls, even the barstools held on to the smoke smell like living tissue. And in our infinite cleverness, the Teachers' *Lung* was born. How many nights we'd spent there, celebrating, or commiserating. Seems a lifetime ago. In some sense, it was.

Just shy of eighteen years.

Your mother promised me she'd let me tell you this story when I felt the time was right, as if there were ever a right time to admit to . . . well, to the thing I would admit to. She said it wasn't her tale to tell, but that if I didn't, she would, and I couldn't have that. I'm thinking now might be that time, when telling you is tantamount to saying the thing out loud. So—here goes.

"Knock, knock."

How about that? Another time then.

"Got a minute?" David leaned on the doorjamb. Arms crossed, his face held a restrained expression of sympathy, lips tucked, eyebrows raised, the nonverbal equivalent of I Don't Know What to Say mixed with I'm Here for You. I was impressed. At least *he'd* been practicing. "How was the first class back?"

"Incredible. Gave them an exercise to push their creative boundaries and experiment with form and function. Stunning work by all involved."

"You gave them a generic prompt and scrolled social media the entire hour while they wrote?"

"Give the man a prize." I closed my laptop and waved him in. He pulled at the waistline of his sagging slacks, all his pants' bands stretched beyond the limits of elasticity by a gut growing at a rate alarming to everyone but David. I gestured to the chair in front of my desk, and he lowered himself into it, hands on thighs, griping as he did.

"They say the first sign you're getting old is you make noises when you sit," he said.

"And how long have you been making those noises?"

"Too long. But my aunt Chrysanthemum used to say—"

"Chrysanthemum?"

"What?"

"You people say we have strange names."

"You people?" I smirked at David's faux horror. "It is strange, but we called her Gigi for short."

"So why didn't you just say that?"

He cocked his head. "I don't actually know. Anyway, she said growing old ain't for sissies. But then she also said it's better than the alterna—"

Finding opportunities to increase David's discomfort was an activity in which I'd always taken great pleasure, though those moments most often manifested when he'd said the word "Black" that while in a manner devoid of malice, I'd tell him he was guilty of yet another racist screed. While he knew these jabs to be jovial in nature, he squirmed nonetheless, checked the room, ensuring no one actually thought *that* of him. Though his tired and poorly planned aphorism about aging was a different type of gaffe, I couldn't, in good conscience, let a chance pass to avoid revealing anything about my true emotional state. I narrowed my eyelids, sending how-dare-you daggers across the space between us. In turn, his eyes went wide, smile disappeared, hands up in defense, ready to rationalize and retract, flop sweat forming at the fringes of his retreating hairline. Unable to contain the quiver in my chin, I broke and grinned.

"Gotcha."

His breath left him in a whoosh as he put his head between his knees, a passenger prepared for an emergency landing. I reached across the desk and patted his back. He flinched and shirked my reassurance with a playful pout. "Too mean."

"Maybe."

"I take it you've had enough time off, then?"

"Enough time . . ." I sat back. "I've been thinking—who measures grief?"

"I'm sorry?"

"I read somewhere that grief experts recommend at least twenty days of leave after the loss of a close family member. How do they figure that out?"

"*You* decided to come back early. I had your classes covered."

"I'm serious, though. Who decides the appropriate amount of time you need to cope? This person or persons have to exist, right? Do they have an actuarial table calibrated for sorrow? Do they factor in standard deviations from the mean? What's the n value? Do they use regression analysis? How do they know that in three or five or ten or twenty days your bereavement should end? That your emotions will stabilize, thus rendered able to return to the full duties of your job? What if that person never experienced their own grief? Do they speak the language of loss? How long is too long to mourn? How short is too short?"

David stared, unblinking, though past me, not at me. I snapped my fingers in his face. He shook his head as if I'd splashed him with water. "I'm sorry, were you saying something?" Mouth open, it was my turn for mock shock. He returned the smirk I'd given him moments ago.

"Good one."

"'The language of loss.' You should write that down."

"Noted. So . . . what is it?"

"What is what?"

"Why are you here, David?"

"What do you mean?"

"I've never known a conversation beginning with 'got a minute' to lead anywhere good. Or take anywhere close to a minute."

He sat forward, leaning his forearms on his legs, a posture affirming my assertion.

"Jokes aside, how are you doing? Good? You seem good. Are you good? I'm saying good too much."

"You are. But I'm all right. All 'good.'"

"Very funny." He eyed the area rug under his feet, finger-combed his thinning grays, then looked back to me. "You don't have to be. All good, I mean. You don't have to be here right now, either. I meant it—you can still take more days, despite your wholly unsubtle knock on our bereavement allotment." He winked, but made a smooth slide into sincerity. "I know you know that, but I just want to say it again."

"Your minute's almost up."

He chuckled. "Yeah, you're all good. *Any*who . . ." He slapped a beat on his knees and glanced around the room, anywhere but at me. "Any bites on the manuscript?"

"There's the rub."

"What rub? No rub. Just a question."

"A loaded one. If you hadn't led with 'got a minute,' I maybe would have believed you. Maybe."

"Come on, it's not like that."

"No? What's it like then? You know you'd have been the first person I told if there was news."

"You're right. I know, you're right. It's just . . ."

"See? There is a rub."

He ran his palm back and forth across his forehead. "So, here's the deal—and this is not coming from me—but if you don't have something soon, a contract, an excerpt somewhere big . . . the committee meeting is going to be here before you know it. You know it's publish or perish here. You knew that coming in."

"Uh-huh. 'Publish or perish.'" I stood and tripped on my messenger bag as I retrieved the paperback of my first novel from my bookshelf and tossed it in his lap. He stuck out his jaw and averted his eyes. "You see that silver foil stamp, Dave? Same award nomination as Richardson's book. How many books did he publish before he got tenure?"

"You don't want to go there, man."

"Anyone show up at his door and give him this talk? Of course I mean *before* he got the tenure you're telling me I'm in danger of losing."

"You know his book was a monster."

"And mine wasn't?"

"A monster? No. In a perfect world, critics' love equals sales, but let's be honest—did that happen?"

I tapped the silver foil badge on the cover. "Nominated for the same national award, David."

"He was also a part-timer for years, several more than you."

"That's crap, Dave. I did my time, too. How long did I adjunct here? How many times did I apply for full-time and get rejected? And I kept coming back like a kicked puppy."

"I know that. You know I know that, but Richardson was also well known by the committee."

I scoffed. "'Well known.' It's funny, man, I hear you giving all the reasons my tenure is in danger but the real one."

"Don't do that."

"I'm just saying, man, all things being equal, all things don't seem too equal." He shifted in his seat. I tried a different tack. "Dave. Come on. This is you and me. What's really going on?"

He pulled free a bit of cuticle he'd been picking at and winced, stuck his thumb in his mouth and sucked the blood bubble that bloomed there. "Look, if no one is biting on this one, maybe you should think about spreading your wings a bit. Maybe stay away from the . . . you know, more incendiary fare."

"'Incendiary'? Is that a code word? What are you talking about? You just said the first book did great, and it did."

Thumb injury managed, he took an interest in the shine of his shoes. "Right, sure, but I mean . . . time was on your side. So to speak. You know what I mean, right?" I crossed my arms over my stomach. "Come on, man. Don't make me say it." I raised my eyebrows. "It's just . . . people have moved on from the racial narratives. And not just with fiction. You know I loved your first one. The mixed-race protagonist struggling with his identity. It was all so topical yet timeless. But . . . well, it's not 2020 out there anymore, you know?"

"I'm sorry, did you say 'moved on'? I mean, did you actually just use those words?"

"Hey, I didn't say *I* moved on. *They* have. You know." He waved his hands in the air at some unseen entities. "*They.* They're kind of . . . over it."

I blinked rapid-fire and shook off the shock of still-worse words falling unfettered from my friend—check that—colleague's mouth. "They're . . . over it."

"What, this is breaking news to you? Do you read the paper these days?"

"No one reads the papers these days, David."

He reached across the desk and slapped my arm. "I know, I was being ironic." He grinned. I didn't. He stopped grinning. "Hey, you *know* me. I'm not saying it's right. It's not. It's fucked. You know I know that. But it's the reality, man. I mean, Christ, they're banning books from schools now."

"Which is exactly why I need to keep writing my story, David. Our stories. You want me to whitewash my work, not talk about the issues in my community because Black folks are no longer the movement du jour? Because some narrow-minded fools want to keep us off the shelves? No, sir. I'm not the one. *You* know *me*. At least I thought you knew that, because I can't believe what I'm hearing. From you of all people."

"Hang on, don't do that. Don't paint me out to the bad guy, all right? I'm here as a favor."

"This doesn't feel like a favor, David."

"Believe me, it is. Look, real talk?"

And now it's time for another spin of Dave's favorite album, Time-Life Records' *Hey Cringe*, Volume One. Whenever Dave wanted connection with me on a more serious level, he dialed up his discography of what he perceived as Black culture's greatest hits.

Swoon to the sultry sounds of track one, "Real Talk."

Slow-jam with the downbeat number "You Feel Me."

Close out your evening with a soaring rendition of "My Man."

"Agree with me, disagree with me, these are the facts. At least as far as the tenure committee is concerned. And that's what matters right now. You feel me?"

Track two.

"Do I feel you? Let's see. If I'm picking up what you're putting down— and please, correct me if I'm wrong here—you're saying that despite the university posting my face all over the website as their latest and greatest diversity faculty hire, if I continue to write about Black issues—sorry, you said mixed-race, right?—that are apparently no longer in vogue, then I'll be shown the door like every other director of diversity, equity, and inclusion as of late. Is that it? Am I feeling you, Dave?"

For a second there, Malcolm, I swore I heard your voice instead of mine.

David gave a sharp exhale, stood, and tossed the book back on my desk. "This would normally be where I'd say you're out of line, that you know I'm as aware of this place's shitty politics as you are, and how I'd fight like a dog to keep you from losing tenure. How I maybe already did but that it didn't matter and that I still had to come down here to have this incredibly uncomfortable conversation with my friend. Normally, that's what I'd do. But these aren't normal times, so I'm not going to say that to you. I know that despite the jokes earlier, you're having a rough go of things and that those jokes are how you deal with things, along with getting just the slightest bit vicious, so I'm going to pretend you didn't imply that I align with those closed-minded idiots, and I'm going to go home before this situation becomes even less normal. Okay?"

He approached the office door. As angry as I was, I sensed no false sincerity in what he'd just said, and I'd not realized how much I'd needed some of that genuine-article compassion until just then.

"Not okay." He stopped and faced me, eyebrows raised. "That explanation was exceedingly expositional. I expect better from tenured faculty such as yourself."

The tension around his eyes relaxed. "Maybe I should sign up for your class then."

"Too popular. Wait-listed. You should maybe remind the committee of *that* fact."

"Who says I haven't?" He resumed his route to the door. "Go home. Get out of the apartment this weekend. Take the rest of your leave. If you need more time, talk to me. We'll work it out. Go find some inspiration."

"Yeah. Maybe I can borrow your jacket with the elbow patches. That's sure to make me feel like writing."

"Jealousy is ugly. Don't be ugly." He sighed. "Tell me you'll at least think about this."

"'You'll at least think about this.'" He frowned. "I'll think about thinking about it."

"All I can ask." He walked back to my desk, arm extended, his pudgy porcelain paw dangling for dap. I gave his fist the once-over. "Come on. Give me some."

No, my brother. You got to get your own.

I obliged with a smirk. And with a finger gun and a wink, he glided out of the room to the dulcet tones of track three, "My man."

Time was, a conversation like that would have sent me spiraling down an anxiety abyss, but with my antidepressant prescription pumped up post-funeral to proportions fit for a pachyderm, I was quicker to another emotion. I flipped open my laptop, opened a blank document, and switched the font.

publish or perish

publish or perish

publics or paris

pubis or pear shaped

plkuxiubtkonzfjnsrogjnldskgm;sLDmfgsPKRGMFUCKYOUDAVE

My hand hovered over the print icon. Send the job to the community printer. See who picks it up. He'd know it was me but could never confirm. But that back-and-forth between us pushed the limits of my tolerance for conflict. I closed the document and slapped the laptop shut. He was right about one thing—I knew the deal when I took the job, but as far as I was concerned, tenure track meant tenured. I'd fought the battle, won the war. Just had to bide my time. And when it happened, I knew, just knew, the wall damming my creativity after publishing the first book would crack then break, releasing the torrent of words sloshing and frothing against the barrier, just high enough to keep them from spilling onto the page. No more writing in the margins of the copywriting gigs and other adjunct positions I'd cobbled together, or in between my weekly visitations with you, Malcolm. Writing would become the day job. Teaching writing would only make my writing stronger. Tenure would remove the pressure of making rent and buying groceries, until I would become so unfettered as to become prolific. But the dam was made of committee work and four-four loads, a foundation I found impossible to break. So, I went back to what got me here in the first place—another novel interrogating a mixed-race man's Black identity, albeit in a different way. And despite my initial resistance to revisiting that well, the creative waters surged, breached the wall, and I swam with the current. Yet those familiar waters had now put me in danger of drowning.

Despite my anger with him, saying he was wrong about all he'd said would have been lying to both of us. I'd seen the slow closing of the door to Black creatives. The corporate backslides on promises for more inclusion. And still somehow—and yes, I'm sure you know how, Malcolm, but I'm making a point—I thought that this reality wouldn't come for me. That I was safe. Immune. I was award-nominated after all. And yes, you're right, I shouldn't have let him off so easy. Yes, I'd gotten angrier with you for less. But was it fair to hold him accountable for the truth I'd asked him for? Besides, I knew (believed) (hoped) David likely *had* tried to help me with the committee, though doubts lingered as to whether his effort matched his narrative. He was younger than the senior faculty, relatively, and far more progressive, though that's far from the compliment he might have perceived it to be. Still, he was a sight better than that proverbial network of truly old boys that ran the roost. At the first university holiday party, your mother and I, tipsy, had joked—a little too loudly as I'd learned in a text from David the next day—that one of their past committees had to be the one where the one-drop rule had been created. Because my hair was—say it with me, brothers and sisters,

CALL: Closer to straight than curly, but
RESPONSE: Curly enough
CALL: My nose not that wide, but
RESPONSE: wide enough
CALL: My skin light, but
RESPONSE: not light enough.

These self-evident truths meant I had no room for error, that they had no time for a diversity hire professor who didn't publish, especially after that diversity hire was hired due to the acclaim of his diversity book, but then couldn't publish because he wrote another diversity book that the zeitgeist had now determined was too diverse. By my count, that's two strikes. And shame on me. Had I no idea how that might reflect upon them? I mean, my God, man, think of the optics. They couldn't be out of step with the times. There was enrollment to consider.

Office hours over, I picked up my bag from where I'd kicked it, and the envelope fluttered to the floor. I'd tucked it so far down into the pocket. How had it worked its way out? Had I kicked it that hard? Or had it made its way out through other means?

Or was it you?

I laughed, perhaps a bit too loudly. That's just crazy talk.

I sat back down, collected the letter from the floor, and scanned it again, still in disbelief at its contents. Then I picked up the phone.

After I made the appointment with the attorney, I sat for a moment with the letter in my hand. A connection to you. Your name on a piece of paper. A keepsake for a shoebox tucked away on a closet shelf full of things meant to tell the story of you, something to retrieve in low moments to remember you fondly, as if fond memories were all there were. These keepsakes for the dead never made sense to me. I don't want a placeholder for your absence. I don't want to remember the happy times because they make me sad. I don't want to remember the sad times because they were my fault. I want my memories of you to decompose and fall away.

I tore the letter to pieces and threw those pieces in the trash. And then I went home.

THREE

He is seven.

And I am spellbound.

He sits on the floor, hips and legs forming a *W*, though his mother has told him often how bad this position is for his knees. I let him be, though, as I'm envious of the flexibility—I couldn't touch my toes at his age—and not because I know it will antagonize Vanessa. Never that.

Action figures from comic books and cartoons of every genre surround him in what appears to be a circle prepared for some kind of ritual—and in some ways it is. He moves from one part of the loop to another, engaging his characters in epic battles whose choreography rivals some action films I've seen. Dramatic dialogue and situations between his dramatis personae ensue, so enthralling that I'm brought close to shouting at them not to be so stupid, don't go in there, don't listen to him, he's got a sword behind his back, a gun tucked in his boot. The production then shifts gears into slapstick as the comic relief makes his appearance.

On this carpeted stage on the floor in front of me, there is happiness. There are tears. Somehow, I find the will to fight the urge to cry out, bite my lip to keep from snickering, and watch while appearing not to watch.

I fail.

"What?"

"*What* what? What do you mean?"

"What are you looking at?"

"Me? Nothing." I hold up a book. "Reading. For work."

"You haven't turned the page yet."

"Yes, I have."

"No, you haven't."

"Play with your toys."

"Stop watching me."

"I wasn't. *You* stop watching *me*."

"Whatever."

His face, full of playfulness and disdain, lingers on me a moment more, assured I've returned to my reading but flattered I've been watching his drama-meets-comedy-of-errors unfold, and he can't tell me otherwise, much as he'd like to. I read the same sentence I've read for the last fifteen minutes, but I can't help myself, either, and peer over the top of my pages once more.

"You're doing it again," he says.

Defeated, I set the book down. "Well, how do you expect me not to watch? You've got heroes from DC fighting villains that are clearly from Marvel. This guy's from Image. And this one over here? What is that? Some kind of cut-rate Transformer? Is that . . . is that a Go-Bot? Did your mother buy that for you?"

"What's wrong with Go-Bots? They're as good as Transformers."

"What's wrong with . . . ? As good as . . . ?" I point to the apartment door. "Out. Out of my house. I'll not have such blasphemy."

He laughs. God, that laugh.

"What's blasphemy?"

"Never mind. Here's the deal—you need a director because I can't do it, I can't take watching this travesty anymore." I rise from my desk, stand beside him, and gently nudge him with my shoe. "Move aside, boy. Let me show you how this is done."

A giggle forms in some joy-filled center in his stomach and ripples upward and out through his bright smile as I make a total fool of myself, acting out my own scenes, playing off the ones he's created, complete with terrible accents, worse sound effects, and melodrama.

"Dad, you are crazy."

He shows me how I'm doing everything wrong. He blocks scenes and improvises dialogue. His dialects are far better than mine. He takes great pleasure in his correcting me.

And so do I.

We play like this for the better part of an hour, though it seems impossible that that much time has passed when his mother arrives. She knocks as she pushes open the door to the apartment and surveys the explosion of action figures around us, hands on her hips, struggling not to beam at us but losing the battle.

"Finally stopped pretending, huh?"

"Pretending what?" I ask.

"That you don't play with toys."

"Excuse me, these are collectibles. And we are not playing." I wink at him. He approximates a wink back, though it is a motor skill he's not mastered, resulting in some kind of tic that makes him all the more adorable for the effort. "We, madame, are creating."

Vanessa puts a hand over her chest in mock embarrassment. "Oh, my, please excuse me. I did not mean to cast aspersions on the masters while they work."

"What are aspersions?" he asks.

"A big word your mother likes to use to seem fancy." She slaps my shoulder. He is confused by our banter, and wears a grin communicating more anticipation than joy. He knows as well as I that mirth can move to malice in a breath, almost always exhaled by me, bearing something stupid. Because it feels real in the moment, we don't take the moment for granted. Groaning from the mouth and joints, I stand, straighten my slacks, and gesture toward our theater in the round. "Clean it up, little man. Time to go."

He grumbles but does as he's told, sweeping his figures into Rubber-maid containers and snapping them shut. Stacked and tucked under one arm, he hugs me with the other, pressing his cheek against my stomach. How much taller he seems each time he's here, though less than the span of a week separates his visits. Vanessa's glance shares the same sense of dis-belief at how quickly he grows. He releases me and takes her hand as she leads him away. I call out to him at the open door.

"Remember where we left off for next time, okay?"

He turns. He nods. "Love you, Dad."

"See you next week, kid."

His smile bends but does not break. The creases in his cheeks shallow, and his face asks me a question, though I believe it's one he doesn't yet have words for, one enmeshed in an emotion he doesn't yet understand, one he doesn't yet have the tools to express.

His mother does, though. There is no ambiguity in her affect, which shouts the question he doesn't know to ask.

But I am not ready to answer it. So I make my smile wider, lips parted, teeth revealed, conveying all the paternal warmth I can produce, and hope my grin isn't the grimace I know it to be.

DEADLIFT

I don't
know how to weigh loss
But I do
know how heavy it is.

FOUR

"Land?"

"Land. Bay front, no less."

"And now it's yours?" she asked.

I cradled the phone between my ear and shoulder as I packed. "That's what he said. 'Written into the inheritance language.' The plot was to go to Malcolm on his eighteenth birthday. Unless that wasn't possible."

A hitch in your mother's breath while I held mine.

"I don't understand. *Your* grandfather. Like, your *mother's* dad. Left land. To our son."

I scoffed. "Damn near next to a country club if you can believe it."

"Make this make sense."

"When it makes sense to me, you'll be the first to know. I'm leaving tomorrow morning to see it."

"Packing your trunks?"

"Oh, you're so funny."

Her smirk was audible. "You still won't get in the water?"

"Still. Always."

"You're perpetuating a harmful stereotype, you know that?"

"I told you, Van, I can swim. I choose not to."

"Mmm-hmm." A pause. "Wow. Your grandfather."

"I know. I can't wrap my head around it, either. The only thing I can think of is it having something to do with when Malcolm worked at the nursing home."

"Oh, come on."

"What?"

"He leaves Malcolm a plot of land to, what, rub it in your face that they had a relationship even though you two didn't? Doesn't that seem—I don't know—a little far-fetched?"

"The man disinvited us from his wife's funeral, Van."

"That's one thing, but—"

"That's one thing? Really?"

She let out one of those exasperated breaths, which signaled I'd exhausted the minimal reserve of her patience for me, a sigh that said this could have been a text conversation. And you know how I am with uncomfortable silences, Malcolm. Got to fill that space. I tried a different tack.

"You should have seen the attorney's face when I turned out to be his ten o'clock."

"Oh?"

"I mean, I don't think he was expecting someone of my complexion."

"Well, you are so articulate." Her tone again betrayed the upward turn of her mouth.

"Gets me in trouble when I pronounce that hard *r*, though."

She snorted. A little bit of self-deprecation went a long way with your mother, especially after I'd said something irretrievably stupid. The smirk in her voice just now told me I'd hit the mark with my ego's immolation, and I envisioned her lopsided smile, the singular dimple, as if she sat right next to me. But as was my standard, I'd no sooner turned back the tide than I'd tripped and fallen face-first in the sand.

"Van, come with me. Come see the property."

Nothing. Then

"Why?"

The question stood me upright. I stopped packing. "Why? I don't . . .
I thought . . . I mean—don't you want to see it? He left the land to our
son."

"Right. And now it's yours. I don't know what that's got to do with me."

"Van, you're being—"

"What? I'm being what? Think very carefully before you answer."

"Right. No, you're right. It was dumb. I didn't consider what that
might mean, asking that of you."

A deep breath. A narrow opening for hope.

"What are you going to do with it?"

There was what I expected her to say, and there was what I wanted her
to say, and what she said was neither.

"Do with it?"

"The land. Are you going to keep it?"

You had been our only remaining tether, Mal. A tenuous thread to
which I'd clung, a climber's belay rope protecting me from the peril of
rocks below. Selling the land would have been a way to say good-bye, at
least in part, to my grief and guilt. I'd rid myself of the inheritance like
the letter informing me of its existence, just another memento mori I'd
hoped soon to forget. But doing so might also have taken a knife to the
last threads of that rope connecting your mother and me, and once cut,
I'd have nothing to slow my fall, with no thought of where I'd land, but
knowing the fall would be hard enough I'd never make the climb again.
But if I let myself fall, maybe I'd stop putting my faith in the false hope
of reconciliation and maybe I'd stop exhausting her. How hard it's been
to count on that line to hold, for me to hold that rope when my hands
were so tired. Sometimes the fraying cords snapped. Sometimes I slipped,
as when I replied,

"Well, like you said, what's that got to do with you?"

"Wow. Okay. You know what? You're absolutely right."

"Wait, I'm sorry."

Saying sorry had become a reflex, a platitude professing neither sincerity nor shame. Sound and fury and all that. I'd been infinitely indelicate
with your mother, making my apologies pollen, an irritant to be forcefully
expelled.

"Don't be sorry. You're right. Good luck."

"Van—"

"I've got to go."

"Yeah, all right."

She ended the call. She didn't say *I'll talk to you later*. She didn't ask me
to tell her after how the visit had gone. She didn't say good-bye, though,
just then I was convinced that was indeed what she had done. It occurred
to me, too late as was my custom, that I was an anchor to her grief and my
petulance had finally been enough to unmoor her. I put the phone down
and finished packing for travel to waters of my own.

FIVE

I don't own a pair of swim trunks. Not anymore. Because I don't like the beach.

I never told you why, for the same reason I never told you why I never went back there with you. At best, the story is embarrassing. At worst, revelatory, and I'm still not there yet. But time alone in the car reminds me of the time you left me alone in the car, and this drive to see this inherited land is a long one with no time for me to go holding up traffic again with another episode. So let's talk.

You see, Mal, I didn't dislike the beach because of the ignorant notion I'd had some melanin-mitigated inability to swim. In fact, when I was a kid, the water held me in thrall. Your grandfather, my dad, had been overweight and a heavy smoker, but turned fitness buff after I was born, and laps at the YMCA pool became part of his weekly regimen. When I was four, he and my mother enrolled me in the Red Cross swimming program at camp, and by the time I was six, I'd freestyled from the shallow to the deep end and earned my Advanced Swimmer card, flashing it like a badge behind its plastic screen with a rip of my Velcro wallet. I'd soon join my father in the adjoining lane at the Y, pushing to match his pace, open palms slapping the water while his hands sliced through. Any time we traveled out of town, my first question was whether the hotel had a pool. Epic were my pouts if no chlorinated oasis lay within. Your grandparents couldn't keep me away from the water—until a trip one summer down the shore the year I turned nine.

Independent and adventurous—yes, you got that from me, sorry—I'd padded down the packed sand to the water's edge, tensing at the cold from that first splash of ocean on my feet, surprised by the change in temperature as it washed over them again, marveling as the water warmed with each approach and retreat until it reached my trunks and sent the cold fabric creeping up my legs, starting the cycle all over again. Up the beach, my parents reclined in their folding chairs. My father napped, an open book on his bare chest. My mother shielded her eyes with one hand and waved at me with the other. I waved back, assuring her she was still within my eyesight, and thus me in hers, then turned back and faced the horizon.

Though my blossoming brain couldn't yet articulate what I'd felt, I was captivated by the sea's boundlessness. I knew enough to understand the ocean didn't stop where the sky met the waterline, but I deduced it wasn't endless, either. What was on the other side of that line? How far would I have to go to reach another beach? I'd take a few more steps forward, turn and wave as I'd been told, then back to the infinite aquatic. The tide was calm and though the water neared my chest, it only pushed me back a step or two as it rolled over itself to reach the shore. The ebb and flow moved me in rhythm, and I dug my toes into the sand. Seagulls wheeled overhead. Just a pair at first. Then another. And another. They stopped their turns and hovered, their cries louder and louder. Then your grandmother screamed my name.

She was much farther away than the last time I'd turned back. Her wave had gone from pleasant to frantic, from one hand to two, palms no longer outward but swinging toward her face. She wanted me back on the beach. I grumbled something about not being a little kid and slapped my hand on the top of the water. And that's when I saw it. A small jellyfish floated listless next to me. I flicked my hand, in hopes of splashing it away, only to have it stay in the same spot. Then another jellyfish came to the surface next to it. The warm breeze slid aside the clouds obscuring the high afternoon sun, and among the twinkling diamonds created by its reflection were more jellyfish still. Spinning in place, I was surrounded by them—and I was alone. Other waders and swimmers had already made their way to shore. A seagull swooped for its meal and splashed next to me. I squeezed my eyelids shut, opened my mouth, and screamed.

More splashes sounded in front of me. Strong hands hooked beneath my underarms and hoisted me from the water. Even so, I kept my eyes closed. The hands held me close and high, my toes skimming the surface, until I felt the grit of sand and broken shells beneath my soles, my trunks heavy with water and, as your grandfather took great pleasure in recounting many years later, no small amount of urine.

"Did they get you?"

I opened my eyes. My father towered over me, his proud Afro round like a resistance fist, encircled by the sun like a halo, the backlighting casting his figure in shadow.

"No," I said, then burst into ragged sobs.

"All right," he said. As was his way, he gave my hair a tousle and turned me toward my mother. He toweled off, returned to his chair, but did not replace his book on his chest. Though by all appearances he lay stone still, I watched him close and saw him shake, the tremors almost imperceptible— but not quite. My mother moved toward him, but he waved her away, moving only his hand, his arm rigid by his side. She understood this unspoken communication then pulled me into her arms and whispered words of calm and comfort. She explained a probable storm had washed in what seemed to be hundreds of jellyfish, many of them dead or in pieces. How I hadn't been stung I still don't understand, as I learned later even the dead ones still had the mechanism to do so. I peeked up from my mother's arms, alternating sobs and sniffles, and watched the seagulls feed. My father lay stiff, breathing in through his nose and out through his mouth. What's wrong with Daddy? I'd asked. Instead of answering, Mom told me she'd take me to the gift shop for being such a brave little man, despite insisting on the car ride to the beach that there would be no toys so don't bother asking. Her reneging terminated my tears. She took my hand and told your grandfather we'd be back.

We stopped in the first shop we saw on the boardwalk. The open entrance boasted novelty T-shirts, fluorescent buckets for sandcastles with their matching shovels, and hermit crabs scaling mesh drums, their shells painted with superhero logos. Mom let me wander while she searched for a postcard to send to Nana, your great-grandmother. Down one narrow aisle, I found a box not much bigger than the palm of my hand that said "Pet Horny Toad: Do Not Open." I'd never been allowed a pet. So of course I opened it. Under the lid I saw a rubbery frog on its back, complete with a cartoon face, bugged-out eyes, and a lolling tongue, spread-eagled, with a massive bright green erection.

Your grandmother rounded the corner, and before I could say a word, she snatched the box, put it back on the shelf, and led me out of the store by my wrist, muttering something about shame to the poor kid behind the counter. She damn near dragged me back to the beach, my flip-flops slapping my heels as I scrambled to keep up with her indignant march. No postcard for Nana. No turgid toy for me.

When we returned to our spot on the beach, my father was gone. Mom said not to worry, that he'd probably gone to the bathroom. When he didn't return, my mother suggested we'd had enough beach for one day and took us back to the hotel. When we arrived, I saw my father on the bed through the door to our adjoining rooms, hissing with pain. There'd been nothing miraculous about his adventure into the water. He'd been stung many times over. He hadn't wanted me to know he was hurting, I suppose. He hadn't wanted to scare me any more than I'd been scared, I suppose. I say I suppose because we never spoke about it. We never spoke about it because watching him lie there, just before my mother closed the door, showing her his pain but not me, my gratitude for his rescuing me turned to anger. We never spoke about it because though I didn't know why I was so upset, I had some intuition of a sense of betrayal, of unworthiness, as though he didn't think me strong enough to witness what he must have seen as his weakness. We went home the next day and never took another trip to the shore because I told them I no longer liked it there, though I didn't tell them why.

A father hiding his emotions from his son? I mean, who would do such a thing? Can you imagine, Mal? I certainly can('t).

All this in mind, you can guess why, when you asked your mother and me to take you to the beach, I hesitated. No, you're right—I'm not being truthful. I flat out said no. But you would not be deterred. I'd like to say I agreed because you were just so adorable in your insistence, your pleading and your puppy dog eyes the remedy to my recalcitrance. I really would like to say that. But I can't. Your mother made happy by my eventual acquiescence, that's what did it. Another move on the chessboard. Yes, I know now what that makes you. That's the point of all this reflection. It occurs to me I knew then, too.

When you made that run for the water, though, that was one occasion when I had my doubts about my motivations. Not while it was happening, mind you. It's rare when I give regard to recollections of the details of complex emotional states, described as if these epiphanies evinced themselves with clarity amid a traumatic event, as anything more than an opportunity for the relater of said recollection to convince the receiver of said recollection how self-aware they are. I'll do you the favor of sparing you such a display of ego by being honest and telling you that when I set down our beach chairs and saw you shin-deep in the surf, I panicked. And I sprinted. I had to catch you before you went too deep, before you made me go too deep chasing after you, before you were too far out to be rescued should you need to be, too far out to be rescued by me.

How you kicked and flailed when I scooped you up, wanted no part of my taking you back up the beach, wanted only to wade farther into the water. When I put you down at your mother's feet, I thought sure I'd be rewarded, the attentive father saving his son from the perils of the dangerous ocean. Instead, I stood before you both, silently censured by your expressions, left to watch as you and your mother walked hand in hand back to the water until it was up over your waist, you squealing with delight as the tides knocked you off balance, washed over you, as Van hoisted you sputtering but smiling from beneath the surf. I'd never seen you so happy. Either of you. While you two played, I went back to our hotel room, never to return to the beach for the rest of the weekend. Or ever again.

Until now.

The business building bar graphs shrunk in my rearview as I exited the expressway. More than seventy miles of straightaway before I reached the beach, a near-empty two-lane stretch flanked by local diners, bungalows converted to gun shops, and fields of corn and grain guarded by massive metallic stick-insect irrigation machines creeping slowly down the rows.

I'll confess this confessing was exhausting when it amounted to my monologuing with no real resolution. Of course, had you engaged in the dialogue with me at that point—or any point, really—I'm not sure we'd have made it to the rest of the story, as my next conversation would have been with a shrink. That said, I was unconvinced of the exercise's continued usefulness, so I eyed my phone on its dash mount. I hadn't called my parents since the funeral. I hadn't called them much before then, either. My father and I had never been phone talkers, but the issue had been forced when Mom's Parkinson's rendered her near nonverbal. Before then, she'd been our interpreter. Though I'd felt betrayed by him at the beach (a betrayal forgiven by pizza and a movie later that day), the truth was he and I had never been outwardly emotive, in particular with each other. Not to say I didn't try, but I learned to read his responses and imitate his actions. When he responded with "you, too" to my "I love you," I learned we didn't say "I love you." When his hands tapped my back while I squeezed him in a hug, I learned to make our embraces ethereal. It wasn't that he didn't care. His affection came in ways I didn't understand until I was a young man. Car rides to and from school were time to talk about what life was going to be like for me having a white mother and a Black father. About how the world would see me, no matter how I saw myself. About how though my hair wasn't like his, I was as Black as he was. About how I could be mixed and Black at the same time, and about how little choice I had in that determination. About how I needed to assume all white folks were racist until they proved otherwise. It was heady stuff for a fourth grader, but I saw the pride in his face when he saw the pride in mine, as if this was his way of hugging me back.

As I grew into adolescence, so, too, grew my resentment for his lack of emotional availability. My athleticism—and that's a generous use of the term—stopped with pee wee football and diocese league basketball in seventh and eighth grade. Your grandfather lacked any of my interest in comic books, professional wrestling, and kung fu theater, and so we had even less to talk about. He'd sit disinterested while I regaled my mother with the latest storylines in the multitudinous mediums I consumed, her feigned enthusiasm no less satisfying than the real thing.

A failed senior-year relationship sent me spiraling in a twister of adolescent angst. I ate little and spent all my free time in my room, buried in books and video games. Mom offered her shoulder and her ears. Dad offered his back. He didn't understand my melodrama, said he didn't understand why I dated so many white girls. I was incredulous at his ignorance, appalled by his apathy when I was in pain, confused by his lack of comprehension at my romantic tendencies, as though I hadn't come by them honestly. And while the tragedy of teenage love subsided, my relationship with my father experienced a shift in the faults, a sliding of the plates that shook the already precarious foundation of our relationship. When they dropped me off at college, Mom pelted my cheeks with kisses. Dad and I shook hands.

When I called home with updates, Mom always answered the phone, ready to relay the information. It's not that I didn't want to tell him how I was doing directly. I wanted to be the one to let him know I'd joined a group of Black writers on campus. That I'd met a nice Black girl who told me she liked my hair and whom I was going to meet for coffee, though I'd never had a cup before. Mom would ask me if I wanted her to put him on the phone, and though I wanted to say yes, what I wanted more was for him to want to get on the phone, and because I was my father's son, I said no, you can tell him. I knew she heard it in my voice, though. That longing. Somehow, she always knew when to tell me when he was proud of me, and I always knew to pretend to believe it, though I knew she never believed me. There was longing in her voice, too.

But Parkinson's rendered my mother's face motionless, left lifeless her vocal cords. As time went on, there would be no more arbitration, no more translation. My father and I were forced to learn each other's language, and we were hard learners. The cordless phone was his last participating stop in technology's march toward the future. He had no cell phone, no tablet, no means for us to engage in nonverbal communication. Even the cordless phone had an old cassette answering machine attached, with an outgoing message I'd recorded for them when I was in high school. Where my mother would always answer calls, he screened them. When I phoned home to tell them about what had happened to you, I talked over the static sound of my teenage voice informing callers we couldn't come to the phone right now but please kindly leave a message—the news of your death rung in with a digital beep.

An ache settled into my arm, my hand still hovering in front of my cell phone. There was no question how the conversation would go.

Listen to the recording.

Dad picks up midway through when he hears it's me.

Update from Mom's last home care visit.

Silence as we think of something to say, same as we did at the funeral, talking about anything but what was there in front of us, of things lost to us, of what could be restored between us, but we didn't because, well, that's just not what we do, so I'd hold back telling him about where I'm going because his reaction will be what I know it will be and not what I want it to be, and I'll be comforted and angered at the same time and I don't want to be any more confused than I already am so I'd say nothing more except see you later and we'd hang up before the answering machine cassette runs out of tape.

I returned my hand to the steering wheel and drove on.

My musings proved sufficient distraction and I arrived nearer to my destination sooner than I'd expected. Fields full of corn and beanstalks now bore seafood restaurants, mini golf emporiums, and outlet stores. Traffic slogged between poorly timed stoplights, lurching forward in long lines despite the early-afternoon hour. The GPS indicated my turn approached, though, at my current pace, it seemed farther away than when I'd begun my journey. I eventually made the turn off the main route and followed the satellite's instructions toward the bay.

The town enjoyed a progressive reputation, the state proud of its blue roots, a modern-day mecca for the marginalized. Yet away from the busy interstate and deeper into the adjacent neighborhoods, I noticed far fewer rainbow flags and a great many more American flags. Flags flapping from the porch. Miniature flags circling trees in the yard. Flags on mailboxes. Mailboxes painted like American flags. Road signs on the main drag advertising support for the latest Democratic candidate replaced by yard signs advocating their ideological rivals on the suburban side streets, all veiled behind the veneer of conscious capitalism. Who was more honest?

The mass of McMansions thinned the farther in I drove, and the copse of trees yielded to an expanse of green flat land. The GPS alerted me that I had arrived at my destination. There was no gravel road to a farmhouse, no well and pump, nor any other landmarks to speak of confirming the terminus I'd intended. The overhead internet image the attorney had provided contained exactly what lay before me—nothing but acres upon acres of long green grass.

I parked and turned off the car but did not exit. Despite not feeling my normal nervousness on the drive, something else brewed. Not anxiety. That was a feeling immediately identifiable, which struck me as an odd sort of comfortable, an ability to give my monster a name. This sensation, however, was a different creature altogether. This beast had a gravity all its own. It sat behind me, arms around my chest, rooting me to my seat, and whispered dread in my ear. Its presence filled the car, enormous, using all the air inside for its own lungs. I felt if I didn't get out, I'd suffocate.

The car gently pinged, a reminder to remove my keys from the ignition as I stood at the open door. A warm breeze dragged gray clouds along the sky, portents of a summer storm, bringing the bay's briny tang with it. Though the closest home was almost out of view, I walked the field, surveying in an attempt at appearing official should any suspicious onlookers be watching with wariness this lone Black man wandering near their neighborhood, whether he wore a shirt and tie or not. Waves struck sand with a whisper, and I moved toward the sound. A narrow rocky beach lined the edge of the property. Across the bay sat the country club, its parking lot along the shoreline. I l wondered what price the land might fetch.

I can't breathe.

I can't sit up.

We're going to be late.

A rushing sound filled my ears, then pressure, then a pressing against my head from all sides. I remembered the first time I'd jumped into the deep end of the pool as a child and the fear I'd felt at the thought I might not make it to the surface. My eyelids fluttered, my field of vision narrowed.

Then the water's lapping was louder. My legs warm.

I stood knee-deep in the bay.

My prescription could not blunt the panic that clung to me as my damp slacks had as I turned and trudged out of the water. A side effect of the medication, perhaps? Consult your physician if you find yourself standing in seawater. The horizon had gone a purplish orange, and I checked my watch.

Two hours. Two hours? How many of those hours had I been standing half-submerged?

Unnerved, I sat on the pebble- and twig-laden sand and drained the drink from my loafers. The pharmacist would be my first call after I'd settled into my room. The temperature had dropped, and a low rumble rolled behind the thickening clouds. Dry or not, it was time to make my exit. It was now well past check-in and rush hour was over, so I headed to the rental for a planned night of endless googling for symptoms of what

I'd just experienced until I found enough confirmation to calm my disquiet. When I opened the car door, I heard a scream, like that of a woman. Tortured. And close.

The fields cast in a fading light, each gust moved the grass, adding gasoline to my fear-fueled imagination. Fear bred by familiarity. I'd heard this sound before.

With you. And I hoped it wasn't that.

Another shriek, but from elsewhere in the field. Whatever or whoever it was, they were moving. Hurt, perhaps. Dragged. Calling out crossed my mind, but equal parts self-preservation and cowardice strangled any sense of heroism. A patch of grass moved out of sync to the wind, in a straight line, toward a clearing. I ducked and peered over the hood of the car.

A fox peeked its head through the reeds, and a relieved cackle left me in a rush. The fox pricked up its ears and turned its head in my direction. My amusement advanced to anger and I clapped my hands to scare it off. It sat and scratched its cheek, then shook its head before trotting off back into the grass.

I got in the car, started the engine, and hoped to God I'd run it over on the way out.

SIX

He is eight, though when I tell others this, he is quick to correct me that he is, in fact, eight and one quarter. I have learned not to argue.

Today ages him further and faster than I am prepared for.

He stands before me, hands in front of his face, balled into little fists, thumbs out. His elbows are raw and his eyes shimmer. I wrap my hands around his and correct their position, tuck his thumbs under. I reach down to his ankles, altering his stance.

"Like this. So you can see them in front of you, so you don't hurt your thumbs. Feet wider for balance."

"But I don't want to hit anyone."

"Don't you want to protect yourself?"

"I guess."

Tears brim, but he wipes them away with the back of his arm before they can fall, fists still held tight. He corrects his hands before I can.

"Like this?"

"Like that."

I don't want him to get it right. Not now, at least. It's too soon, as though there's ever a right time. But he has a lisp and a slight stutter that worsens when he's nervous, neither of which are his fault, but mine. A boy, taller and stronger, mocked him during a break at Sunday school. Malcolm's heart bigger than his body, he stood up for himself, told the boy not to make fun. The boy told him,

"You're my slave and I can do whatever I want,"

and pushed Malcolm to the ground so hard he slid, flaying his forearms on the asphalt. Malcolm dutifully told the instructor, who later asked Malcolm, in front of me, no less, how she could better support him when things like this happen, a thinly veiled assumption this would happen again. An eight-and-one-quarter-year-old boy tasked with deciphering the emotional complexity of being told you belong to someone else, asked as though he were the one who'd done something wrong.

I hate this. I hate that I can't tell if the fear on his face is there because of the boy or because of me. I hate how I can't take this moment away from him. I hate that from this moment, things will never be the same. I hate that I'm teaching him to hurt when he doesn't want to. I hate knowing that I have to. I hate watching his eight-and-one-quarter years roll down his cheeks. I hate that someone else's hate has fostered the same emotion in me. I hate watching my son's soft heart harden.

I am in my father's car again. Except now I am driving.

I kneel on the carpet in front of him, my eyes level with his. "What's that show you like again? Forest Rangers?"

"Dad," he says, drawing out the *a*. "*Power Rangers.*"

"That's what I said."

An eye roll. A smirk. A sniffle. His shoulders relax.

"Imagine I'm one of the bad guys."

"Like the Putties?"

"Putties? Really? They sound . . . not so scary."

"There's usually a lot of them."

"Putties it is. Okay, I'm the chief Putty. Show me what the Forest—"

"Power."

"*Power* Rangers would do."

He squares up, then drops his hands. "I thought I was supposed to turn the other cheek."

He hasn't thrown a punch, yet I am struck.

"That's true. But not in this case, Mal. You can't."

"Why?"

"Because sometimes you have to fight back."

"But why is it okay sometimes and not the other times? I don't understand. Won't I go to hell if I fight back?"

"Hell? What? No. Why would you say that?"

"Doesn't the devil take you if you don't listen to God?"

"It doesn't—the devil isn't, he doesn't, like, work for God."

"He doesn't? It seems like he does."

"It's complicated, Mal."

"You say that a lot."

"That's because it's true, smart guy." His smile seems meant only to appease me. "Now come on. Pretend I'm a Putty."

Hands up to protect my face, I don't see the front kick coming. Malcolm is tall for his age, but his long limbs have little muscle between the skin and bone. Still, the tip of the cowboy boots for which he'd developed an obsession earlier in the year, a fixation his mother was all too happy to oblige despite (because of) my objections, lands just below my sternum. The force is not great, but the accuracy, coupled with the surprise, is enough to bend me over. On his face I see expectation. I want him to feel strong. I think of my father again.

Clutching my stomach, I drop to the ground, fetal and gasping for air. Eyelids pinched in exaggerated agony, I peek up at him, hoping to see his arms in the air, bouncing from foot to foot in victorious celebration. Instead, I see despair. Tears fall. He goes to all fours, brings his face to the floor, and his soft palm on my cheek nearly breaks me.

"Daddy, I'm sorry!"

Hoping humor will bring him back from the brink, I halt my heaving and open my eyes wide.

"Gotcha."

Malcolm pulls back. His brows converge. His lips tense. Fear becomes fury. Before I can rise, he jumps on me, and my surprise at his heft leaves me in a short-lived laugh. He is heavier than he should be, gravity fit to pull him straight through me, his weight belonging to the man he's been forced to become. I have earned the painful punches battering my back, the palms pressing down on me, I am the proxy for his pain, and though I am larger than him, stronger than him, I cannot move, and his fear becomes mine.

"Malcolm, let me up."

He punches still. He is heavier still.

"Malcolm, I can't breathe."

He punches on. His legs squeeze my ribs, and my voice rides the air from my lungs.

"Malcolm!"

He stops. Coolness spreads across my spine as he stands. Relieved, I roll to my back and take a deep breath. He stands above me, fists clenched, slight striations lining the lengths of his forearms, muscles normally masked from view, revealed by rage. I hazard a glance at his face and wish that I hadn't. Eight and one quarter years old no more. Under Malcolm's scowl, I am the child, every bit the boy who took something that didn't belong to him.

"Malcolm, I'm sorry."

"Why?"

His timbre belies the tremble in his limbs. His question arrives with the force of his kick and his hunger for an answer hollows me. Why are you sorry? Why did you do that to me? Why did the boy say that to me? Why do I have to hurt when hurt? The whys are legion, the answer singular. I come to my knees in front of him.

"I don't know."

Malcolm's shoulders ease away from his ears. His fists open. He steps toward me, and I lift my arms to embrace him. He puts a finger in my face and growls behind his teeth.

"You scared me. Don't ever do that again."

I want to tell him I won't. I know he wants me to tell him I won't. We both know it will be the first of many lies between us if I do. I will have to scare him again if I want him to survive this world. So I say nothing at first. He drops his hand to his side. He knows. Then I say worse than nothing. I lie.

"I won't."

"Promise?"

"Promise." Another question lingers, but he hesitates. "What is it?"

"Do I have to go back?"

"Do you want to go back?"

"No. And yes."

"I get it. But we can't let bullies keep us from the things we want, right?" Nods. "You've made friends there, haven't you?" Pauses. Nods. "Don't you want to go back and see them?" Longer pause. Nods. "Then can you give it one more shot?" Longer pause still. No nod. "For me?" At that he lifts his head, then his chest. Stiffens the upper lip. Crinkles the chin. One curt, forceful, proud nod. And he should be proud. I should be proud, too.

Of him, I am.

I hold my hand out for five. He gives it a slap and turns his palm upward. I return the smack, and before I can bring my hand back, he steps in with a fierce hug. His arms shake, from the effort or from some residual anxiety or anger, I can't tell, and I am afraid to ask why, because I fear the answer will yield more questions for which I am both ill-prepared and ill-equipped. Instead, I pat his back, signaling it's time to let go. He does.

"Want to break out the action figures?"

"Dad." He rolls his eyes. "I'm too old for those."

"Already? When did you get so big?"

He shrugs. But I know. I've just watched it happen.

"So . . . what then?"

"*Street Fighter*?"

"Your mom lets you play that?"

"You scared? If you're scared, we don't have to."

"Oh, it's on." I get into my stance and do my best Hadoken. He waves me off.

"E. Honda's going to slap the sh . . . mess out of you."

"What did you almost say?" He goes wide-eyed, and though I front an angry façade, it cracks. "You better get over here!" I jump at him, and he shrieks with joy as I chase him, happy he doesn't realize that not only am I scared, I am terrified.

SEVEN

Though I had wanted to stay as far away from the beach as possible, only scattershot rentals remained available, and the one I reserved was reasonable considering the time of year. Few parking spots sat open on the main drag leading to the boardwalk, but I eventually located a space a few blocks away, parked, and walked. People passing by smelled of sunblock and booze as they made their way back from the water. Mopeds and motorized scooters buzzed up and down the thoroughfare. Nag champa wafted from shops with fu dogs guarding the door and windows advertising henna tattooing and crystals, the owners either unaware or caring little for the cultural contradictions. You would have called them out right away, Malcolm, and though I was still shaken from what had just occurred at the bay, I had no difficulty imagining your righteous indignation. In my inattention, I kicked a water bowl left out for the coterie of canines walking their humans up and down the sidewalks. The shop owner told me no apology was necessary though her tone and the set of her mouth said otherwise. I walked on.

When I reached the address, I thought sure I had it wrong. I hoped

I had it wrong. In front of me stood a small bar, The Thirsty Scholar. At least I assumed that's what it was called, because the hand-painted window sign read Thristy, not Thirsty. Not all that scholarly.

Familiar and not entirely unwelcomed smells rushed out the door as I opened it. I'd spent enough time in bars like this one to know Murphy Oil Soap had been applied to the burnished wood bar top that morning, along with a brass rail polish, but the fryer grease hadn't been changed in a while, and the bartender needed to give the floor under the rubber mats behind the bar a thorough scrubbing due to what I assumed were countless beers spilled back there that had seeped beneath, hiding, transforming into some combination of liquid, solid, and gas on the underside of the mats where the hose spray couldn't reach.

My eyes adjusted to the darkness, the space illuminated by yellowed fixtures, as if light were simply a suggestion. Empty two-tops lined the wall opposite the bar where a young white couple in beach gear and an older Black man dressed far too warmly for the season sat with several seats between them. I approached the bar but didn't sit. The bartender held up a finger to me as she topped off a draft glass and placed it in front of the older gentleman while clearing his empty one. Her tight auburn curls bounced as she walked over to me.

"You know your sign out front is misspelled?"

She tilted her head down. "You know your pants are wet?" My slacks had not yet dried since the bay. No wonder people stink-eyed me on the walk here. "I'm kidding. I'm sure it's a good story." I held my hands out to my sides and searched my mind for a witty retort but came up empty. She threw a life preserver. "The sign's my tourist detector," she said. The older man snorted into his beer. She smirked at me. I stayed stone-faced. "That's a joke, too. Well, sort of. When we first opened, the sign painter messed it up. I thought it was kind of funny and quirky, so we kept it. When anybody tells me about it, I know they're from out of town, because everyone else around here knows about it. Tourist detector."

"Very clever."

"I thought so. You clearly don't, though."

Another snort from the older man. I pulled my cell phone from my back pocket.

"Wondering if you can help me? I'm looking for this rental address, but it brought me here."

She leaned over the bar. I caught a whiff of hair oil and cocoa butter and thought of your mother. She brightened.

"You're my tenant!"

I cocked my head to the side, and she pointed upstairs. I grumbled.

"Of course I am."

"Problem?"

"No. No problem."

"*That* sounded convincing." She turned and retrieved a ring with two keys from a drawer underneath a liquor bottle–stocked shelf. "If you go back out the front, there's a door on the right side of the building as you're facing it. That opens to the steps which'll take you up to the apartment. Top floor. Great view of the beach." She slid the keys across the bar. "First one for tenants is on the house. Bourbon guy, am I right?" Before I could protest, she turned and pulled a bottle from just below the top shelf and poured two fingers. I smelled it before she placed it on the bar in front of me, watched the amber legs lingering along the inside of the glass from where it had splashed when she set it down. She watched me watch it, head tilted in wonder.

"Sorry, do you not . . . ?"

"Can I get a water back?"

"Oh. Sure."

She poured water from a soda gun into a matching highball and set it next to the drink. I stood. And I contemplated. Contemplated and stood. Save the occasional shooter of cough medicine, mouthwash, and the accidental rum ball at a holiday party, alcohol hadn't passed my lips since shortly after you were born, and with good reason—the Teachers' Lung.

Yes, it's time.

My teetotaling was a promise originating as a loosely held vow of solidarity with your mother as my proclivity for drinking held sway while she was pregnant. In all fairness (to me), your mother was no lightweight when it came to booze, but she quit cold turkey when we found out about you. My penchant, on the other hand, she'd said, was more my problem than predilection, to which, of course, I protested with verve. I'd gotten better, I'd argued. Fatherhood wasn't something to be taken lightly, I'd told and told myself, near the point of believing. Responsibility was my new mantra, so much so that when she'd discovered she was pregnant and decided she'd nurse, I more or less moved in with her for the first six months to help her care for you, our unintended, especially in the late and early feeding hours.

After a piece I'd written—the dreaded personal essay, the one where I'd succumbed to my colleagues' all-too-well-meaning advice and talked about my mulatto-ness in all its tragic glory, knowing full well I'd be theretofore conflated with the fictional biracial protagonist I'd planned to write—gained acceptance to the pinnacle of creative nonfiction literary magazines, I'd raised my glass with my fellow adjuncts, but not too many, because I was a Responsible Father now, and I had to get home to my son and not-girlfriend, but yes, one more, just for the road, publications like these don't come every day, even though I felt as if I'd sold my soul and even though that sale meant that this acceptance might be the start of something, so, of course, one more in celebration, not in mourning for a lifestyle lost to fatherhood, and definitely not in avoidance of accountability, sidestepping even temporarily a life that terrified me, one I wasn't prepared for (the writing or the fatherhood?), no, definitely not that, who would do that, not a man, and I was a man, wasn't I?

Time went slick and slid me late to your mother's apartment, slipping my key into the deadbolt only to have the knob pulled from my grasp as she opened the door, cradling you, wearing her weariness as a shawl on her shoulders, though whether it was me or you who bent her back, I couldn't quite tell.

That's not true. I know who it was. So do you, I'm certain.

Maybe it was the fatigue that clouded her judgment in handing you to me. It was for certain the bourbon that clouded mine in taking you from her. She pointed me to a warmed breast milk bottle on the bathroom counter and shuffled down the hall to her bedroom for a new mother's deep slumber. I took you into the nursery and though I plopped down a bit too quickly in the glider chair, your expectant eyes glimmered with unearned trust.

How long I slept before I dropped you, I'll never know. You lay faceup on the thick-piled carpet, on the other side of the ottoman, arms bound, screaming. Had the ottoman not been there, chances are I'd have buried you much sooner than last week. The yawn of your shrieking mouth immobilized me, my arms resting on my legs, still holding the empty space you had only just occupied. Your mother appeared in the doorway with such speed it was as if the entrance were a portal through time, and she scooped you into her arms, disappearing with the same immediacy. She didn't ask what happened. She didn't have to. And I never had another drink.

But as time does with all things both good and terrible, the horror of that night wore away, faded but ever present, and though I never returned to the bottle, I found myself missing the bars, their smells and sounds, the camaraderie with colleagues, and all the other rationalized reasons. Nostalgia was the soil in which temptation was planted, but my guilt over dropping you blocked out all sunlight, never allowing that seed to grow. Yet the seed remained. Your mother and I went from co-parenting to co-existing, never in the same room at the same time unless we had to be and even then, not one minute longer. When she could manage the nights and mornings without me, that's exactly what she did. We arranged a visitation schedule, and I tried to fill the hours without you—okay, yes, *her*—with work. But the seed was thirsty, and nostalgia's dry ground begged for drink. I watered the seed with meetings in a church rec room. Then every Sunday in the pews of the same church. Then church group functions. Replaced the spirits with the spirit. Hands around a glass or pressed together in prayer, both scratching the same itch.

How strong the itch now. And there I was, in my church.

I held the bourbon and water glasses in each hand, closed my eyes, brought the bourbon to my nose, and inhaled deeply, then took a sip of the water. In my nascent sobriety, I had tried all the tricks to drink without drinking. Nonalcoholic near beers were too bitter to bear. One sweat-soaked anxiety-ridden night, an internet search yielded a find, a supposed sensory misdirection. I never took the method for a test drive because there was no way I would buy bourbon I wouldn't drink. But this bourbon was free.

Swallowed. Breathed. And tasted only water. When I opened my eyes, the bartender's head sat skewed, her face relaying as much bemusement as confusion.

"That's a first. Does that actually work?"

"No." I set down the water and held the bourbon from the underside of the glass, turning it left and right. The bartender exchanged squints with the old man. Pinned on the wall behind the bar hung a screen-printed T-shirt emblazoned with the face of some white-bearded philosopher, the rendering just bad enough to obscure his identity, with the misspelled logo from the window arced above his head. A Post-it pinned to the shirt read $10.

"Shirt's misspelled, too."

"I know, but I'm committed to the bit at this point. Plus, the irony is chef's kiss, you know?"

"My son would have loved one."

You would have.

She turned and retrieved a folded stack from a shelf, then placed them in front of me. "What size is he?"

Your mother was always better with sizes, always took you school clothes shopping. At least you let me take you to buy your suit. The only one you had. The only one you'd ever wear. Forever. The one that would stay the same size while your body shrunk, withdrew from it.

That size I knew. That size I remembered.

I shook my head. She understood.

"Oh. You said 'would have,' didn't you?"

I nodded.

"I'm so sorry."

A hum of affirmation was all I offered in return. I chewed the inside of my lip, lifted the glass toward the shirt on the wall, then took a sip.

To you, Malcolm. Aren't you proud.

The bourbon left a smoke trail down my throat and lit embers in my chest I thought long burned out. Unable to suppress a new (born-again?) drinker's clichéd cough, I cleared my throat, then finished the rest of the drink with one swallow. Pins pricked my face, my nose watered, and with a hollowed exhale, I breathed fire and wiped a tear from my cheek.

"You okay?"

The old man regarded me with raised eyebrows. She did, too. I pushed the empty glass toward her. I sat.

"Another?"

"Please."

She poured and placed it in front of me. This time, I did not hesitate. And I was knee-deep in the water again.

The white couple seated along the wall left after the first hour. Others came and went, but most all were one and done, seeming to buy a drink out of obligation for having walked in and not wanting to be rude for not staying. The small bar lacked the beachfront kitsch of pastel paint and wooden sea life mounted on the walls. No Caribbean music or thumping house jams on rotation. A happy hour menu of beach-body-unfriendly fried foods. No specialty coffee drinks. On occasion, a stray from the herd of street traffic cupped their hands around their face and peered in the window only to shake their head and fall back in step with the pack.

"How does this place stay in business?"

She excused herself from her conversation with the old man and walked to my end of the bar. "Wow. Almost two hours without a word, and then you insult my bar?"

"The bar's yours?"

"Whew, it's a good thing you don't have far to go tonight. Misspelling on the window? Tourist detector? Remember?"

"No, I know, but you said 'we.'"

"Ah, right. Should have expected that."

"Expected what?"

"That you'd pick up on semantics like that. I'll have to be careful, I guess. Not every day you get an award-nominated author sitting at your bar."

The old man perked up. "You say author, Freddy? Who?"

I turned and, with no small amount of effort due to my decreased facial sensation and declining motor control, pushed my lips out in a fleshy duck bill, and pointed two thumbs at myself. "This guy."

"You know James Patterson?"

"Not personally, no, sir." He grunted, waved me off, and went back to his beer. I turned back to her. "'Freddy?' Parents *A Different World* fans, huh?"

She smacked her palm on the bar. "Thank you! So few people get that reference."

I rolled my eyes. "Millennials."

"Right?"

"I was a Whitley man, myself."

"Whatever. Cree Summer could get it."

The old man's baritone boomed from his end of the bar. "Don't sleep on Kim, now. You two light-skinneds over there showing your asses."

We shared a smile, then a laugh, an honest-to-God laugh, the feeling almost forgotten, but so, so welcome.

"So, you read my book?"

"I did."

"And?" She trained her eyes on the ceiling. "Oh, no. You didn't like the book. You didn't like my book?"

"I didn't say that."

"You didn't *not* say that."

She turned away. "How you doing down there, Comrade Clarence? Ready for another one?"

"Oh, come on. For real?"

She cupped her hand around her ear, focusing on the nonexistent refill request. "Be right there. Excuse me."

I turned to he who was now called Clarence. "Why'd she call you comrade?"

Freddy walked down to the old man and poured him another pint. "Oh, lord, why did I say anything? Please, Clarence. Spare me. And him."

"Hush, Freddy." To me. "It's because of my last name."

"Which is?"

"Tartovsky."

"Tartovsky. Your name is Clarence Tartovsky."

Freddy placed the pint in front of him. "Here it comes."

"What, you ain't never seen a Black Russian in a bar before?"

Freddy gave an exasperated sigh. "How does that joke keep getting worse?" Clarence outright guffawed as I grimaced and finished my drink in another gulp, regretted it, and held my empty highball up with a contemptuous throat clear. Freddy walked back to me, moved to pour another, then stopped.

"Are you okay?"

Fist to my mouth, I held back a belch and swallowed the same drink a second time. "I shouldn't have finished that so fast."

"Maybe time to dial it back a bit, yeah?"

"Did you know that, before tonight, I hadn't had a drink in seventeen years? Seventeen!"

I'd reached the stage where I'd lost volume modulation, and she winced at my shout.

"Wow. What are you celebrating?"

Both elbows on the bar, I leaned in and wagged a finger at her. "Changing the subject. I see you. But I can do that, too. I haven't forgotten you hate my book. But it's fine. It's fine." The last two words bled together. I tucked my lips and sucked in my cheeks, hoping I'd return feeling to them, then sat up in a show of mock pride. "I inherited a piece of land."

"No kidding? Here?"

"It's not mine, really. It's my son's. It was supposed to be his. But he's dead, so . . ." She peeked at Clarence, then back to me, her discomfort apparent. "No, no. No sad faces. It's fine, really. I'm fine. He didn't like me so much, I don't think. It's okay, though. It's fine. I said that already. Maybe I'll put a-a-a baseball field on it, and then he'll come back, and we'll have a catch, huh? If I build it, he will come." She didn't get the joke. Or didn't like it. Either way, her eyes went wet with pity and that made me angry. "Whatever. Can I get that drink or what?"

She replaced the bourbon bottle on the shelf. "I think maybe that's enough for tonight, what do you say?"

"Come on. I'm celebrating, right? That's what you said. I'm just going upstairs. Only a danger to myself. If I kill myself falling down the steps, I promise I won't sue you."

"Freddy, what time's Jordan getting off work?"

Clarence gave me a wary once-over. I whipped my head back to Freddy. "Jordan? Boyfriend?"

"Partner."

"Right. Should have figured."

Clarence took a sudden interest in his beer. "Uh-oh."

Freddy crossed her arms over her chest. "Should have figured?"

"No, hang on. That's not what I meant. It's, you know, this town is known for . . . you know, it's a destination spot for . . ."

"Jesus, you can't even say it." She made for the POS machine behind her, the screen lighting her face as she closed my tab. She ripped the receipt free and slid it over, pen attached. "You have yourself a nice evening."

"But I'm still thristy." I turned to Clarence. "Thristy? No?" Clarence shook his head, hissed through his teeth. I stood and steadied myself on the bar, feeling like a cartoon thermometer, the liquor I'd consumed standing in for the red mercury filling the bulb that was my head. "Thought we were friends, comrade." Freddy watched me as I added a tip and signed the receipt. I considered another joke, but whatever portion of my brain that hadn't been battered by bourbon sealed my lips and suffocated any remaining sass in my mouth. Freddy took the slip and placed it in a drawer and walked back to Clarence. I pulled the keys she'd given me earlier from my pocket and made for the door but stopped. "I didn't mean . . . Yeah. Okay, I'll go. Sorry. Good night."

Neither answered. At the door, I turned back one more time, giving a half wave, and though I'd just crossed several lines, concern creased Freddy's face, if only for a moment. The door closed behind me. An ozone smell carried on the breeze and heat lightning illuminated the night sky, crawling through corpulent clouds full to bursting. I considered going back and expanding on my apology, but my hold on my resistance to gravity increased in its tenuousness and there were steps to climb.

The close walls of the stairwell acted as pinball bumpers, my shoulders bouncing from one side to another, knocking loose chipped paint, searching for support as I made my ascent. Several curses at the lock later, after attempting entry into the apartment with my car keys, I remembered that while I'd brought my laptop and shoulder bag with me, I'd left my overnight bag in the car. Another low rumble sounded outside and the window in the stairwell vibrated. Drops spattered against the frosted pane. Retrieving my roller bag would wait until morning, on a walk of shame with plenty to be ashamed of. My face went freshly flush recalling what I'd said to Freddy. She had to know I didn't mean anything by my comment. You would have known what I meant, right, Mal? I know what I'd told you before about the difference between intent and execution, but come on. Countless customers must have made their share of inappropriate comments about all kinds of things, lubricated by a little liquid honesty. I'm sure I was no different. Except I'd made it personal, maybe lashed out a little because she didn't like my book. But she never actually said that, did she? Seventeen sober years and with one drink—okay, yes, you're right, several drinks—I reacted to a perceived slight like a child. See how much I've evolved, Malcolm? Christ, I'm lucky she didn't cancel my reservation right then and there. Best to slither into bed before she changed her mind.

I groped the wall for a switch, and when I found one, an amber light glowed from a polished brass lamp. The studio apartment was small and clean, art prints abounded, along with a not unreasonable number of houseplants, the walls painted in warm reds and browns. Reclaimed wood floors let out a pleasant creak depending on which board my foot fell. A writing desk sat in front of a picture window. Freddy was right. Despite my distaste for the beach, the view was indeed beautiful. A sage green recliner sat situated in a corner of the room not far from the bed. Freddy had taken great care to make the space feel lived in. Muted thunder rumbled again, followed by a flash of light that filled the room. The storm moved closer.

The rain fell harder, breaking the silence, an interruption for which I was grateful. Even when things became challenging between you and me, even when we'd argue until one of us had emptied our endurance, until resolve gave way to fatigue, resolution an impossibility, even when we'd thrown our hands up in disgust, expressed our sarcastic sadness at the other's obtuseness, pitying their inability to understand, we were never silent. Not until the after.

In the after, every footstep, every exhale echoed off my bare apartment walls, off the bookshelves, the bonsai clinging to life without you here reminding me an excess of care would kill it. Each ambient noise amplified, the quiet decibels deafening. I ate out instead of ordering in, walked the shorter distances to places I'd normally drive, anything to evade the volume of the void you'd left. But it was inescapable. Despite my well-developed sense of misanthropy, I told myself I needed the human noise of conversation. Except that wasn't it. Not at all. It was conversation with *you* I needed. Even admitting that, I still couldn't reconcile that need with how rough things had been between us toward the end.

And now here I am, in the quiet again. The unhappily forever after.

Determined to make my own noises, I sat at the desk, retrieved my laptop, and opened a browser, distracting myself with a search for a possible scientific explanation for my episode at the bay, far too late to call my pharmacist or physician. No internet connection. I'd not asked Freddy for the Wi-Fi password and wasn't about to head back down to the bar, considering the show I'd just put on. I scrolled through my cell phone for the reservation email. The words on the screen went in and out of focus and the soft lighting lent no assistance to my ailing eyes suffering from drunkenness and the worsening nearsightedness of aging. The simple effort required to keep one screen from becoming two was herculean. Everything in the room vibrated. My respirations ran rapid and sweat sequined my upper lip. I hated vomiting, so I made for the bed. In through the nose, out through the mouth. Note to self: ask Freddy the name of whatever that scent is in that diffuser. So calming. In the nose, out the mouth. In. Out.

Daddy.

I opened my eyes but couldn't see clearly. Something obstructed my view. The pillow. On my stomach. Had I fallen asleep? Was I still sleeping? A dream. Your voice. A whisper, the way you'd call for me, standing outside my bedroom door when you'd had a nightmare, always enough to rouse me, not enough to pull me from that liminal space between waking and dreaming. I'd stir, lift my head, see an interruption of the light coming in under my door, your legs casting long shadows. The second call a little louder, I'd put feet to floor and accompany you back to your room where I banished the beasties under the bed.

I wanted to push up from this bed, to bring the apartment door into view, but couldn't. I opened my mouth to shout, but managed only a mangled moan. Couldn't turn my head. Couldn't move my arms. My legs. Fear spread in my chest, brain asked mouth and throat to shout for help, but my tongue lay thick and immobile in my mouth.

Then, just within the borders of my periphery, I saw it. Someone in the room. A silhouette. In the recliner. Sitting. No, not sitting. Crouching. Perched.

Another attempt at a scream. Nothing. Lift my head, lift anything. Only my eyes moved from the recliner to the blackness of my pillow and back again.

Gone. Whoever—whatever it was. Gone.

Was I asleep? Was I still sleeping?

No. Something on my back. Pressure. Hands. Pushed me down into the bed. My face turned sideways, deeper into the pillow. Further and further into the mattress until the frame creaked under our collected weight.

I can't breathe.

I can't sit up.

We're going to be late.

Please let me be dreaming, and if I am dreaming, let me wake.

Daddy.

My eyes opened. I screamed.

"Malcolm!"

I sprung to all fours, took a deep panicked breath, then several more. I said your name out loud again, grateful my words had returned. The recliner empty. I searched the studio. Slid open the closet door, not knowing what I'd do if I found someone—*you*—there. The door to the apartment remained locked. Unconvinced, I took to the stairwell, then opened the door to the side street. Rainwater gushed from a gutter. Warm wind blew mist in my face. No mysterious figure running down the street. No wet footprints on the steps behind me.

Back in the apartment, I sat on the edge of the bed and unlocked my phone. Someone had been in here. You had been in here. Except that wasn't possible. So it had to be something else, something that made it so I couldn't move, couldn't talk. That couldn't have been a simple nightmare. It felt so real. Except sitting there, phone in hand, contemplating a call to Freddy, your mother, maybe even the police, I felt the details of what happened already slipping away, like forgetting a dream soon after awakening. But that pressure. That touch. I heard my cries. I felt those hands push me down and it wasn't the first time. You remember.

Adrenaline dump diluted, my head throbbed. I tossed the phone on the recliner and shuffled to the kitchen sink for a glass of water. I downed the glass in a few glugs. My forehead broke out in a sheen of sweat. A cape of fatigue fell over my shoulders, and I dragged it back to the bed with me. I pulled back the comforter, paused, then went down to my knees and clasped my hands in front of me. Your funeral was the last time I'd prayed, though not a prayer of my own making, instead a response to the priest's direction, the rehearsed incantations of ceremony, devoid of passion or purpose. Not now. Now I prayed with fervor, felt the necessity in my words, until it was no longer a prayer but a plea. A prayer unanswered is expected. A plea unanswered, terrifying.

My mind and body spent in equal measure, I climbed into bed, still fully clothed, and pulled the sheets up to my chest. Though warm outside, cold consumed me from inside out, and though my lids grew heavy, and my eyes burned, there would be no sleep again that night. I wondered if there ever would be again.

EIGHT

He is fourteen.

And I am running late. Again.

Malcolm wanted a job as soon as he'd left thirteen behind. Van and I had been determined not to let him make the same mistakes we'd made in our youth with money. That meant to Malcolm we were stingy. Attempts to play us off each other for increased allowances or cash for video games failed, so he filled out his working papers the day after his birthday. As I drive him to school, he points out a sign posted on the front lawn of an assisted-living facility advertising a solid wage for dietary aides.

"What about that?"

"Uh-uh."

"Why 'uh-uh'? It's right down the street from your apartment. I could walk there."

"You could. But you're not."

"So I got to get a job, but I can't get that one? That pays better than bagging them damn groceries."

"Watch your mouth. And I said no."

"Why not?"

"Because I said so."

"I knew you were going to say that."

"Then I guess you could have saved us both the trouble of this conversation, huh?"

"Man, I can't wait to go back to Mommy's. Shoot."

He puts his forehead on the passenger window and watches the world go by, arms crossed, jaw jutted. *Mommy.* It never fails to aggravate me and he knows it. Van eats it up. I pretend not to care. Told myself it was only right a boy his age called me "Dad," convinced it was immature at best for him to speak of his mother like a child. He's not a baby, Van, I'd say. Stop treating him like one. She didn't argue, but she didn't correct him, either. Truth is, I'm all male bluster. I wouldn't have corrected him, either. I did enjoy the "Daddy" days. Every time he calls her "Mommy," especially as a profession of parental preference, I act as if it doesn't hurt by pretending I'm annoyed. Can't let him see the jellyfish stings.

I sigh. "Your great-grandfather lives in that facility."

Into the window. "So?"

"So I don't want you working there because I don't want you spending time around him."

"Thought y'all were tight when you were a kid."

"We were. And then we weren't."

"What happened?"

"It's complicated, Malcolm."

"There you go again. 'Complicated.'"

"Fair enough. Let's just say he turned out to be someone other than who I thought he was."

"Some racial shit, huh?"

"Your mother might let that slide, but cuss again and watch what happens." He covered his mouth. "Good. Yeah, it was definitely some racial *stuff.*"

"Huh."

"What?"

"I don't know. Seems kind of like if I don't get a job there because he's there then he's kind of . . . winning, you know? Like . . . me working there is his problem, not mine, ain't it?"

Among the many things unknown before becoming a parent is how to handle when the child becomes the teacher. They proffer up parental pearls dispensed to them, and while thinking they'd fallen on deaf ears, the child delivers them back with a simplistic effectiveness using their own words instead of the ones we fumbled and stumbled over, attempting to sound sage. He pulls his head away from the window and leans across the console, grinning with the knowledge he's dismantled my argument. My lips tremble, resisting a swell of pride, and I wonder if this is how all the other fathers feel.

"What? Stop staring at me, boy. Trying to drive."

"So?"

"You're on my last nerve, you know that?"

"That's a 'yes.' Man, I can feel that PlayStation controller in my hands already. Turn this car around, Hoke. I got a job to apply for."

"Hoke? You better act like you got some damn sense, Miss Daisy."

He pointed at me. "Ooooh." He pointed at the sky and tsked. "You blasphemed."

"See what you made me do?" I crossed myself and he rolled his eyes. "And that's not blaspheming. I didn't use His name. Get it right. You owe Him some absolutions on Sunday, you little heathen."

"Yeah, yeah. And hey, don't worry about your grandpa. I get that job, I'll make sure the old man gets some special sauce in his oatmeal. You know what I'm saying?"

"Malcolm! Lord, what am I going to do with you?"

"*Now* you blasphemed! Five hundred Hail Marys—now!"

He threw his head back and laughed. And as I turned the car back toward the nursing home, I laughed, too.

NINE

Morning found me with a brain two sizes too big for my skull, swollen with last night's liquor and lingering questions. Standing in stages, hoping to hold back the inevitable pounding in my temples when I reached full vertical, the plan broke down halfway through the process as an intense need to vomit superseded ideas of avoiding the headache I'd earned. I threw open the bathroom door and put a dent in the drywall and my security deposit. Bile blasted the bowl, and I was thankful I'd not ordered any happy hour snacks. Nothing left to heave but hot air, I closed the lid, flushed, rested my arms on top, my head on my arms. Stomach muscles fatigued, throat raw, temples thrummed.

I rinsed my mouth of sick at the sink and went back to bed, exhausted. A betta fish I'd not noticed last night swam in a glass bowl on the writing desk. The sun shone through the bowl and cast a shimmering reflection on the ceiling, interrupted by the fan blades' slow spin. The night's terror came back to me in a rush. Despite my drunkenness, I'd not slept, fearful of another episode of . . . whatever that was. In the light of day, any thoughts of some sort of supernatural visitation (whether it was you or something else made no difference in my discomfort) gave way to ones far more realistic, though no less frightening. Strokes had occurred on both sides of my family, as had cancer. Another relative had a brain tumor. And I'd inherited my anxiety issues from my mother, unable to sidestep a history of mental illness.

My family doctor returned my call within the hour. I led off with the incident at the bay.

"And you don't remember walking out into the water? At all?"

"In my dress slacks? Yeah, no, I don't remember doing that."

"And you didn't have a headache beforehand? No vertigo or anything like that?"

"You're thinking a stroke? I wondered that, too, but no, no headaches. Nothing."

"Hmm."

"Nobody likes when a physician says 'hmmm,' Doc."

"Fair. Sorry. It *is* possible you're adjusting to the increase in your medication, though that would be rather soon, all things considered. Even so, what you'd experienced—that'd be the first I'd heard of that sort of presentation." A pause. "I suppose there's something else it could be, but it's a stretch. Was there a storm by any chance?"

"Sort of. Mostly heat lightning and a little bit of thunder at the time. Why do you ask?"

"Well, what you're describing in some ways sounds like an epileptic episode. While it's exceedingly rare, it's possible you had a photosensitive fit."

"What, a seizure? From the lightning? That's a thing?"

"It can be. But again, it's *very* atypical. Did anything else strange happen yesterday?"

I hesitated. Telling her about the . . . visitation, I guess? . . . would lead to more questions. More questions meant admitting I'd fallen off the wagon, although in fairness (again, to me) one night of drinks didn't constitute a fall. More like the wagon hit a rut in the road and I'd slipped off the edge but regained my grip before my feet hit the ground. No way I'd let myself feel again like I felt that morning. Of course, I wouldn't. I didn't have to tell her any of that. When it's that easy to lie to yourself, lying to someone else is light work.

But I had to know what that was, and you couldn't tell me. I described to her the inability to speak or move, the feeling of a presence in the room, of pressure on my back. I left out that it felt like your presence. Your pressure. That I'd heard your whisper. She affirmed each explanation with an assured "mm-hmm" as if she'd heard them many times before.

"Welcome to the world of sleep paralysis."

"I'm sorry?"

"It's far more common than you might think, though it's still not all that well understood. Without getting too technical, it's a condition where your REM sleep and waking cycles overlap. You end up stuck between waking and dreaming."

"And the pressure? The . . . thing in the room?"

"Part and parcel for the condition, believe it or not. The anecdotal evidence points more to a feeling of something sitting on their chest, not their back, but everyone is different."

"So, what makes me the lucky one to have this?"

"All the hallmarks are there. Take your pick. Stress."

"Check."

"Medication."

"Check."

"Not drinking, though."

I paused.

"Right."

She paused.

"Not drinking, though?"

"That would be pretty dumb of me to do on medication, wouldn't it?"

"Yes, it certainly would be."

"Right."

First a brief lecture about the dangers of mixing alcohol and antianxiety meds, then a suggestion I see a neurologist. Hangover headache in full swing, I agreed with zero intention of following through. I felt some sense of relief hearing her list of factors and was content to leave this strange episode behind me. As if reading my thoughts, your whisper echoed in my ears, mocking the ease with which I dismissed your possible presence. You never understood what you perceived as a contradiction in me, my embrace of both science and God, said it was hypocritical, given our debates over my devotion to the latter. God was as real to me as any formula or calculation, my continued sobriety as much evidence for His existence as any photograph. Maybe my expectation you'd understand at your age was unrealistic. You were smart but you didn't know everything. But then maybe I didn't know everything I thought I knew, either, because if my abstinence was my proof of His being, then last night marked my fall from grace.

Somewhere in the middle of my silent solipsism, my doctor made one final plea for therapy. False promises made, I ended our call. I then called the number for the local real estate office my grandfather's attorney had given me. They said they'd send an agent to meet me at the property in an hour. Showered, shaved, teeth brushed, I went downstairs. The bar was dark, not opening until early afternoon. No eye contact to avoid, no awkward apologies to make, not for now. Maybe today would be okay.

You might not remember, but one of my visitation weeks, I took you to your favorite pizza spot, only to find they'd changed their hours and closed early on Sundays. You were so mad as to be inconsolable. I'd never cared for their pizza, I feel I can tell you that now, so I said "Oh well, man plans, and God laughs." You rolled your eyes back so hard I only saw the whites and truly thought you were about to slip into a fit. Well, if it makes you feel any better, I'm certain God had himself a hearty howl when I arrived at the site. A car sat parked sideways at the end of the gravel trail, the real estate brokerage logo emblazoned on the driver's side door. Freddy leaned against the hood. Her curls pulled back into a tight bun, she'd traded last night's jeans and black T-shirt for a sleeveless blouse and a pair of linen slacks. She waved as I approached, confirming my fear that she was the agent I was scheduled to meet. Her face dropped when my car pulled close enough for her to see the driver.

I parked and cast my eyes skyward. *Seriously?* I tilted my rearview and checked my hair, breathed into my hand, no vomit odor, good, wait, what am I doing? As I stepped out of the car, her face went tense, her lips battling between polite grin and grimace. My ears went hot, and flop sweat pooled on top of my head.

Don't be clever. Apologize. Don't be clever. Apologize. "We've got to stop meeting like this, huh?"

Damn it.

"Mmm."

"So, you half Jamaican or what?"

"Excuse me?"

I dipped into a poor man's patois. "How many job you got?" *You're doubling down now? What is wrong with you?* "You know. *In Living Color?* The Desmonds . . . how many job . . ." *You are an idiot. Stop talking.*

"No, I get the reference. 'Excuse me' means I'm unclear as to why you're talking to me like we're friends or as to what makes you comfortable enough to ask me if I'm half anything."

"Wait. So you're not . . . ?"

"Is that your business? And what does it matter if I am or not?"

No answer for a question I'd never been asked. I'd spent my life seeking out other mixed-race folks, prided myself on my ability to know my own. In unfamiliar settings, finding someone like me offered an immediate icebreaker, a comrade in arms with whom to navigate the white spaces I'd often found myself in, where I'd count the seconds until someone made *that* face, ready to ask *that* question. Finding a kindred spirit, having someone to exchange smirks with when a white person acted the fool, joking about which half of ourselves liked this show or that musician, was the warmest, most comfortable security blanket I could imagine. Freddy's question ripped that blanket from my shoulders, left me exposed and shivering. I'd never imagined *my* question as another version of *the* question, but inadvertent or not, I'd asked exactly that—what are you?

"You're right," I said. "That was too familiar."

"Should have listened to her. She said don't go. Should have listened."

"Her?"

"My wife. You know? The one you 'should have figured' I had."

I cringed and massaged my forehead. "About that . . ."

"Yeah, about that."

"There was—is—no excuse for what I said. I'm just . . . I'm going through some things." She put her hands on her hips. "And that sounds exactly like an excuse. I swear, I don't mean it to be. I'm embarrassed to be standing here in front of you, considering my behavior last night, and even now, I can't stop putting my foot in my mouth. I'm uncomfortable, and when I'm uncomfortable, I make bad jokes. Like, really bad."

"You weren't joking last night."

"You're right. I got defensive about you not liking my book, and I lashed out. I don't know what to say."

"Sorry would be a good start. A real one. Not a half-assed one you toss my way when you're one foot out the door."

"As many times as you need me to say it."

"One would work."

"I'm very sorry. You didn't deserve that."

The skin around her eyes smoothed. Lines around her mouth receded.

"Thank you. I appreciate that. But if that's the bag you go into when you feel attacked, you might have some things in that bag to unpack, and I'm not going to do that for you."

"You're right again. And understood."

We both took a deep breath. A corner of her mouth turned up.

"And I have three jobs. We also own a bike shop in town."

"Okay, wow. Really doing the most, huh? How'd you two end up running things in this quiet little beach town?"

"Jordan runs the shop. I handle the bar. She lived down here already. My dad is—was—from here. He owned the Scholar. I was working in tech when he died. He was big on Black folks owning real estate so he left the bar to me."

"You must have left behind some good money."

"I did. But I love my father." I shoved my hands in my pockets and shifted my feet and wondered if you were listening just then. She noticed the change. "Shit. My turn to apologize?"

"No, no, it's fine. So, why the bar *and* real estate?"

"You said yourself the bar isn't exactly lighting the world on fire." I cringed and opened my mouth to apologize again but she waved it off. "No, you were right. I'm well aware we're not a destination location. Anyway, transferring the building to my name, I really got into the whole real estate process. A few sales here and there keep us afloat. I know my dad wanted it to stay open. Makes it worth it."

"I'm sure he's proud."

She took a deep breath, then let it out short and sharp. "We should probably get into it, you think?"

"Please."

We walked the property, stepped over puddles where water had collected from last night's downpours. The sky was bright but gray, the air smelled of grass and mud. Seagulls whirled over the water, skimmed the surface, cried out over the shush of small waves washing up on the beach. We came closer to the shore, and I stopped short, recalled my trancelike journey into the bay the day before, not wanting to go any farther lest it happen again. Freddy walked on, unnoticing.

"You've got a few hundred acres here, maybe more and . . . Hey, are you okay?"

"What? Yes. I'm fine."

"Why did you stop?"

"I did stop, didn't I? Sorry. I saw something. A fox, I think."

"A fox? Around here? Doubt it."

It seemed I'd accumulated some goodwill, so I decided against squandering it by telling her I'd seen one last night, hearing how the explanation sounded like mansplaining in my head. Know what that is, Malcolm? Growth.

"So, a few hundred acres?"

"At least. I didn't have time to do a records search before I came out, but I'll verify that number if you decide you're listing the land. This lot will fetch you a prime price. Bayfront property is a hot commodity. You sure you don't want to hold on to it and build a house here? There are some pretty great financing options these days . . ."

Her voice trailed off and I mumbled affirmations, to what, I didn't know. I was transfixed by the beach. The waves. There was no storm now. No lightning flashes. But I felt a pull toward the shore, strong enough that I would not take another step for fear of ending up in the water again. I faced down the waves, as if turning my back to them would grant them the opportunity to drag me back toward them, their crests claws pulling me into their undertow.

"Hey. Seriously. You all right? You keep kind of spacing out."

"Hmm?" I watched the water while I responded. When I realized she hadn't answered, I saw her staring at me, eyebrows connected in a worried arch. "Me? I'm fine."

"Okay. It's just you were mumbling something to yourself. And you seemed like, I don't know, like you were somewhere else."

"What was I saying?" I asked.

"Don't know. Couldn't make it out. Hey, are you sure you're ready for this? You don't have to decide here and now. This can be a tough decision as it is, but under these circumstances? Dude, I get it if you need time."

"Do you?" She raised her hands in defense. There had been more edge in my voice than I'd intended. "I didn't mean to snap, Freddy. Sorry. Again. It's just this whole thing has me a little upside down. Thinking about things I'd rather not think about."

"That's not unusual. There can be a lot of emotions tied up in this process. Especially when family is involved."

"True, but . . ."

She waited for me to finish. When I didn't, I saw she wanted to ask 'but what?' and I wanted to tell her. I wanted to say out loud what happened yesterday and last night, to have someone who didn't know me, who had no reason to spare my feelings or tell me what I wanted to hear, how all that had happened was strange coincidence, that I was overthinking things, that I'd had a very vivid, very specific, very realistic nightmare, that you hadn't been in my room. But then she might not say that and then what?

"But?"

"You're right. I maybe do need some time to sit with this."

"I think that's smart."

"If we were to move forward, what would we do next?"

She explained she'd have to go back to the office for listing paperwork and arrange for testing of the ground, something about water runoff, and that she could meet me back at the bar to sign the necessary forms. So simple and easy. I should have agreed then and should have ended this all with a few pen strokes. All I had to do was say yes, but the decision felt too final, even though a close to this chapter—your chapter—was what I'd told myself I'd wanted. As Freddy drove away, the remembrance of you at my door calling me in the middle of the night to be your monster slayer returned, replayed on a loop in my mind's eye, and not completely unbidden. My body remembered the feeling when you showed your concern and admiration as I put my face to the floor, scouring with my hand beneath the bed frame, despite your warnings a creature could dart out a slimy, taloned hand and pull me into the void. My body remembered how I hugged you afterward, how all the fear you'd held in your muscles melted away when I told you there were no Balrogs under the bed.

Maybe I didn't want to be free of this. Maybe I'd work my way to a place where the memories brought only the feeling that being a hero to your child can bring, especially when, toward the end, I was anything but. Maybe there would be a time when that sense memory was stronger than my grief, my guilt, not only over what happened, but over the fact that I wasn't always happy to be your hero. That sometimes annoyance at your asks was my initial instinct. Maybe being here let me see things through a clearer lens. Maybe being your father was what I was meant to be. Maybe this land was a gift.

Maybe I was full of shit.

Daddy.

"Jesus!"

I spun but saw nothing. No whispering wraith. You weren't there. Except you were. Because I wasn't drunk or half asleep. Wide awake. No seizure. No stroke. Your voice in my ear turned every reassurance my doctor had given me to dandelion seeds in the wind. Every ounce of unease poured back into me. I called Freddy on my way off the property. No rose-colored reminiscence would change my mind. This chapter needed to end.

Clarence lifted his chin at me when I walked in the door to the Scholar.

"Colson Half-Whitehead! What's happening, brother?"

I waved him off and sat at the bar. The door opened behind me. A couple peeked their heads in. Freddy offered them a friendly greeting, but they waved and backed out.

"That happen a lot?" I asked Freddy.

"More than I'd like. If it wasn't for Clarence here, I'd probably shut it down."

Clarence raised his glass. "We got to watch out for our own."

Freddy blew him a kiss, which he caught. She then grabbed a manila folder from the shelf behind her and slid it to me. Colored stickers showed me where to sign. Freddy said something again about a groundwater test and the cost coming out of the settlement fees once the property was sold. I'll confess I half-listened while I signed. I just wanted it all to be done. I worked my way through the pile, evened out the stack, and handed them back to her. She reviewed them, then told me the contractor was one of her few regulars and that he'd head to the site tomorrow. A little digging, wouldn't take more than a few hours. Then the land would be listed.

Freddy offered a celebratory drink, but on the drive over, I'd decided I'd check out of the room after the papers were signed and head home. I'd reserved the room through the weekend, thinking a change of scenery might stir the creative juices, but I had no desire to set foot in that room again, even to pack, let alone spend another night there. I entertained, just for a second, leaving the bag in the room altogether. As I was about to share this decision with Freddy, my phone buzzed in my pocket. I held up one finger while I unlocked the screen.

An email from my agent, Emily. Another pass on the novel. We'd exhausted the list of big houses and their imprints, as well as a few of the larger independent presses. Not time to panic, she said, but time for another conversation, and that maybe we'd given readers enough of this theme in the first book, that perhaps this one was too didactic, too much finger-wagging, that readers didn't want to be preached to—not that you're preaching and well, we can talk about it but don't get anxious, but call her as soon as I can, and I was back in my office with David all over again. I pulled up her contact, hovered my thumb over the call button, then locked my phone and set it facedown on the bar.

"Yeah, I'll have that drink."

Freddy tilted her head toward my phone. "Celebrating or mourning?"

I put my credit card on the bar. "Keep it open."

"That bad?"

"You hiring?"

"Ouch. There's always real estate."

I stood and walked to where Clarence sat. I gestured to the stool next to him, and he pulled it away from the bar, making room for me to sit. Freddy brought a bourbon neat with a water back. The highball with water stayed full. The glass with bourbon did not.

Funny how fast habits take hold again. My head buzzed after the third drink and my early exit plan exited. I'd have to stay one more night. But that room. Not in that room. More booze might have guaranteed a restful night, but then again, it might not. I swirled the swallow of bourbon. Freddy stood in front of me.

"You good?"

"Me? Sure. Actually, no. Can I ask you something? Both of you?"

"I'm glad you finally brought it up," Clarence said. "That shirt is all wrong for your body type, son."

Freddy flicked her towel at him. "Clarence! You want to be cut off?"

"There you go. You high yellows always sticking together."

Freddy turned back to me. "Ask your question."

"Okay, for the record, I'm only asking this so you can tell me I can relax, that nothing is wrong with me, or that maybe something is wrong with me, but it's a completely normal wrong with me, the kind of wrong with me where I might need help, but that's okay because it's the kind of wrong with me where I *can* actually get help, okay?"

Freddy shook her head, dazed. "My eyes just went crossed, but sure, okay."

Clarence leaned in, and Freddy rested her elbows on the bar. I took a deep breath then talked until I was out of said breath. The sudden immobility, the pressure on my back, the shadow in the chair, your voice—let all the crazy out. Freddy didn't appear the least bit fazed.

"So, you have sleep paralysis?"

"Wait, you've heard of this?"

"Jordan gets it sometimes."

"You're serious? You're not messing with me? You know what this is?"

"Not messing with you. She even jokes she has a sleep paralysis demon. Sees it in the room. One night was creepy as hell. She was making this awful sound, and I couldn't wake her up right away. When she did finally snap out of it, she told me she was trying to say 'help.' She was actually mad at me for a minute because she thought I was ignoring her."

"Oh, man. Oh, man, oh man, oh man, Freddy, I want to pull you across this counter and kiss you."

"Please don't."

"You have no idea how much better this makes me feel. I thought I was losing my mind."

"Glad I could help." She faced Clarence and her light dimmed. "What's wrong with you?"

Clarence sat, mouth tight, eyes clear, despite hours of drinking. "Y'all call it what you want but sounds to me like you got a haint."

"A what?" I said.

"Do you know anything? A haint. A ghost."

Freddy threw up her hands. "Don't listen to him. With his drunk ass."

Clarence's eyes went from clear to electric, and he aimed their charge at Freddy. "Don't you do that. Don't you make fun of me or say I don't know what I'm saying."

"Go on, then. Go on and tell him about that Louisiana voodoo bullshit."

"It ain't bullshit, Freddy, and you're not right letting him think it's something else."

"No, *you're* not right. Look at him. You already got him petrified."

"I'm okay. Say more, Clarence?"

"See? He don't need you sticking up for him. This is a grown-ass man sitting here." He leaned in again. "This ever happen to you before you came here?" I shook my head. "Mmm-hmm. And you say you heard your boy's voice?" I squeezed my lips together and nodded. "And that land you selling. Said it was supposed to go to your boy. What you know about it?"

"Just that it was in the family."

"The white side?"

I nodded. Freddy spoke through a clenched jaw. "Clarence."

"So what do you *really* know about it?"

Freddy slapped the counter. "Uh-uh, Clarence. Too far."

"I'll tell you something I bet you *don't* know. You know what the name of this city means? 'Somebody of mixed European and African origin.' Now why do you think that is?"

"Clarence! Enough!"

Clarence leaned back in retreat from Freddy's ire. I wanted to know more while not wanting to hear another word. Clarence shrunk into himself and grumbled into his glass. "Just saying."

"I'm sorry about that," Freddy said, ignoring Clarence's pouting. "You okay?"

My eyes stayed on Clarence, rotating the drink in his hands, a scolded child. Conflicting thoughts slid slippery through my mind. "I'm fine. I'm . . . yeah, I'm going to go. Good night. Night, Clarence."

Clarence nodded. Freddy admonished him on my way out the door. Something about how I was hurting. Fragile, maybe. I hadn't realized my cracks were showing.

A warm mist floated outside. The sky snarled a warning of another storm to come. I rounded the corner and entered the stairwell to the apartment. At the top of the steps, that damned door. My heart pounded.

Were you behind that door? If you were, then you'd violated the agreement we'd made, or rather, the agreement I'd come to you on your behalf, wherein I'd say what I needed to say, what needed to be said, and you don't respond because you can't. I mean, what am I supposed to do with that, Malcolm? You talking when you're not supposed to be able to do that. How does one react when God answers?

But maybe it wasn't you. Maybe Clarence was right. Maybe behind that door was a haint. Something unsettled from the site, something I'd brought back with me. Except the idea was patently ridiculous. There are no ghosts. No spirits.

Not even holy ones, you'd ask.

That's not the same, I'd say.

Not different, either, you'd say.

You're not supposed to be talking, remember, I'd say.

And it was quiet again.

Minutes passed standing, staring at that door. I had to sleep, but I knew I wouldn't. I knew more drinks would help, but I didn't want to go back to the bar. I know how much this sounded like an excuse to get drunk again, Malcolm, I know, but I promise you, that wasn't what I was doing. I honestly didn't know what else to do. And then I did. A few of those little airplane-sized bottles would be no different from popping prescription pills. When they're gone, they're gone. Just dragging my toes in the dirt off the back of the wagon. Tomorrow I'd pull my legs back up and in and keep them there.

I opened the map application on my phone and searched for the closest liquor store, found one a short car ride away, yet too far to walk in the impending rain, and I was not sober enough to drive. I ordered a rideshare and waited in the doorway. The storm set foot on land before the car arrived, wind howling past in gusts.

As I sat in the back, my buzz amplified my usual car sickness. I rested my head against the cool of the passenger's-side window and closed my eyes. The tires' hum buzzed loud in my ears, so I pulled away to open the window an inch. The mist on my forehead, the breeze made cool by the car's velocity calmed the bubbling in my gut, the spins in my head. I closed my eyes again.

I woke to the crack and pop of gravel and dirt replacing the paint-roller sounds of wet asphalt beneath the tires. The car slowed and I sat up. The driver turned on his high beams.

"You sure this is the right address, man? There ain't shit here."

"You were supposed to take me to the wine and spirits store."

"Wine and spirits? That's not what I got here." He tapped his phone on its mount. I fumbled for my phone. A joke, surely. Or something more sinister. Was this guy going to rob me? I pulled up the rideshare app and saw I had entered the location for the property. Impossible. I opened my notes and pasted into them the last thing I'd copied. A phone number. Not the address. I'd typed the address of the property into the rideshare app.

When . . .

When had I . . .

When had I done that?

Had I . . .

Had I done that?

The driver slowed to a stop. He watched me with a wary eye while I wondered how we'd arrived here, then told me he didn't carry cash. I reassured him I was neither of the mind nor the physical capacity to rob him. His substantial shoulders pulled away from his cauliflower ears. He asked should he take me to the liquor store when a flash of fur ran across his headlights and into the reeds near the shore. "You see that?"

"See what?"

"Drive ahead."

He looked me up and down, then crept the car forward. I searched the tall grass for movement, eyes fooled by the sway caused by the increasing wind speeds. Best to take him up on his offer to reroute to the store and drink myself into some semblance of slumber before the storm swelled. But I had to see if I saw what I saw. I asked him to park. He was reluctant. A sizable cash tip was my promise for his time. To ease his reticence, I flashed cash to prove I wasn't lying and after some further hesitation, he agreed. I got out and walked toward the reeds. He called out from his open window, arms hanging over the door, asking what I'd seen.

I shushed him and moved forward. Another flash of orange and brown bounded away from me, closer to the sand. I ran after it. When I reached the beach, I removed my dress shoes and socks and rolled up the cuffs of my pants, not wanting to get sand in either. The glow from the headlights spanned a short swath of shore. I scanned up and down, back to the reeds, saw nothing, and dropped my arms in defeat. A car door closed behind me. Gravel shifted underfoot as the driver jogged down to me.

"Hey, man. I know you're tipping, but I'm not sure whoever owns this land is going to be cool with you taking a nighttime stroll out here, you know?"

"It's mine."

"What is?"

"The property. It's mine."

"Oh. Right on. Like, all of it?"

"A couple hundred acres. Or so I'm told."

"You don't know?"

"Long story."

"Well damn, maybe I should rob you." His tone lacked mirth, but his playful punch to my arm allayed my fears, no malice in his goofy grin. "Is there, like, a house or something?"

"No."

"So, what do you do with a couple hundred acres?"

"Sell it."

"For real? Man, I'd totally build a dope little beach house here. Or one of them, what do you call them, tiny homes, you know? I'd be out on that water every day." The lights from the car amplified the glimmer in his eyes when he talked about the water. His enthusiasm reminded me of you. He saw me staring and shifted his feet. "Anyway, we should probably go. This rain's about to get serious. You can smell it."

"Just one more minute." I stepped closer to the water. "I know I saw it. She's wrong."

"Saw what now? Who's wrong?"

"Maybe it went down to the water. Do they do that?" His question registered on a delay. "Sorry. A fox. Someone told me they're not around here."

"A fox? On the bay? Nah, man. Doubt it. Whoever told you that is right."

His response deflated me. Twice denied, by two locals. If not a fox, then what? I saw something. "Do you believe in haints?"

"What's a haint?"

"A ghost."

"Oh, nah, not really." Wind blew a length of long hair into his face, and he pushed it away. "I got an aunt who's real into tarot cards and whatnot. Crystals, all that stuff. Says she's a witch or some shit. I don't know. It's real enough to her, I guess. Wasn't ever really my thing."

"And what about God?

"Man, is this going to be one of those things where you ask me if I've accepted Christ as my lord and savior? Because that ain't worth the tip."

"No. No, it's not that."

"I don't know. Maybe? I mean I don't go to church or nothing. I sort of pray sometimes, but that just feels like I'm kind of talking to myself, you know?" I did know. "This is probably going to sound corny, but, like, if there is a god, like with a capital *G*, I hope it doesn't matter if I believe in Him or not. More kind of hoping He believes in me."

"How would you know?"

He took a beat. "I don't know. Never really thought about it until you asked. But I think maybe that's what faith is, yeah? Not exactly believing in God, but believing He believes in you." He blew out. "Fuck, that's deep, huh?"

I opened my mouth to answer when I heard that scream in the distance again, this time from behind the car.

"You hear that?"

The driver turned and peered into the darkness. "Hear what?"

On my second plodding step back up the beach, a searing pain shot through my foot and quickly traveled up my calf. The intensity dropped me to the ground on my rear. I grabbed at my leg and yelped. The driver ran to me and crouched down.

"You all right, man? The hell happened?"

"I don't know. My leg is on fire."

We surveyed the sand and saw nothing. He told me to sit tight and made his way back to the car, returning with a small flashlight. He swept the beam back and forth, then stopped. A prismatic reflection gleamed off a translucent glimmering glob. I knew what it was before he said it.

"Fuuuuck. Jellyfish. Jesus, they're everywhere. Storm must have torn them to pieces and washed them up. Man, talk about unlucky. Should have kept them wingtips on, I guess."

My teeth ground grit between them. The pain in my foot and leg was excruciating, like nothing I'd ever experienced. I remembered your grandfather, silent and shivering on his bed in the hotel room, what it must have felt like to be covered in stings, entire body alight with invisible flames.

"Can you walk?"

I nodded and accepted his help getting to my feet. "You heard it, right? The fox? You heard that scream?"

"Only scream I heard was you hollering just now."

The briefest moment on the ball of my foot sent pain lancinating up my limb, sapping my will to argue about my phantom fox. He offered his shoulder and wrapped his arm around my waist as I hobbled to the car. I sat back and helped my leg in. He closed the door while I buckled up. The gears sung as he reversed and turned onto the gravel road. The sting throbbed in time with my pulse, and I hissed.

"You want me to take you to the ER?"

"And sit there for hours? No, thanks."

"I don't know, man. Some of those stings can be nasty, depending on the type."

"I'm not worried. Liquor store. I'll self-anesthetize."

He agreed. As we drove down the road, I placed my head against the window again. Crouched off to the side of the dirt road, tail curled around its paws, sat the fox. If the driver had seen it, he showed no signs of having done so. Though expecting it had vanished, out the rear window I saw the fox illuminated red by the taillights' glow. I watched him until he disappeared into the darkness, then resumed my position in my seat. Swollen drops of rain spattered against the windshield, intermittent at first, then in a deluge. The driver half turned his head toward me. We remarked on our fortunate timing, but the rest of the ride passed in silence. We pulled back onto Route One. I watched the neon lights go by, surf shops and beach bars lending their luminescence to the night sky. We reached the wine and spirits store. Mini bottles of bourbon in hand, I returned to the car and sipped from one as we made our way back to Freddy's apartment. A space was open in front of the building, and he pulled alongside the curb.

"So, do you believe?" the driver asked.

"In?"

"Ghosts. God. Either. Both."

"I'm not sure."

"About which one?"

"Either. Both." I pulled the door handle, then stopped. "Hey, man, I never asked your name."

"Mo."

"Thanks for the conversation tonight, Mo."

I dug into my pocket for my wallet and pulled out two twenties. He folded them, nodded thanks, and put them in his pocket. I stepped out of the car onto my stung leg, and the pain buckled my knee. He opened his door and circled around the front, but I waved him off with my free hand. He stood for a moment in front of the car, needles of rain filling the headlight beams. Another wave from me and he got back in the car, then drove off with a hybrid hum. Droplets dripped from my earlobes, my nose, the now saturated paper bag. I cradled the sack from the bottom, not wanting the bottles to tear through. I downed the bottle I'd opened in the car then sneered at the door to the apartment stairs like it had done me wrong. In a way, I guess it had. Thunder cracked and the rain fell harder still. I limped for the entrance. Once inside, I regretted sending the driver away. The pain in my foot made negotiating the steps slow going. I dragged my shoulder along the wall. The handrail squeaked and wobbled with each step, threatening to pull free from its anchors.

The blessed banister held, and I reached the door to the apartment. My leg pulsed, the skin tight, feeling full of fluid. An insidious itch crawled through my foot and ankle joints, as though the venom had burrowed into my bones. I hand-walked my way to the bed and sat, opened another bottle, sipping at first, but sitting seemed to increase the pain, so I downed that one, too, enough to take me across the threshold. I lay back. The edges of my vision vibrated, then dimmed. I welcomed oblivion with arms spread across the mattress, embraced the sensation of slipping into slumber.

The itch in my leg roused me often. I woke not to scratch, but because of the pain induced by my quick, deep scratching. Trapped somewhere in between waking and dreaming, I scratched until my leg went wet, until my fingers went deeper, past the flesh, flaying fascia, pushing past muscle, twanging violin strings of tendon and nerve, until my fingertips scraped bone, and still I dug, rooted until I'd pulled that itch from the marrow. The grate of my nails against tibia and fibula reverberated through my hand up my arm until I felt it in my jaw.

I sat up, frantic, and pulled back my pant leg. Raised purple streaks snaked up and across my calf, tracing a poison path along my nerve fibers, but the skin was otherwise intact. Reddened from scratching, but no broken skin. No torn muscles. No bright white bone nestled in a nest of gore.

Another nightmare. But the scratching, the digging, had felt so real. The images so clear in my mind, even in those waking moments. My fingers covered with blood. The shimmer of connective tissue as it stretched,

then gave way, revealing the organic mechanics beneath. My limb was a wonder. I could not reconcile the pain and my mind's eye images with the fact my leg remained whole.

I breathed a relieved sigh, swung my legs to the edge, then threw up on the sun-dappled patch of floor at my feet, undulating light again filtering through the fishbowl. I'd slept through the night but felt anything but rested. I hobbled to the kitchen for paper towels and a trash bin to collect my mess, then changed out of my clothes, damp from the rain or sweat soaked from my nightmare, I wasn't sure. The sheets were wet as well. I stripped the bed, worried I might still discover blood on the sheets, thankful to find none.

My leg throbbed as I stood at the mirror and brushed my teeth. The pain cut through the hangover fog, my mind clearer than it had been in the last twenty-four hours. With that clarity came anger. At myself for throwing away nearly two decades of sobriety. Again. At Freddy, fair or not, for enabling my backslide. At my grandfather, for leaving this land to you, and therefore me, given all that had passed between him and me— between you and me. I spit my disdain into the sink and washed it down the drain. In a matter of time, all this would go swirling away as well. I only had to turn on the faucet.

I limped back to the bedroom, stuffed my wet clothes into my carry-on, and made for the steps. The rain clouds had cleared, and I shielded my eyes against the high morning sun. I took a deep breath and shuffled down the street to my car. Some passersby saw my ungainly gait and gave me a wide berth. Those who didn't flashed annoyed looks and mumbled under their breath when I made no move to step out of their way. I didn't care. Evacuation, not accommodation, was the mission at hand.

The effort needed to reach my car and the resultant discomfort swept sweat down my forehead. As I sat, my leg pulsed harder, the sock elastic constricting my calf, my foot feeling as though it were spilling over the sides of my shoe. I loosened the laces, wiped wetness from my face, and started the car. The hustle and bustle of the main drag shrank in my rearview, and I let loose a breath I hadn't realized until then I had been holding.

Away from the beach, back in farm country, Emily called. I knew the conversation that awaited, but I was already antsy about the impending quiet of a long car ride, and I wasn't ready to talk to you again as I hadn't yet forgiven you for breaking our agreement, so I answered her call. Her tone was awash in worry.

"Are you okay?"

"Why wouldn't I be?"

"No, it's just I emailed you yesterday about the manuscript passes and you didn't get back to me. You usually answer pretty quickly."

"Yeah, no, some things came up and I've been head down dealing with them the last few days."

"Oh. Anything you want to talk about?"

"Not particularly, no."

"Oh. Okay."

A protracted pause followed, one with which I'd become intimately familiar since your death, one in which the other side of the dialogue weighed their options about what to say next—more condolences, more small talk, or get right to business, if there was business to be gotten to, or maybe that was too cold, too uncaring so go with more small talk, but maybe he's tired of small talk, and more condolences only bring up the things he's trying to move past. Sometimes I spoke first to break the silence and spare them their existential crisis. Sometimes I let them stew in the discomfort of their indecision, even if their uncertainty came from a place of genuine caring, which it almost always did. This day, however, a lack of patience and a waning pain tolerance served Emily a snap she didn't deserve.

"What is it you need, Emily?"

"Right. Sorry. Are you driving?"

"Does that matter?"

"No. Well, maybe. Did you see the list for the next round of submissions? I sent it this morning."

"Haven't seen it, no."

"Oh. Okay. There are some good houses on there. Again, a little smaller

than we'd hoped originally, but still reputable. They've got solid distribu-
tion. We can still get some coverage in the trades. If we get picked up."

"If?"

"Hey, I'm as surprised as you are that we're having trouble selling this.
I mean, I am and I'm not. The second book, it's tricky work and readers
are fickle these days."

I chuffed. "These days."

"What's that?"

"Nothing. So what's next?"

"Let's just see how this round goes."

"Yeah, but then what?"

"Like I said, let's just see how this goes. I haven't given up yet."

"You sure about that?"

"Sorry?"

"My tenure is at risk, Emily."

"What? Since when?"

"Since the department head said the new manuscript is too Black. That
the first one rode the wave of the moment, and now I'm drying out on the
beach. Like you just said."

"Wait, hang on. When did I say that?"

"You didn't say it, say it. Not in so many words. But don't worry, message received. Too Black. *Got it.*"

Another call beeped. The display read Freddy.

"Hang on, Emily. I have to take this." She sighed loudly before I
clicked over. "Hey, Freddy."

"Where are you?"

"On the road. I have classes to teach tomorrow."

"You need to get back here. Right now."

"What? Why? Oh, the wall. I'm sorry, but the door slipped out of my
hand. You can take it out of the security deposit, right?"

"The wall? No. Meet me at the property. How far away are you?"

"Freddy, what happened?"

A beat. "You just need to get here as soon as you can, okay?"

TEN

He is fifteen.

And I am anxious. And I am angry.

I sit at the dining room table, drawing endless circles on an envelope until the spirals turn into one dark blue blot, until the paper becomes so saturated with ink that it gives way, and the ballpoint digs into the wood beneath. I curse at having marked the table and add it to the list of grievances I will unleash when he walks in the door. *If* he walks in the door. Because I have no idea where he is.

Footsteps echo in the hall, slowing as they approach the door to my apartment. A key slides home. I put aside the pen and envelope, sit straight, remove any sense of worry from my face, and replace it with fury. He cannot see I was concerned. Not now. Consequences first. Compassion after.

His shoulders drop when he sees me at the table. His backpack slides off and he leaves it on the floor near the door, a habit he knows drives me crazy. He avoids my scrutiny, which is good, because I'm not sure I'm sufficiently suppressing the outward expression of my relief at seeing he is alive and unharmed. His sudden interest in the floor tells me I've made my desired feelings clear.

"Let's hear it."

"Hear what?"

"Boy, if I have to ask again."

"If you have to ask what again? You ain't *asked* me anything." I stand, hands in fists, knuckles on table, making brief his bravado. He side-eyes, arms crossed over his chest. "I was at the mall, okay? I stayed after to talk with Pop-Pop for a little, then Trevor drove some of us over to hang out at the food court."

"I'm sorry, you stayed to talk to whom?"

"Pop-Pop."

"Who is Pop-Pop?"

"Seriously? Great-granddad."

"Uh-uh. No. Pop-Pop? No, you don't call him that."

"What? Why?"

"Excuse me? Because I said so, that's why." He shoves his hands in his pockets and whispers, chin tucked to his chest. "Speak up, you got something to say."

"I said he's just a lonely old man."

"Right. Sure. Okay." I scoff. "See, this is why I didn't want you working there. I knew he'd get his hooks in you. Manipulative prick."

"Hooks? You act like he's dangerous or something."

"He is, Malcolm."

"Whatever, man."

"What is with you, Mal? Huh? You've been like this since you started that job. Is this from your little friends working there? This attitude? You so cool you don't even call or text to tell me where you are? Or even ask if you're allowed to go?"

"My phone died."

"So, you charge it, and you text me, you understand? And who is Trevor?"

"Mommy knows him. She said it was fine."

"Stop calling her Mommy!" He shrinks from my shout. I take a breath and lower my volume. "You are fifteen years old, Malcolm. You're a young man. You don't need to call your mother that. It's childish."

"If I'm such a young man, why you keep treating me like a baby, huh? *Dad*?"

There is toxin in his tone, and the poison goes right to my heart. He knows it. No longer does he avert his eyes. His intensity I can hardly withstand, but I keep my eyes on his, no matter how much I want to dodge his disdain. We hold this standoff for what feels like minutes, waiting each other out, seeing who breaks the stare first, who speaks first, who rolls over and shows their belly. He walks toward me, then past, in the direction of his room.

"Did I excuse you?"

He stops, turns, and puts his hands on his hips, head cocked to the side, tongue pushing against his cheek. I don't want this, but I don't know how to change this. He is so smart, smarter than I was at his age, and he sees all the angles, finds the weakness in any argument, of which as of late there have been plenty. The change happened so quickly, and I keep asking myself how I could have prevented it, and if there is a way to make things as they once were. I want to say this to him now, to drop all pretense of anger, to hug him and have it mean something to him, to let him know that I am his daddy, and he is still my little boy, and this is why I am angry, because I want to protect him still and always, if only he'd let me. And as much as I want to believe that, as often as I tell myself to believe this about myself, this notion of perfect fatherhood, something about the idea feels false. I am conflicted, and my hesitation hampers my better judgment. I step toward him, and he straightens his head, and his arms drop to his sides, and I think maybe he wants to say these things, too, to feel the way we used to feel. Or maybe he feels the same conflict.

Then I hear music. A ringtone, and not mine. One of the side pockets of his bookbag lights up. He rushes past me to retrieve his bag from the floor and ends the incoming call.

"I thought your phone died."

"It did. I charged it in Trevor's car."

"Don't lie to me, boy."

"I swear."

"Even if that was true, and I know it isn't, you didn't think then to return my calls? To text me and let me know you were alive?"

"Don't be so melodramatic, Dad."

"Melo—? Malcolm, go to your room. Now."

He talks to himself again.

"What'd I just get through saying? You got something to say, say it loud. Don't be no chump."

"I said, 'gladly.'"

"Good, well gladly go on then. And you *are* going to church tomorrow morning, so don't be up all night on that phone, talking about you're too tired to go, you hear me?"

"Why? Why do you keep making me go? I don't care about that crap. That's your thing."

"Crap. Wow. Something important to your father is crap. Real nice. Well, I'll tell you why. You ready? Because I said so. I don't owe you an explanation."

"And you say Pop-Pop is manipulative. You know, he said you'd do this. Overreact. Make it like talking to him was a bad thing. He's been nothing but nice to me, even when I wouldn't talk to him at first, because you said not to. So how come he's been right about you, but you been wrong about him, huh?"

We stand face-to-face. He holds his shoulders high. I'd never raised my hand to Malcolm, but his eyes tell me he is prepared for just that, and it confuses and saddens me that he thinks me capable of that, just as it enrages me to hear him say those things about that man to me.

"Do me a favor, Malcolm. Go away. Go to your room. I don't have anything else to say to you. Not right now."

His body language says he is on the precipice of an apology, that he knows he took things a step too far. If he does, I will accept it, and hold him, because it's all I want in this moment, and for the moments that follow.

I think.

But it is in those following moments that his body speaks a different language, His eyes narrow and he lifts his chest. He walks past me, brushes his shoulder against mine. I don't turn to watch him go. I cringe, prepared for the slam, but his bedroom door closes with a quiet click.

fought it. The need to leave the town and the experiences of the last two days were as strong as any emotion I'd ever felt, and yet there was this tension, a stretching that occurred with each mile that ticked on the odometer. I had been tethered to a place I never wanted to be. Freddy's call came when the truss had reached its limits of elasticity, where it would either snap, or rebound with violent force. As I turned the car around, my path back to the beach felt predetermined, a roller-coaster car on a track, towed toward the top of the hill, then released, building speed until the ride reached its end.

Dense traffic slowed my arrival. Freddy jogged toward my car as I drove down the gravel trail. In the distance, red and blue lights flashed. I slowed to a stop and lowered my window.

"Freddy, what's going on? Why are the police here?"

"The contractors found something."

"Found what, Freddy?"

"You'll have to park a little farther away than last time. They need room."

"Freddy, what did they find?"

"Come on. I'll walk with you."

"Freddy."

She pulled away from the window, arms crossed, focused on the road toward the police car and a pickup truck emblazoned with the contractor's logo. I waited for her to face me, to tell me what she knew, to spare me a dramatic reveal. She refused, going so far as to turn her body away from me. I laughed in disgust and pulled the car off the trail, parked in a patch of grass, then joined her back on the trail. She spoke softly.

"What happened?"

"I was going to ask you the same thing. Again."

"No, I mean the limp. What happened?"

"You wouldn't believe me if I told you."

"You'd be surprised by what I'd believe at this exact moment."

I stopped. "Freddy, what the hell is going on?"

She put her hands on her hips and turned her head toward the fields. "What do you know about this property?"

ELEVEN

Water destroys. It runs relentless over rocks until it smooths them, erodes them, breaks them down. Water seeps into walls, let loose from leaky pipes until it saturates the drywall birthing black mold, feeding it like mother's milk, sustaining lethal life that brings illness and death to the vulnerable. The smallest wave has the power to push and pull a person under its weight until their world is reoriented, unable to tell up from down, until they breathe liquid, returned to the womb. We obsess over our daily consumption of water, carry it around in thermoregulated bottles, bathe our children in it, and count the days until summer when we can stand at the edge of its endlessness and pretend it cannot swallow us whole. This awesome, powerful, formless thing. It is heartless. It is cruel. And yet it pulls us toward it as the moon pulls on it.

You felt that pull. I saw it in your face the day you ran into the ocean. You didn't resist. You succumbed to the sea's siren song, unafraid. So much of your mother in you. Your fearlessness frightened me, your willingness to give in to the water's wiles.

As I drove toward home, I experienced the water's pull, too. But I

"That it's a few hundred acres, but you were going to confirm that."

"I'm serious."

"So am I. I'm saying that's all I know. But apparently there's more. So can we stop with the mystery now?"

She lifted her head. What I saw in her face went beyond fear. Frayed at the edges. Coming apart.

"There's something in the ground."

"What do you mean there's something in the ground? What kind of something?"

"Come on."

She walked on. I didn't. A bottle of Ativan sat in my suitcase, a rip-cord should I find myself in a situation where the levels of Lexapro in my system weren't enough to block my senses from serotonin and keep me sane. Turn back and get them, I thought, but now well within the police officer's view, any backward movement might make him think I'm running away. Yet I couldn't convince myself to move forward. A few hundred feet ahead of me stood a different life, one I'd not asked for, one I'd not worked toward, one I'd never even considered, one that, even if I stayed rooted to that spot, would come for me one way or another. Would you stand here with me, Malcolm? If all was about to change, I would savor these last few moments where I had some final scraps of control. Freddy noticed within a few strides that I was not by her side. She returned to me, and her words came with a surprising tenderness that made me feel selfish and comforted.

"Hey. I'm scared, too. If that helps."

"What's down there, Freddy?"

She cocked her head, beckoned me to join her. We walked. The lone officer took notes from the contractor, who appeared as shaken as I. The officer saw us approach and excused himself from his interview. The contractor, seated on the tailgate of his pickup, put his head in his hands. There arose in me an unusual urge to apologize to him. The cop held out his hand in my direction.

"Officer Ryan. You're the owner?"

"That's correct."

"And, sir, how long have you owned this property."

"I came into possession of the deed last week."

"And how did it come into your possession?"

"The property was left to my son by my grandfather."

"Your son? So, it's not yours?"

"His son passed away," Freddy said. "The land was turned over to him as next of kin."

I thanked Freddy with my face. She returned a tight-lipped nod.

"Are you aware of whether or not your grandfather had a criminal history?"

"I'm pretty sure that old man was capable of anything. Wouldn't surprise me if there were bodies in his basement walls."

"Sir?" His expression told me he took my jape as truth and I had best course correct.

"I'm sorry, Officer. I'm a duck on the water right now." His head took on a canine tilt that would have been amusing in any other circumstance. "You know, calm on the surface, feet paddling a mile a minute below?" He nodded in recognition, unimpressed by my metaphor. "What I'm trying to say is I'm quite anxious about what's going on here, and when I'm anxious, I get a little glib to cover up how uncomfortable I really am."

"Understandable, sir, but you need to understand that everything you say right now is incredibly important. Maybe now isn't the time for jokes."

"I'm sorry, but just what is happening here? Do I need a lawyer?"

He flipped his notepad closed and tucked it in his breast pocket. "Follow me."

Freddy mouthed "yes" to my question as we followed in step with the officer. He stopped. To his right was a large pile of dirt. He stepped aside. Within the fresh pit the contractor had dug were the intact skeletal remains of an arm and hand. I jumped back.

"Whoa, what is that? Are you kidding me right now? Is that real?"

"As far as I can tell, yes, sir." He gestured past me. "They'll tell us for certain."

Gravel crunched behind us. Two additional police cruisers rolled down the road, followed by a black SUV. Two officers exited their vehicles while the driver behind them fished around in her open trunk. She set something akin to a high-tech lawn mower on the ground and pushed it toward us, trailed by whoever had been riding with her in the passenger seat. They all exchanged familiar pleasantries with the interviewing officer and walked around Freddy and me as if we weren't there. The SUV driver's windbreaker said "Forensics" on the back. She flipped a switch on the mower and walked a methodical line away from us, head down, watching an LED screen. Her partner, dressed in the same attire, opened a leather-bound case full of tools. He knelt at the excavation and gingerly brushed dirt away from the exposed extremity, eventually revealing a full arm. Officer Ryan squatted at the edge of the pit.

"Is it real?"

"Oh, yeah. Definitely."

At that affirmation, I lost all sense of alignment. The sky became ground, the ground the sky. I was weightless and I was heavy, floating yet anchored. I listed into Freddy.

"Hey, whoa. You okay?"

She squeezed my arm, and her touch restored my sense of place. I felt the earth push back under my feet again, but my legs trembled.

"I think I need to sit down."

She guided me to where she'd parked her car, opened the back driver's side door, and held my elbow as I lowered myself to the edge of the seat.

"Are you all right?"

"Bet you're glad you took on this listing, huh?"

"I mean, I can still walk away."

I flashed her a weak smile and she returned one. She considered the officers, then turned back to me. "Did you have any idea something like this—"

"Are you kidding? No."

She blew a raspberry. "Do you have a lawyer?"

"You really think I need one?"

"Don't you?"

I clasped my hands and brought them to my forehead. Tell me what to do here, Malcolm. You always knew what to do, what to say, always a step ahead. When you didn't answer, I thought of praying, out of need or out of spite, not sure it mattered which, until one of the officials called out.

They'd found something else.

Freddy offered her hand, but I stood on my own and hobbled after her back to the dig site. The contractor jumped from his truck bed and also walked over. The man in the pit brushed away dirt, but the officers were standing with his partner, observing the screen attached to her machine. Officer Ryan looked up at me.

"What?" I asked. The woman operating the machine gave him a curt nod before he turned back to me. "What?" I said again.

"There's another one."

The man in the pit called out. "Ryan, come take a look at this."

Ryan walked the few short feet back to the pit. Further brushing revealed one side of the rib cage and half the skull, to which the man pointed.

"See that there? That broken orbital bone. It's unhealed. Premortem. And I can tell you this much, the injury isn't recent. You're going to want to put a call in to the archaeological society."

I stared at the skull, the shards of bone around the socket.

My bloodied face in the rearview mirror.

An itch in my cheek, just below my eye.

Dirt thumping on a coffin lid.

I can't breathe.

I can't sit up.

We're going to be late.

"Sir? Are you local?"

"What? I . . . What? I'm, no, I'm not."

"You'll understand if we're going to have to ask you to stick around town the next few days? Sir?"

I backed away from the pit.

Bits of glass in my face.

Blood running into my eye.

Cool air blowing on open cuts.

Rain dripping from the branch.

"Sir, can you hear me?"

I can't breathe.

"I can't breathe."

The man in the pit climbed out. Officer Ryan and the other two officers moved toward me. I backed farther away and into Freddy. She gripped my wrist and spun me to face her.

"Hey, are you all right?"

The flashing roof lights. The woman's lawn mower contraption pinging away. The accusatory eyes.

The bones. The small waves hissing as they broke on the shore. My leg throbbing.

I moved away from Freddy and pulled air into my closing throat, asked my heart to slow, asked the sweat on my forehead to stop, asked the pins and needles to please push themselves from my fingertips.

All the old familiar faces. In all the old familiar places.

My knees buckled. Freddy's grip tightened.

"Uh-oh, okay, come on. Let's sit you down."

I licked my dry cracked lips and tasted blood. Somewhere in the field, the fox screamed. If anyone heard it, they didn't show.

"Not going to make it, Freddy."

My arm slipped from her grasp, and she clung to the slack in my sleeve. Something tore. She shouted for help. The edges of my vision went dark as the ground rose to meet me.

I didn't know where I was, except I knew I was in a bed. There was a mattress beneath me and a sheet on top of me, but the familiarity ended there. The room was dark, but none of the shadows took the shape of anything I recognized. The chair was not my chair. The bed was not my bed. I knew this because my bed did not have a footboard, and that footboard certainly never had a silhouetted figure perched on top of it.

The footboard had a silhouetted figure perched on top of it.

For whom I screamed, I don't know, nor would anyone else, because all that sprung forth was that same labored lament from the previous night. Again, only my eyes moved, rolled back in my skull with the attempt at lifting my head. Nothing doing. Arms and legs. Same. When my eyes returned home, I saw only the bridge of my nose. The figure was gone. Then pressure on one ankle. Then the other. The pressure lifted, then came down again on one shin. Then the other. The mattress sunk between my parted legs. Whatever this thing was, it was crawling up me. I moaned louder still, pleaded with God, grant me the power to move my lips and tongue, fill my lungs with air, so I can scream for help, but His mercy did not arrive, a habit of which He'd become increasingly guilty. The thing's weight moved up my thighs, over my stomach until it sat atop my chest, and it did not move. Flat to the bed as I was, I could not see it, but it was there. If it had a face or eyes, I did not know, but a mouth it most certainly possessed, because I felt its breath against my skin as though we were face-to-face. I imagined a malicious maw, all jagged teeth, saliva clinging to the tips, hanging centimeters from my face, ready to drop, before the thing buried them into my cheek, my throat, clamping down to rip it out.

But all the thing did was breathe. Not the searing, sulfurous exhalations of some demonic apparition. Instead, warm and sweet. Familiar. Like baby's breath.

Like *your* baby's breath.

The thing's (your?) soft sighs moved closer, its (your?) pressure on my chest pushing life from my lungs.

Let me breathe, Malcolm. Please.

And then I was awake. *Awake* awake. Not somewhere in between. The room was still unfamiliar, but I knew exactly where I was. The fluorescent lighting buzz, the monitor's rhythmic beep, the squeak of sneakers on the hallway linoleum, the antiseptic smell, the stiff starched sheets. The first movement I made was to bring a hand to my face. I searched for bandages, stitches, relieved to find none, to find I wasn't still dreaming, reliving the worst day of my life, instead discovering a tender spot on my left cheek, the other side, the one without the scar. I hissed in pain. The sound startled someone next to me, which in turn startled me.

Your mother had been sleeping in a chair next to my bed, seated far enough behind my periphery to escape my view. She ran two fingers down the sides of her mouth, clearing away signs of sleep, and stretched her arms overhead. I tried not seeing the sliver of stomach revealed by her rising shirt, but old habits and all that. Sorry, that's more than you need to know, isn't it? Maybe it helps to know that no matter how slick I thought I was, she always caught me, always held that annoyed expression until I was brave enough to meet her eyes.

No? Yeah, I guess not.

"You're awake," she said.

"Am I? Then how are you here? Because you being here feels like I'm dreaming."

"You still have me listed as your emergency contact."

"I hadn't realized."

I pushed myself to a seated position and regretted the quick change in posture. My head throbbed and my vision narrowed. A dry-erase board hung on the wall across from my bed. My nurse was Sharon. Hello, Sharon. The words blurred, doubled, and slid across each other. "I'm going to lie back down." I fished for the remote and elevated the head of the bed. "Hey, you, uh, didn't see anyone else in here, did you? No one, say, on the bed?"

"On the bed?"

"Yeah, never mind. So . . . the way you said 'still.' I guess you want me to change the emergency contact?"

"You're the wordsmith. How are you feeling?"

"Do you care?"

"Don't do that. I asked."

"You also asked me to remove you as my emergency contact, Van."

"Did I say that? Did any of those words come out of my mouth?"

"You did and you didn't."

"I'm here, aren't I? I came when they called."

Lord, you were your mother's son. I was talking to you as much as I was to her.

"My head hurts."

"What?"

"You asked how I was feeling. I'm telling you my head hurts."

"I'm sorry."

"That you asked or that my head hurts?"

She sighed. "How did you hit your head?"

I reached for her hand. "I'm glad you're here."

Her hand stayed by her side. "I'm glad you're glad."

She chewed the inside of her cheek. The way her lips pursed and collected on one side of her face sent a shiver of longing through me. Seeing the tremor, she asked again if I was all right, and I dismissed the shaking to a chill in the room. I told her what I remembered leading up to the panic attack, excising the incriminating details like cancerous lesions. In this story, I'd not mixed alcohol with medication. I'd not been visited by chest-sitting haints. I'd not been having conversations with you. My tone and timbre lent drama to the tale, her brow uniting and separating, lifting and falling at all the right spots, though her face was framed by condescension, the sincerity of her expressions feigned for my placation. She succeeded, as I would take what I could get. Half-truths told, I put on an expectant face. She returned one of confusion, clear she was unclear as to what it was I expected. My leg itched and I scratched, gentle at first, then furious as the sensation spread, intensified. She watched with curiosity. The irritation irritated me. With my leg. Then with her.

"What'd I do now?" I said.

"You're bleeding."

Red spots dotted the sheet over my calf. I stopped scratching and set my jaw, willing some calm into my noxious nerve endings. "It's nothing.

I'm fine. I'm sure you must have somewhere else to be, right? Certainly somewhere more important than here."

She took a deep breath, set her mouth tight, and stood, slinging her purse over her shoulder. As she did, a physician tapped his knuckles on the door and entered before I bid him do so. He talked to himself in fragments as he reviewed my chart, reported in rehearsed cadence that my X-rays were negative for fracture, and while the MRI was negative, I'd best behave as if I had a concussion. At that fact his voice stiffened, scaffolded by severity, and warned me against continued drinking while on antianxiety medication. I informed him, with a voice absent any assurance, that I didn't drink on the regular, the alcohol in my system a one-time occurrence, unable (read: unwilling) to face either him or Vanessa in that moment, due to an acute awareness of their disbelief and disappointment. He concluded his sermon with a set of discharge instructions. As he passed them to me, he took note of the blood by my leg. I informed him of the sting, and he pulled back the sheet. Another series of erudite rumblings. A rubbing of his hairless chin. An adjustment of his glasses. A recommendation for an antihistamine. My pleading for something stronger for the pain. His mistrustful mien, one that spoke to his suspicion of drug-seeking behavior, or more likely, a disbelief of my pain altogether, followed by an insistence on the effectiveness of said antihistamine, and a promise to send a nurse (would it be Sharon?) to dress the wound. My reluctant acceptance of a prescription. His exit laced with less alarm than accompanied the entrance. Vanessa followed.

"Wait, you're leaving?"

"You had an emergency. They contacted me. I'm going home."

"You drove hours."

"I know how long I drove."

"Well then go back tomorrow. I know what he said, but I'm not drinking again. It was just one time." She side-eyed me. "Okay, technically, twice."

"'Technically.' What does that even mean?" She scoffed. "One time, two times, every day. Do what you're going to do. I don't care."

"You don't look like you don't care."

"What do I look like?"

"Angry."

"Shouldn't I be?"

"Then you care."

"About the drinking? No, I honestly don't. You are—arguably—a grown man. You have only yourself to answer to about why you stopped and why you started."

"Okay, what then, Van? Why are you angry at me?"

"'What then?' What then is you brought me back to a place where I had the best and worst days of my life. And it never even occurred to you. That's what then."

A silent moment. Her words a mirror making a reflection I refused to see. How often she'd shouldered me, never having to be asked, yet how often I'd asked. I lowered my head and thought of the poetic ways I could apologize. Tap into that writer brain. Conjure similes never before conceived, magnificent metaphors that broke all molds, sweep her off her feet with a soliloquy of contrition, signifying all the growth she thought me incapable of. But she wore her weariness with me unabashed, and true regret reigned for the lies I told myself, told her—told you—past and present.

"I'm sorry."

And then her palm on my cheek. Not a slap. Brief, but soft. Her thumb traced the curved contour of my scar. Worry ringed the rims of her eyelids, then regret for that worry, translated by a gentle push, a push I allowed to turn my head to the side as she walked out of the room. Her hand left her smell on my skin, her warmth lingered on my cheek, and I brought my hand up to contain it. I held my breath, knowing that within seconds, my senses would adapt, and her scent would disappear. When it did, I realized her gesture for what it was—a good-bye.

And just like that, Malcolm, I'd lost her, too.

I scratched my leg again. Another rap at the door. Anticipating the nurse, I unleashed a curt "what." Freddy stood at the entrance, two coffees in a cardboard carrier, a pyramid of creams and sugars in the center.

I waved her in. She pulled the adjustable table over the bed and set the coffees down. She dumped countless creamers into her cup and stirred.

"Just saw the doc leave. What'd he say?"

"Possible concussion. I hit my head?"

Her eyes widened. "Dude. So hard. Like you'd stumbled on a patch of land with extra gravity or something. I never saw someone fall so fast. I tried to catch you, but your sleeve ripped. If this is going to be a thing with you, think about buying better shirts."

"I'm in academia."

"Point taken."

She sipped her coffee. I removed the lid from mine and blew ripples across the surface.

"I saw a woman leave after the doc, too."

"Uh-huh." I drank. Freddy smirked.

"Black, huh?"

"Sorry?"

She raised her cup. "Your coffee."

"Right. Yes."

"Like we like our women."

I shifted in the bed. "Okay."

"Oh, come on. You're too easy. Who was she?"

"Jealous?"

"Of her? Not hardly. But you?"

"Freddy, what would your wife say?"

"That I'm married and not dead."

"Fair. She's Malcolm's mother."

"Your wife?" I shook my head. "Oh, sorry. Ex?"

"Not exactly."

"She seemed upset."

"She was."

She moved to sit on the edge of the bed. "Shit, what happened to your leg?"

I swallowed a too-large sip of my too-hot coffee, scalding my throat, and aahed, sounding like my father used to at the pleasure of his first sip of beer. Nothing, I told her. A sting. Scratched too hard, too long. I'd be fine. She nodded and hummed. The resultant quiet surprised me with its comfort. Maybe it was the way she drank her coffee, eyebrows raised, asking without words, "tell me more," that made me want to tell her more. Maybe it was the way she asked about my leg with care, true, genuine, unsolicited care, that untied the loop around my larynx. Whatever it was, I launched into it, and I mean everything.

Mal, I'm going to need you to leave the room for a moment.

When I was sure you had, I told her how Vanessa and I'd met in undergrad in a senior literature seminar. How quickly we'd bonded over the almost alarming similarity in our favored and disdained authors and their works. How I'd misinterpreted with a quickness her friendly affection for the romantic kind. How one night after too many drinks I convinced her we should give it a shot, that relationships that began as friends were often the strongest, the longest lasting. How we'd decided that even though she was on the pill, I'd pull out, and how we both decided in the heat of the moment I wouldn't (Freddy's face conveyed her doubt in this mutual agreement), and how it didn't take long for the morning sickness's arrival. How she decided that though we'd made a mistake, she wanted to keep the baby, and how even though I was by no means ready to become a father, a baby kept me connected to her, sowing seeds of both gratitude and resentment for Malcolm, seeds that grew like crabgrass, rampant and out of control, forever trying to find a balance, until it was too late to do anything more about it.

You can come back now if you want.

Telling Freddy these things left me with a sense of breathlessness, as though I'd sprinted an impossible distance. Her expressions all the while were honest, made no attempts to conceal her sympathy, apprehension, contempt, or understanding. I saw she wanted to know more but guilt set in at revealing intimate information about someone other than me, so I stopped. The silence that followed was then quite uncomfortable.

The promised nurse Sharon entered, donned gloves, and pulled back the sheet. She remarked on the lines tracing up my calf, the inflammation of the wound, then sprayed saline solution and dabbed at the wound with gauze. Strands stuck to the skin as she pulled the pad away. She picked one away when she retracted her hand with a yelp. Her jump caused Freddy and me to do the same.

"What is it?" I asked.

She bent at the waist and peered at my leg. Fingers in pincer position, she spread the borders of the skin I'd scratched open. "Is that . . . is that a hook?"

"A what?"

"There's something poking out here." She retrieved a pair of tweezers and removed a pointed tip of . . . something and dropped it into a stainless-steel tin with a quiet yet musical ping. "Never saw that before."

"That's it?"

Her disinterest was almost comical. "Probably just some debris. Sharp, though. Stung like hell."

I faced Freddy. "You hear that, Freddy? Probably just some debris. In my leg."

Freddy shushed me. As though she'd not just removed a foreign object from my bleeding limb, Sharon dressed the wound, then told me I could leave when I was ready, though her tone implied the hospital would like me to leave when *they* were ready, which seemed to be right then. I tossed her a thank-you, yanked back the covers, pinched my gown at the rear, and stood. Blood rushed to my stung limb and the painful pressure pushed outward. I bent my knee and went up on my tiptoe. I must have appeared close to falling, as Freddy shot up, ready to catch me again, but I waved her off. She resumed her seat but watched with caution.

"I'm fine. I won't fall again."

"Pretty sure you didn't think you'd fall last time."

I paused, then asked, "Why are you here, Freddy?"

She tossed a key on the table. "Hotel rates are crazy this time of year. Since the cops are saying you got to stick around for a bit, I thought I'd extend your stay. If you want."

"Really? I've been kind of a shit."

She pointed and covered her mouth. "Swear word!"

"Put it on my tab. But seriously."

"I don't know, man. Yeah, you said some stupid stuff, but you seem all right. Spend enough time in the bar, you get a read on people. Mine on you is pretty good."

I pulled on my pants under my gown and put the key in my pocket. "That's kind of you. Thanks."

She gave me a thumbs-up. "Don't mention it." She took another sip of coffee. Then another. And then another.

"What?"

"Huh?"

"Come on, Freddy. There's something else. Give me the tea."

She puffed her cheeks and let the air leak out. "Before I say what, let me just tell you, I'm nosy by nature, so I'm sorry. But you were going to find this out one way or another."

I pulled the curtain between us. "Uh-huh." I took off my gown and saw how soft my stomach had gotten. Except I didn't think I'd gotten *that* soft. And so quickly? I sucked my stomach in, then pushed it out, then tried to hold it at some range in between. Meanwhile, Freddy's silhouette paced.

"Right. So, I went back a little further in the ownership records. Before, I just had to do a title search, make sure your grandfather was the last owner, that kind of thing. But after a little digging—pun intended—I, uh, found more."

"Don't."

"Don't what?"

"Don't tell me."

"Why?"

I pulled back the curtain. "Because if you say the thing, I'm going to know the thing, and knowing the thing changes everything."

"You say that as if you know what the thing is."

My leg throbbed, so I sat where your mother had waited for me to awaken. The cloth-covered cushion sighed and brought with it the citrus notes of her perfume. She never wore much. Always did that thing where she sprayed it into the air and walked through it. Subtle as it was on her, I knew when she had been in a room long after she'd left it, and it filled me with a yearning for her presence, a sense of absence as real as hunger, as strong now as it was then. If she were here, I could pretend to be the kind of man who could handle whatever it was Freddy had to tell me. Instead, I was the kind of man who found himself alone when he needed her most. Because I always seemed to need her most. How tired she must have been, because I was tired of myself. Who are you when no one is watching? She wasn't there, though.

You were. And so I told Freddy,

"Fine. Tell me the thing."

She did. And I was right.

Everything changed.

TWELVE

It is at this point, Malcolm, where things get quite strange.

THIRTEEN

I am seven years old.

And I am confused.

Mom and Dad are not getting along. They aren't arguing or yelling, but they don't seem to like each other that much lately. The social work team at the hospital doesn't have enough people, so Dad works a lot of overtime and extra shifts. His beeper goes off all the time. Sometimes it wakes me up at night. He sleeps on the couch, not because he and Mom are fighting, but because he doesn't want to bother her when he has to leave or come home while she's sleeping. She says it isn't a problem, that she wants to have him in bed, but he says it's not fair to her, and he wouldn't sleep because he'd be worried about waking her up. She stops pushing, but I can see she still wants to. She says he still makes time to go to the gym, where "she" works out. I don't know who she is, but I can tell by the way Mom says "she" that "she" is not someone she likes. Dad calls her paranoid, says if he doesn't take care of himself while working all these extra hours that he'll get sick and then what. This makes sense to me, and I almost come from the living room where I'm watching cartoons to tell her so, ask her why she won't leave him alone about it, but then she does, so I stay put. I notice they only talk about these things when they think I'm not listening, so I think I'm smart to keep pretending.

They keep talking. She suggests a date night. He says we go to dinner every weekend. She lowers her voice and says she wants a night with just the two of them. My cheeks get warm, and she says something about passing ships, feeling like roommates. Dad agrees, and now my ears are prickly hot. I am angry at them for wanting to go out without me, but I am also glad that they are agreeing about something. It seems to make them both happy, and that makes me happy. I think. Dad asks how they can pull it off. My sitter has gone back to school, and they never got around to finding a backup. Mom suggests my grandparents and Dad's voice changes. His face does, too. Then so does Mom's. They are back to not getting along again, but I don't understand why. Grandpa calls me every birthday. He asks what toys I like, and he remembers them. He got me a Snake Eyes figure when they were sold out everywhere. He buys me things Mom and Dad won't. He listens when I tell him about my comic books, like really listens, doesn't pretend the way Mom does. Dad doesn't even try.

Dad says they have talked about this, and he doesn't want to have this conversation again, especially now. He moves his head in my direction. Mom doesn't seem to hear him. She says she understands why he feels this way but doesn't see another solution. Dad says they need to find one because he's not leaving me alone with them. I don't think they have ever left me alone with Grandma and Grandpa, at least as far as I can remember. I want to ask why this is, but they are still talking. Mom says her parents love me and isn't that what's important. I want to agree, but then Dad asks her if it's okay that they don't like him. She says he knows that's not what she means, that of course they like him, but the way she says it makes me wonder if that's true. Dad laughs but doesn't smile. It's weird how he does that and it makes me uncomfortable. How can he trust that they won't say things I shouldn't hear, he asks Mom. How does he know they won't say bad things about him to me, as if I would ever let them say something bad about my dad. They aren't like that, she tells him, not that way. She uses the word "conservative," which I've heard before but still don't really understand, but it has something to do with what Dad doesn't like about Grandma and Grandpa, because he says they are more than just conservative, and he asks if he has to remind Mom of the flag plate on the bumper of Grandpa's Buick. Mom reminds him Grandpa went to school in Georgia and loved his time there. Dad asks her if she doesn't think it's strange that he doesn't have a flag of the school, then tells her the state flag has long since changed. I am confused again because the flag on his car looks almost exactly like the one on the top of the car Bo and Luke, the Duke boys, drive, the General Lee, one of the toys Grandpa brought me that makes the horn sound and everything, and then I remember that Dad doesn't like when I play with that car, when it plays that song, or when I pretend to be Bo or Luke. I figure he just doesn't like the show, but now I wonder if there is another reason.

Mom doesn't know what she's said wrong to make Dad so upset. Dad is upset because she doesn't know what she's said wrong, or, more importantly, he says, what she doesn't say right. That's not fair, she says, and he does that weird laugh without smiling thing again, and Mom's face goes red. I don't like being laughed at, either, and feel bad for her, but Dad makes a different face when he laughs this time. The first time, he wrinkled his nose like something smelled bad. This time he seems so sad, like he might even cry, but also confused, like he doesn't know what's happening. He opens his mouth like he's going to say something else, but then he closes it. Then he asks Mom what she wants for takeout. She does a weird laugh of her own, then wipes her nose and calls me from the living room to ask me what I want for dinner. I usually love when we order food out and always ask for more than I can ever eat but they always get it for me. We set up the tray tables in front of the couch and pick something to watch together on television, most times *The Jeffersons* or *Sanford and Son*, and they love when I sing along with the theme. This time feels different. This time it feels like they're ordering food out, feels like they've called me over to their conversation because they don't know what else to say to each other. I don't like how that feels. And I'm not hungry.

FOURTEEN

"Huh." I said.

"Huh? That's it?"

"Oh. I mean . . . yeah, wow. Crazy stuff. Really interesting."

"Interesting? Are you okay?" She snapped her fingers in front of my face, as I'd taken to watching some undefined space beyond her.

"Me? Yeah. I'm fine." Freddy doubled her chin. "I mean obviously not *fine*. Who could be fine with news like that?"

"Right?"

"Yeah, I mean, it's really, really interesting."

"You said that already."

"Did I? It is, though, isn't it? Interesting?"

"I just told you that you inherited a plantation from your grandfather. That's interesting?"

"Well, and weird, right? Definitely weird. Definitely."

She slapped her hands on her thighs, stood, and shook her head. "Right, well you're clearly in shock, so I'm going to go."

"You're leaving?"

"My guy, you need some time or space or whatever to process this."

"I guess that sounds right."

"You guess? You guess. Yeah, I'm absolutely going to go. Don't forget the key." She made for the door when it hit me.

"Hey!"

She turned.

"What time do you open the bar?"

"Oh, my God. Bye." Her footsteps faded down the hall.

"Don't know what she's upset about," I said to no one (you?). "Not like she owns a plantation."

And then what should have hit me, what Freddy didn't understand wasn't hitting me, sidled next to me, tapped me on the shoulder, and slapped me across my fool face.

"Jesus, Lord. I own a plantation."

I stood to go after Freddy, to tell her that her joke was the furthest thing from funny, because what she said couldn't be anything *but* some ill-conceived prank, to tell her to come back here and explain herself, but my ankle buckled when I gave chase. The over-the-bed table being the closest support, I reached for it, but the wheels were unlocked. It skated from under my flailing hand, and I fell across the mattress. The table tipped, hovered like a falling tree, then cracked off the tile floor. Nurse Sharon appeared in the doorway, face awash with alarm, then drooped with displeasure after seeing I was unharmed. After apologizing, I asked if the hospital could supply me with an ankle brace, and maybe a cane, since they wouldn't prescribe anything for the pain in my leg. With no lack of condescension, she informed me insurance wouldn't cover it because my leg was not why I was admitted and handed me a xeroxed copy of local drugstores that sold medical equipment. She was out the door before I could offer my sarcastic gratitude.

Worried I'd pulled loose the dressing, I pulled up my pant leg. The gauze was intact, but wet, and not with blood. My finger was centimeters from touching it when something moved under my skin. Long and threadlike, like a vein, but I was not so physically fit as to have visible veins in my legs. I retracted my hand, blinked, and watched. No more movement. I reached for the bandage again, but the vein didn't twitch. I touched the wet spot on the gauze. There was no resistance to my pressure from the skin and muscle beneath. I pressed harder. The gauze was saturated with whatever clear liquid had initially filled its fibers. The tape pulled away from the skin as I pressed harder, the gauze puckering as I pushed it into a hole in my skin, the clear fluid flooding out, hitting the floor with a splash. I cried out. Sharon appeared in the doorway again with an expectant, impatient frown.

"This is not my leg."

"Sir?"

"My leg. Something is wrong with it. It's not mine."

"Did you mess with the bandage? It should be fine if you don't touch it. I can send you home with some extra pads."

"Can you please just check instead of rushing me out of here?"

She sighed and walked heavy-footed to the bed. "It's just a little spotting. That's normal. You scratched it pretty deep."

"What?" The dressing was intact. A few red dots of blood. Nothing slithering in my calf. No mess on the floor.

"I can re-dress it if you want, but it's probably already stopped bleeding."

I'd been staring at the bandage and hardly heard her. "What?"

"The bandage. Do you want a new one?"

"I . . . no. I'm sorry. I didn't mean to . . ." I stopped. "I think there's a tentacle in my leg."

"It's fine. You're not driving, correct? I wouldn't advise it."

I shook my head. "Did you hear me?"

"You said you feel out of sorts. That's normal, too. The attending gave you Ativan so you might feel a bit woozy."

"What? No, I said—"

"Your discharge paperwork is in the bag with your prescription. Have a nice day," she said, with zero hint of hope or care that I would have a nice day, and almost jogged out of the room.

What the hell was happening?

I rolled my calf from side to side on the bed, searching for the tiny tendril I'd seen shift beneath the surface, the gaping hole into which my finger had disappeared, finding nothing. It seemed so real. Real enough for me to say something ridiculous, and yet that wasn't real either, turns out. So then maybe I hadn't heard what I thought Freddy told me. Maybe instead she told me there were back taxes owed on the property, something about a septic tank, and my lorazepam-lubricated limbic system manufactured the plantation narrative. Reasonable enough. Sure.

I hobbled down the hallway toward the elevator. Outside, I pulled my phone from my pocket to hail a rideshare. Someone had turned my phone off, and when I revived it, it buzzed and buzzed. Texts, missed calls, voicemails. The only number I recognized was my agent. Each voicemail from her had increasing amounts of desperation, worried she'd offended me on her last call, promising she'd work harder on selling this book if I truly believed in it, and please, please, *please* call her back as soon as I got this because she didn't want anything she'd said to have been misunderstood.

Delete, delete, delete.

I pulled up the rideshare app and called for a car. A familiar hatchback slowed to a stop at the curb, and I maneuvered into the backseat.

"Hey, I thought I recognized that name," Mo said. "What's up, jellyfish man!"

A static charge ran across my arms, the hairs standing stiff. "What did you say?"

"My kid loves that movie. The turtle with the surfer voice? Jellyfish man! Isn't that it? Something like that. You never saw that one?"

"I did, but why did you call me jellyfish man?"

"Out on the bay. You got stung. That was you, right?"

"Yeah, that was me. I just thought . . . You know what? Never mind."

"Looked like that hurt like hell. You still limping, huh? Surprised you want to go back."

"What?"

"That's where we're going, right? That's what it says on my app."

"No, I . . ." Hadn't I typed in the address to the bar? I checked my phone. I'd done it again. Or you had. "I mean, yes, I guess so."

"You all right, jelly man? That was it. Jelly man."

"Please don't call me that."

His grin disappeared and he faced forward. "My bad, dude."

His intentions were good, and I hadn't meant to snap, but I had neither the energy nor the inclination for an explanation. Instead, I sat back, willed away the pulsing in my lower leg, and watched buildings blur into one another outside my window.

Cream-colored tent tops poked through the horizon as we drove down the trail. The local police had set up a barricade. An officer approached the car, holding one hand out palm up, the other attached to his belt by his thumb. Mo slowed to a stop and lowered his window. The officer rested his forearm on the roof and leaned down.

"Help you?"

Mo thumbed to me in the backseat. I lowered my window. When the cop saw me, he asked for ID. I showed it, and he spoke into the radio clipped to his shirt. A voice crackled back, and he gestured for me to exit the car and instructed Mo to go back the way he came.

"Watch your step this time," Mo called out. I stopped him before he pulled away and handed him a twenty from my pocket.

"Do me a favor? Don't go too far?" He considered the bill for a moment, then took it, nodding. I waved as he drove off then limped behind the officer toward the site.

"How are you feeling, sir? You took one hell of a spill yesterday."

"Yesterday?"

"Sir?"

"I'm sorry, I thought you said yesterday."

"Right. I did, sir."

"I fell today."

The officer stopped and narrowed his eyes. "You okay, sir? You hit your head pretty hard."

"Define okay." He opened his mouth and let out choppy sighing sounds, a sign I'd short-circuited him with the directive. "Never mind. Yes, I'm fine." He closed his mouth and gave an appreciative nod. While we walked on, I checked the date on my phone. How had I lost a whole day?

The tents came into full view as we crested the small hill. Men and women clad in more denim and khaki than I'd ever seen in one place flitted from one place to another, hiking up their cargo shorts as they lifted their work boots over taut grid lines. The officer called out to a blonde with a pixie cut and an honest-to-God red bandana tied around her neck. I'd have taken a student to task for writing such a cliché. Only thing missing was Dr. Grant scaring a husky kid with a raptor claw. Pixie Cut jogged over to us. The flecks of mud and dust on her face did little to mask her youth.

"Is this . . . ?" she asked the officer. He nodded. "Oh. Wow. Huh. Okay."

"Is there a problem?" I asked.

"No, no, no problem. It's just when they said the owner was here—"

"That's me. I'm the owner."

"Right, I guess I just expected—"

"Someone taller?"

"Huh? Oh, ha. I get it. No, not someone taller."

I turned over my hands and held them out, handing her the rope with which she might hang herself, but she wouldn't take it. She fidgeted on her spot, a child needing the bathroom but unsure how to ask. When I'd tortured her enough, I volunteered the information it seemed she'd dared not speak out loud.

"My mother is white."

"Sure, of course, obviously."

"Obviously?"

"Oh, no, I don't mean *obviously*, obviously. I just . . . I imagine this all has to be really weird for you, huh?"

"The situation or this conversation?"

She clasped her hands behind her back. "Yeah, I'm not doing so well here, am I?"

"You're trying. Maybe start over."

She brightened and extended a grimy hand. "Hi, Ellie Sattler. So nice to meet you."

We shook. "Same. Wait. Ellie . . . Sattler?"

"I know, I know. My parents loved the movie, and then I was kind of obsessed with it, too, and well . . . here I am. Before you ask, no, Alan Grant is not walking around with fossilized claws, scaring husky kids."

"Get out of my head, Dr. Sattler."

"Sorry about that," she said.

"Dr. Sattler is the head of the state archaeological society," the officer said.

"How are you?" she asked me. "I heard you had a fall yesterday?"

"I'm here, which is better than being there, I suppose."

She crinkled her chin and pursed her lips. "I hear that," she said, though it was clear she had no idea what I meant but was determined to be agreeable after her shaky start. That natural urge to amplify someone's discomfort in such situations clawed at me, but I saw she meant well, and exercised what little restraint I felt capable of because there were things I needed to know, and she was the most probable person possessing that knowledge.

"So, what am I dealing with, Dr. Sattler?"

Her eyes went wide, and she vibrated with unbridled twentysomething excitement. "It's really unbelievable. Follow me." She led me further into the property, back where the contractor had made his initial discovery. Two pits had been fully dug, a third in progress adjacent to them. Two additional denim devotees sat in the pit, brushing dirt from bone with fastidious attention.

"I've never seen remains so close to the water this well preserved. It's incredible. They've already told us so much."

In the two pits laid the complete skeletal remains of two human bodies. On their backs. Hands placed over their hips. The one with the broken eye socket's jaw hung open in a silent scream. The rain clouds from the days before had cleared and I considered the angle of the sun.

"Facing east."

"Mmm. And the hand position. If you understand the grave orienta-
tion, I'm assuming you know what that means."

I nodded. "Christian burial."

She tilted her head and gave them a dreamy, piteous assessment.
"Doesn't seem quite fair, does it."

"And why is that?"

Returned from her reverie, she said, "Oh. I didn't mean any offense. It's
just . . . do you not know?"

As far as I knew, Freddy and I were the only ones who knew the history
of the land, an apparent misapprehension under which I'd been laboring,
Dr. Sattler seemed fit to tell me. "That depends, I guess, on what it is you
think I don't know."

Deep breath. Pause for dramatic effect. "Because the remains were in
such good condition, we could retrieve nondestructive samples for DNA
analysis. Since the police were involved in the finding, they asked us to
rush the results, to ensure these weren't new bodies." She leaned in and
put one hand to the side of her mouth. "Though anyone with a couple
of brain cells to rub together could tell you those remains aren't from
this century. Cops, am I right?" I gave her my best while-your-solidarity-
is-appreciated-I'd-like-you-to-get-to-the-blessed-point smirk. She continued. "At any rate, the fast results came back this morning. We'll need to
do some further digging to get more information, but—"

"Dr. Sattler. Please."

Another deep breath. "These two individuals are West African in origin."

"They were enslaved."

Dr. Sattler bit her lip. "Most likely, yes. We're going further back into
property records to see if there's anything that can rule that in or out,
but . . . yes."

My leg throbbed. "I own a plantation. With two enslaved West Africans on it."

"Are you all right?"

"No, I'm very much not all right." I supported myself on my knees.
"Can I have a chair?"

She quick-stepped away from the pit and retrieved a folding chair from one of the nearby tents. She pressed the edge against the backs of my knees, and I sat. One half of the denim duo in the third pit spoke in a whisper.

"Oh, man."

Dr. Sattler stood at the edge of the dig. "What?"

He eyed me, then her. "I think this is a kid."

I stood stiff from the chair and limped over. A leg was uncovered, significantly shorter than those belonging to the two in the adjacent graves. The skull was not visible, but its outline was clear under the remaining dirt.

I can't breathe.

Dirt falls on your coffin lid.

I can't sit up.

Red and blue reflects in the shattered rearview mirror. High beams blink brighter as they pull behind the car.

We're going to be late.

I backed from the pit's edge, then walked away from Dr. Sattler and her team, stopping on a small sand dune not far from where the sea touched the shore. The bay's small waves, roughened from the recent storms, crawled up the beach as though reaching for me, then receded when realizing I was beyond its grasp. The sun's reflection, fractured by the water, sent shards of light toward my shielded eyes, with which I saw out past the bay's borders and there a ship of some sort, a trawler, a tugboat, who knew what, but the longer I watched the vessel, vertiginous, my vision vacillated, showed me a ship, centuries old, set sail with stolen souls, some slipping free their fetters, seeking salvation from slavers, sent themselves soundless, scared to the sea, hearts holding hope for homegoing, returned, reunited with those from whom they'd been ripped. Standing sent slicing sensations down my leg, but I could not walk. I could not turn my eyes away. Though I remained awake, paralysis gripped me again, unseen hands held my head face forward, toward a waking horror, my ancestors on the ship abandoning their lives rather than suffer at the hands of my ancestors who stood on this spot where I had taken root, awaiting delivery of their cargo. Nothing moved save tears down my cheeks.

Light flashed in my periphery. My motor functions restored, I turned and saw a short young man, black hair jutting through the opening of his backward baseball cap, wearing a faded band shirt, a high-end camera around his neck. Next to him stood a brunette slightly older than he in a pencil skirt and blouse, a long braid over one shoulder. She walked toward me, arm outstretched, not with a hand for shaking, but holding an audio recorder.

"Good afternoon. Am I correct in assuming you're the owner of this property?"

"I'm sorry, who are you?"

"No, I'm sorry. I should have introduced myself first. I get a little eager sometimes. Laura Hunter, reporter for the *Delmarva Daily*. Would it be all right if I ask you some questions?"

"No."

"Come again?"

"I said no, Miss Hunter."

"Mrs."

"Fine. No. It is not all right if you ask me questions. This is private property. There are barricades back that way, with all the police cruisers and officers. You might have seen them."

Dr. Sattler came up beside me, leaned in, and whispered. "Hate to tell you, but the police are probably how she knows you're here." Absent a speck of subtlety, she rubbed her fingers together indicating money and winked.

I nodded and wiped the tears from my face. "Mrs. Hunter, let me be clear. I've just left the hospital, and my leg is quite uncomfortable, and you've caught me in a bit of an emotional moment, and I'd prefer not to be rude, so if you don't mind." I walked away from her, but *Delmarva Daily*'s Hunter trailed close behind, followed in step by her photographer.

"I'm so sorry to hear that. What happened to your leg?"

"Leave me alone, Mrs. Hunter." My foot found a loose stone and my ankle rolled. I stumbled but did not fall. Mrs. Hunter persisted in her chase.

"You're right. Your body, your business. Let me shift gears. Is it true you've inherited this land from your white mother's family?"

I picked up my pace as best I was able. Muscles in my shin fatigued fast and my foot slapped the ground with each step. I called out without turning back. "Go away, Mrs. Hunter."

Her steps quickened and she caught up with ease. "And is it true this land is a plantation?"

I stopped. "Who told you that? Look, I'm asking you, please leave me alone. I'm in pain and this is harassment." I yelled past her. "Can someone help me? Dr. Sattler!"

"So you confirm it's true?"

Wade in the water.

"What? What did you say?" I hadn't paid attention to where I'd been walking. The water washed up the sand, stopped short of my shoes.

"You're confirming this is in fact a plantation?"

"No, not that. The water. What did you say?"

"Water? I didn't—"

Wade in the water.

Malcolm?

"I don't want to."

Hunter persisted. "I understand these are tough questions, but this is an important story, Mr.—"

"I wasn't talking to you."

Wade in the water.

I can't. I'm afraid.

"No. I can't go in there."

"In where? Honestly, if you'd just answer my questions—"

"Get away from me. Officer Ryan! Someone! Please get this woman out of here."

"People are going to want to know what it's like for a mixed-race, award-winning—sorry, nominated—author writing about race to own a plantation."

"How do you know who I am? Please, please just leave. Dr. Sattler! Ellie!"

Malcolm, help me.

God's gonna trouble the water.

You're not Malcolm.

Wade in the water.

You're right. I'll go.

I dragged my leg behind me toward the bay. My foot hit the water. I expected fire as saltwater bathed exposed fascia and nerves. But the pain never came. Instead, it stopped. I took another step, the water at midshin. No pain from there down. Up to my knees. Fire extingushed. My heart rate slowed. My breaths deeper, controlled. Hunter stood beyond the reach of the tide, frustration pulling her face tight. Her photographer's shutter snapped shot after shot. I didn't care. My slacks clung to my legs, cold water working its way toward my waist. I didn't care. The pain, gone. The voice, gone. A calm no medication had yet brought me, something I hadn't experienced when in the water since I was a child.

In the distance, Dr. Sattler directed one of the Denim Duo to a tree I'd not noticed before. There he broke off a low-hanging branch and jogged with it in my direction and gave the photographer a shoulder bump as he passed. He called out to me from the shore and waved the stick in the air.

"Ellie thought you could use this," he said, "for support when you get out."

I'm not getting out. Not now.

"Just a few questions," Hunter pleaded. "Then I'll leave you alone."

"No, you won't."

"I'm going to write this story, regardless. You can contribute and have some control of the narrative, or you can take your chances on what I'll say."

She was right. There I was, fully dressed, standing thigh-deep in the bay, appearing to have done so to avoid her questions, which I'm sure is how she'd have framed it if I'd let her. With the lack of pain came an embarrassing amount of clarity regarding my present predicament. How I'd process all I'd just learned, I had no idea. The idea of reconciling this horrific history seemed an impossibility, made more so if I let Hunter tell the story for me. So little left in my control that the notion of even a modicum managed compelled me to move.

"All right," I said.

Sattler joined her colleague on the beach. I gave a curt nod in Ellie's direction, and she walked to meet me at the shoreline. My slacks grew heavier as the sand rose under my feet. Water drained out of my pant legs in a rush, gravity pressing down on my leg with each step, the pain creeping back in. Sattler held out the thick branch. I grasped it and dug it into the dirt.

And I am in a room with no door or walls, only windows, seeing out.

Not windows. Eyes. They are mine, but they are also not mine.

With these eyes, I see a house where there was not one before. Bigger than any house I have ever lived in, white wood siding dressed by a wraparound porch with two rocking chairs flanking a storm door. A well rises out of the ground. There is a tree with a wood-and-rope swing attached to its strongest branch, and on that swing sits a young white child in a cream-colored dress who sings as she kicks her stockinged legs back and forth, gaining height and momentum, pendulum-like, and just as hypnotic. I know this child is my daughter. But I also know that is not possible. I do not have a daughter and yet I know that is who she is. She sees me watching her and digs her feet into the ground, bringing her to a stiff stop. She jumps from her swing and breaks into a run toward me. She is screaming but I cannot make out the words.

It is then I realize I am seeing past something. Someone. I bring my focus to the forefront. Before me stands a man, his lips cracked and split, curly hair unkempt, the skin of his dark brown face dry and ashen, save two straight lines down his cheeks where tears have marked their path.

This body's mind tells me I am the cause of his state, his dehydration and fatigue, his fear. He holds one hand out in front of him, calloused palm up, trembling but strong. His other arm extends back, keeping behind him a young boy. His clothes are as tattered as the man in front of him, his shirt oversized, his pants cinched at the waist by rope. He does not share the fear in the man's face. The boy's eyes, alight with anger, are trained on this me who is Not me, unblinking, unrepentant, unforgiving. He is not afraid of Not me. I wonder why he would be afraid to begin with, why the man feels the need to protect him from me.

The answer is in my hands. The branch I held in my hands moments ago, in this place, in another time, is now a finely crafted walking stick, heavy, with an ornate pewter handle. But I am not using it to support my weight. I am brandishing it. I scream at this body, tell us to put it down. I hear myself ask, plead, why are we doing this, scaring this man and child who are my brothers, but my voice only echoes in this room I am in. My hands are not mine, and yet like the daughter who isn't mine, they are. They are as white as if they've never seen the sun, thick blue veins tracing paths over tendon and bone, under skin taut with the ferocity of my grip. I will this body, this mind, to be calm, but this self, that is so foreign and yet familiar, does not yield to my will.

Speak then. Tell them they have nothing to fear from you, that while you do not know what is happening, you know they are your kin, and you theirs, though you may not appear so, and that you will not harm them. Still this body does not bear my entreaties. This body knows they are not his kin. The man's fearful face only brings this Not me unmitigated rage, and the more fervently I desire to quell this anger, the less capable I become of doing so. That his ward does not fear me incenses me further. In a voice not my own, I say to this man,

I warned you, which is more grace than I ought ever have given you. I set it upon you to liberate that boy of his paganistic ways, and yet again I discover him spitting in the face of the Lord, our God. I thought myself to blame, allowing my beloved to teach you people to read, as if such a thing were possible, sooner teach a pig to plow, but how else to bring you to the way and the light?

I roll the stick in my hands.

Perhaps this is the only way.

The boy, in all his audacity, peers out from behind his protector and snarls, lips tight, gums bared,

Better to reign than serve, ain't it?

And I am incensed. The varnished wood of the cane squeaks inside my grip. I caress the heavy handle.

This stone you will not refuse, child.

My daughter screams from the field through which she runs. She is begging. Pleading for me to back away. To put down the walking stick. I can see she means to throw herself between me and them. My mind is machine parts, grinding at each other, determining the source of her need for their salvation. So desperate are her cries that I wonder if one or both have been familiar with her, and I brim with yellow and black bile, ill-tempered and melancholy, and I must be free of these humors, and I am certain I will find that release in the death of these animals before me. The thought simultaneously excites and reviles me, and I command my hands to release the stick, but they instead raise it until I am holding it as if it were an axe and they trees for felling. My daughter's screams turn to anguished cries, for she knows as well as I that she shall not reach me before I complete my swing. The man's tears stream in rivulets down his face, but the child holds me in his defiant gaze. If there was time for him to be afraid, it is now, but if he is, he will not show it. He has more minerals than I thought one of his making capable, and respect glimmers amid my fury. One final plea from my brain to this body falls unacknowledged, and my arms rear back and my torso twists like a snake coiled upon itself. I swing. The man's mouth opens, but, like me, his scream is not his own.

I stood over Mrs. Hunter. She was on the ground, one hand reached out in front of her in a defensive posture while the other scooted her backward, away from me. She screamed, tearful and frightened. Her photographer, on his feet, backed away in sync, not helping her to her feet, but snapping photos in rapid succession, the shutter sound only just exceeding the pace of my heaving breaths. My hands hurt. I held the stick Dr. Sattler's man had retrieved for me like a bat, and it was then I understood Mrs. Hunter's fear. Her image mirrored that of the man I'd just seen cowering before me, protecting the child. I held my stick over my head, ready to swing. At him. At her.

With the realization of what was happening, I dropped the branch into the sand and walked toward her, apologies tumbling from my twisting tongue, when something hit my side. My diaphragm seized and my breath left me in a graceless grunt. I spun as I fell, the side of my face dragging in the dirt. Then a knee in my back. A sweaty palm on my wrist, wrenching my arm behind my back. Then between my shoulder blades, a focal point of pressure.

So much pressure.

My father crying on the floor. In bed, stung and shivering. You, Malcolm, on my back again. Your baby's breath on my cheek. A wraith perched on my chest. My son.

My son.

My son?

Am I going home? Will you be happy to see me?

My other arm flailed, desperate not to have them both pinned behind me, knowing that if I didn't push myself up, I might never rise again. Sand and dirt filled one nostril and I strained my neck, hoping to lift my head. The harder I worked to keep air filling my lungs, the more often the refrain of "stop resisting" fell into my open ear. I thought to do so, but then not resisting only led to more of the same. One eye pressed to the ground, my open one searched until I found an incredulous Hunter. Officer Ryan found my free wrist and applied leverage, forcing that arm behind me as well. More air left my lungs than came in. His free hand pressed against the side of my face, the side I fell on the day prior in his presence.

I can't breathe.

I can't sit up.

"Please."

Hunter's incredulity morphed into something else, what it was, I don't know, but it was enough for her to say quietly

"Stop."

When the pressure remained, she shouted, "Stop! Let him up!"

More pressure. Less air.

Dr. Sattler now. Her colleagues. "Get off him! He can't breathe!"

Vision narrowed. Photographer stepped closer. Snapped pictures. Pressure abated. Then relieved. Inhaled deep, then again. Vision back into focus. Pulled by my cuffed wrists to kneeling. Dr. Sattler and the Denim Duo at her side moved to help me to my feet, but Officer Ryan warned them back. He spoke to the photographer as he yanked me upright, sending knives through my shoulders.

"You're taking pictures of me?" Officer Ryan then barked at Hunter. "He was going to swing that stick at you."

She stood and brushed off her skirt. "I know what he did."

"But you're going to have him take photos like—" He saw Dr. Sattler holding up her phone. "Are you recording me? Put that thing away, or I swear to God—"

"Or what?" Sattler said. "If I were you, I'd stop talking."

"You people are unbelievable." He puffed up his chest and tossed a sarcastic tone at Hunter. "Would you like to press charges, ma'am?" He spat "ma'am" as though it were bitter in his mouth. Hunter considered me, then Sattler and her crew, then me again. Her hesitation hovered interminable over my head, put my heart in my mouth, swallowed back behind my ribs when she shook her head. "Your lucky day, huh?" Ryan unlocked the cuffs.

I faced him. "Yes, I feel so very fortunate right now."

The corner of his mouth twitched. "You should." I failed to suppress a shiver. He saw it, then spoke past me to the group and tipped his hat.

"Ladies." The photographer sloughed off the attempted insult as Officer Ryan walked back toward his cruiser parked at the barricade. When I approached Hunter, she took a step back. I stopped and put my hands up.

"Thank you."

"Thank . . . ? Fuck you. Stay the fuck away from me or I *will* press charges." She walked off with her photographer in tow. Dr. Sattler's crew trailed behind them and went back to their digs. Ellie stayed back.

"You okay?"

"My face hurts. Both sides now."

She touched two fingers to my chin and guided my head to the side. The tips were rough. "It's pretty scraped up. You'll want to clean that out as soon as you can." I nodded. "So, that was . . . something."

"Yes, it was."

"Has anything like that ever happened to you before?"

"You mean my threatening a woman with a tree branch or almost being suffocated by a cop? Because no, neither."

"To be fair, she wasn't close enough. You wouldn't have hit her from where you were standing. And you did ask her to leave you alone."

"Ellie, if you're trying to make me feel better, could you please stop?"

"Right. Sorry. So are you okay?"

"You asked me that already."

"You didn't answer."

"Well, let's take account, shall we? I apparently almost clubbed a reporter, which if I had, I could have killed her. Then I got tackled and nearly asphyxiated by a police officer who not ten minutes ago had been asking about my well-being, who might not have let me up if that photographer hadn't been snapping pictures, even with all of you watching. So, am I all right? No. No, I don't think I am."

"Apparently?"

"You said 'apparently' you almost swung at her. Like you didn't know you were doing it. Wait. Did you not know you were doing it?"

"You wouldn't believe me if I told you."

"Tell me anyway."

What did I have to lose? "I don't remember threatening her. I know this won't make any sense, but that wasn't me."

She didn't scoff. No surprised expression. "No, I believe you."

Her belief unnerved me. I decided I'd test it. "I don't mean in the sense that I'm not a violent person, though I'm not. I quite literally mean that wasn't me."

"I know."

"What do you mean you know?"

"I'm not really sure how to explain this. In fact, even the thought of saying it out loud sounds just as ridiculous as it does in my head."

"I've been living ridiculous the last couple of days. Try me."

"Okay, but you're going to think I'm nuts," she said.

"Say it, Ellie. Please."

A deep breath. "Whoever was going to swing at her head? That wasn't you."

"Isn't that what I just said?"

"And I'm saying you're right. Your face. Jesus, I can't— It wasn't yours."

"Come again?"

"I thought I was seeing things. Everything happened so fast. But when you grabbed that stick . . ." She reached for my face, and I shrank back. She pulled back her hand, then moved it toward me again, slower. "This scar? Wasn't there. Your hair was different. Your skin. It was like . . ." She breathed out through pursed lips. "Like the bones of your face had melted, then hardened into someone else's. But then it weirdly still looked like you." She laced her fingers on top of her head and paced. "I know how bananas that sounds, but I know what I saw, even though it was so quick. Oh, God, please don't tell anyone I said this. They're going to think I'm on drugs."

She'd seen whomever those hands, that voice had belonged to. Her admission left my legs light, and I thought my knees might buckle again. She reached for the stick and offered it to me again.

"No!" She flinched. "Sorry. I didn't mean to shout. I'm fine. I don't need it." I would never touch that timber again. She eyed me, then tossed the branch back to the ground.

"What are you going to do now?" she said.

"At this very second?" I pulled my phone from my back pocket, the screen cracked, most likely in the scuffle. I pulled up the rideshare app and hailed who I hoped would be Mo. "I'm thinking very seriously about getting blind stinking drunk." I gestured to the dig. "What's next here?"

"We'll continue excavating." She held her hand out for my phone and tapped at the screen when I gave it to her. "I put my number in there and sent myself a text. I'll give you updates the minute I have them."

"Thank you."

"For what?"

"Being kind."

She tilted her head toward the barricade. "Walk you out?"

I nodded. Pain snaked up my calf with every step. At the barricade, Officer Ryan sat in his car, scrolling away on his phone. When he saw us, he set his phone down and watched while we waited for my ride. I was relieved when Mo was behind the wheel of the car cruising down the path. I thanked Dr. Sattler and approached the rear driver's side door. Mo adjusted the rearview as I buckled up.

"Shit, the hell happened to your face, Jelly Man?"

"Me and gravity had another disagreement. And please don't call me that."

His disbelief was clear, but he didn't push it. "App says back to the bar. Sure you don't need to get your face checked out?"

"Get me to the Scholar quickly and the first one's on me."

He draped his arm behind the headrest of the passenger seat and twisted as he threw the car in reverse. "A little early for me, chief, but I'll get you there as fast as I can."

Pebbles popped under the tires as we made our way back to the main road. I turned, wondering if Officer Ryan would follow. Though his car remained parked, there was a sense of his presence behind me, as close as if his knee were still on my back. When I faced forward, orange flashed again. A fox—*the* fox, I was certain—sat on the side of the road, in front of the tall grass, unmoving even as the car approached. We watched each other as the car crawled past, and we kept watching each other until we were both out of the other's sight. Dirt and sand and mud mixed in a mask over my shoes. I moved to brush it away, then stopped. Consideration for Mo's interior aside, I worried touching remnants of the ground would take me back to a place where Not my body spoke in Not my voice and did things I would never do. Despite that fear, whatever Ativan remained untouched by the adrenaline flood did its job, subdued my sense memory and constricted the connections that produced all the emotions I should have been feeling in the moment. My heart did not race. No tears fell. But I shook the entire drive back.

FIFTEEN

What lies in the dirt?

When you were lowered (tossed?) into the loam, when its warmth melted flesh and muscle and tissue from the bones that bore it, did it absorb the trauma now etched inextricable into the rungs connecting your paired helix, no longer to be passed to your offspring because the opportunity to do so was removed from you like a malignancy, but to be fed to the flowers, passed to the grass, transported to the trees, their roots the grasping fingers of a child desperate not to be separated from its mother, clawing at her breast for sustenance, unaware of the pain and horror held within her bosom, tainted not only by the intangible scars of maliciousness meted, but also the makings of the men who meted it, the pleasure they took in the inflicting of their afflictions, their supposed superiority expressed by placing you in servitude, and eventually in the ground, the dirt a womb that held no life, only the truth of what ended it, and the sickness that led to its end, an ungodly nature that feigned godliness by resting you in repose fit to enter a kingdom that would not have the man who placed you there, who would be blinded by the light of the new day he forced you to see.

What lies in the dirt.

SIXTEEN

Mo dropped me in front of the Scholar at the same time Clarence was arriving. He held the door open as I exited the car and called out to me.

"Hey, Phony Morrison! What's the haps?"

I stopped for a moment. Wrong in thinking I was ready to face him or Freddy, I veered toward the door to the apartment. He covered his teeth, brow creased with confusion at my detour. How long he stood there waiting, I didn't know, and I didn't care. I hadn't processed all that had occurred in the last few hours, let alone the last few days, though that thought gave me just as much pause. Maybe what I really needed was to say these things out loud to these new acquaintances. Truth be told, Freddy was the closest thing I'd had to a friend in some time. Maybe I needed to hear the preposterousness of all I'd experienced (or thought I'd experienced) laid bare, to confront the reality of the reality in front of me, and not these delusions that felt so real as to supplant this reality I'd not yet faced, not truly, because who could possibly face that reality and not suffer delusions? Who could not be broken by it, cleaved down the middle, not cleanly, but both halves jagged and macerated? Still, a bar stool confessional would have to wait.

I climbed the stairs to Freddy's flat. At the desk, I opened the last remaining miniature bourbon bottle and finished it in two gulps. I wanted more. Needed more. I didn't want to think. I didn't want to process. I didn't know how. All I wanted was to sleep, thinking things would be clearer after some rest, that I could make sense of all this in the morning, but the idea of sleep had become a cruel joke and my leg ached and throbbed.

Then I remembered the water, how standing in it had relieved the discomfort in an instant. The bathroom behind me, I thought about the last time I'd taken time for myself in a tub. It'd been awhile. Worth a shot.

Hot water streamed from the faucet. The vanity fogged as I traced indistinct patterns in the rising water. Full enough, I stripped. The medical tape, soaked from my venture into the surf, had all but lost its adhesiveness and the gauze pad hitched a ride with my pant leg as I peeled off my slacks. Purple lightning bolts traced their way upward from foot to knee. Still no evidence of the tentacle I was sure I'd seen at the hospital. The wound appeared less angry, but still inflamed. I tensed, anticipating agony as I lowered my leg into the tub. But again, I felt nothing. No, better than nothing. Better, even, than relief. A sensation damn near euphoric. Both legs in and the feeling spread. Wanting more, I slid down the porcelain until only my head remained unsubmerged and closed my eyes.

He is sixteen. And he is trying my patience.

I sit in the car outside Vanessa's apartment, checking my watch repeatedly as though he can see me and know that I am frustrated with his lack of punctuality. He knows that five minutes early is on time and on time is late as far as I am concerned, and that he is now no longer early nor on time is a fact he must realize, and likely relish, given the quality of our recent relations. When the front door opens, he is still late because it is Vanessa approaching, not him. She puts her hands on her knees as I lower the passenger side window.

"Hey," she says.

"Where is he? Services start soon."

"He says he's not going."

"*He* says? Since when is that his decision? This is my weekend."

"I'm aware."

"And yet you're standing here, not him."

"And what exactly would you like me to do? Pick him up by his belt? Drag him out by his ear? He's a foot taller than me."

"You're his mother. He's not going to physically resist you."

"You say that as if I'm going to put hands on him. If he doesn't want to go to church—which he doesn't—that seems to me something the two of you need to work out."

"You're enjoying this, aren't you?"

"A little bit, maybe."

"That's great. Why do I always have to be the bad guy?"

"You don't have to be. You could maybe listen to what he has to say. He's a smart kid."

"He thinks he's smart. There's a difference."

"You would know, right? Or would you?"

"Funny."

"*I* thought so. So, either you're coming in or you're coming back later. Maybe you can convince him to go with you, but I'm not getting in the middle of this."

"Fine." I open my door and follow her up the walkway. I take advantage of her back being turned and take her in, her curves cauterized in my subconscious. I can trace them blindfolded. Her perfume trails behind her, the scent taking shape via a beckoning hand, and I am Pepé Le Pew, minus the assault-adjacent advances, but no less unwelcome. She glances behind her, and I aim my eyes between her shoulder blades instead of her rear, though I'm certain in the split second it takes to do so, she witnesses where they'd rested. Inside, I hear Malcolm's music echoing in the hall before we reach her apartment. My face tenses and my ears pull back when she opens the door, flinching from the bass blast. "Why do you let him play that so loudly?"

"Because I like it, too? Lord, when did you become such an old man?"

"Please. I look good."

"Doesn't mean you're not old."

"So you admit I look good."

She shifts on her spot and I think I know I am maybe certainly on to something. She sees me thinking I know this and stands rod straight. "Go talk to your son." She points to his room.

I hover my fist in front of his door. "To be continued?"

"Talk. To your son."

I put on a playful pout, then knock. No answer. I thump. No answer. I pound. The music turns down. He opens the door a crack. The cage of bone around my heart is no shield to the knife of disappointment that is his face collapsing upon seeing me. There are so many means for me to stitch the wound we suffer together, but I have convinced myself that the edges are too old, the skin necrotic, too fragile to knit, no matter how much thread I use. His disdain is a time machine. While my body remains here in the present, my mind is transported to an adolescent age where I react to agitation and perceived slights with my own in kind. He walks away from the door, leaving it open only inches. I push it wide and stand with my hands comically firm on my hips. The ridiculousness of my pose doesn't escape him. He smirks and lies back on his bed, arms behind his head, as if he cares for nothing in the world, including me.

"Are you about to use your heat vision on me or something?"

I remove my hands from my hips. "Let's go. You don't have time to get changed."

"Why would I change even if I was going?"

"Because you look homeless, and you are going."

"One, that's fucked-up, and two, no I'm not."

"Boy, I'm not going to tell you again about your language."

"Mommy doesn't care. She said as long as it's justified, it's cool."

"And you think just now was justified?"

"You think calling me homeless is?"

"I said you looked homeless."

"Right, because focusing on semantics makes that comment less horrible. Good for you, Dad. Really."

I hide the fact I am proud he used "semantics" correctly in a sentence, even as a clapback. "We're wasting time. Let's go."

"I'm not going to some white man's church."

"White man's . . . Malcolm, it's a Black church!"

"No such thing."

"Excuse me?"

"You all out of excuses, Dad." He stands and pulls *The Autobiography of Malcolm X* from the bookshelf across from his bed, then has the temerity to toss at it me. "You bought me this. You know exactly what I'm talking about."

I hold the worn paperback in my hands, run a thumb over the portrait of my son's namesake on the cover. He's dog-eared the pages, some refolds of the same pages I'd marked when I read it at his age. The swell of pride pushes against my petulance but loses.

"So, what, you're saying Islam was the original religion of our people? The Nation wasn't even—you know what? I'm not doing this. I know you're smarter than this and you're just trying to push my buttons. Well, mission accomplished, Mal. Buttons pushed."

"See there you go speaking for me again, making stupid assumptions. I didn't say Islam was the original religion. I don't care about Islam. Or Christianity. Matter of fact, I don't give a shit about religion. At all."

"Right, because you're too cool for all that, huh?"

"Whatever. You wouldn't listen even if I told you the reason. But what makes me mad is you're standing here trying to force the church on me when Christianity was forced on our people. You know, the ones that didn't throw themselves off the ships."

"Okay, Killmonger. That's enough."

He points at me. "See? Why do you always do that?"

"Do what, Malcolm? Call you on your crap?"

"That! Disrespect me when I'm trying to be real with you. Ain't this the stuff you write about? I mean, isn't everything all about being Black enough for you?"

"Be careful, Malcolm."

"Why? Why do I got to be careful, but you don't? You come in here trying to make me go to church when I don't want to like you the overseer himself. Must get that from Grandma's side, huh?"

I close the distance between us with one quick step and bring my nose to his. Fear sends his eyes searching back and forth across my face. I've not seen him this way before, and though I should be ashamed he fears me, I revel in it, because it's the closest approximation to respect for me coming from him in some time.

"What did you say to me?"

He does not step back, but he does not step forward. "You need to get out of my face."

"Or what, little nigga? What you going to do?"

And at that, his fear disappears. He sees something in my eyes, hears something false in my bravado, and I am naked. And he knows it. Now his nose presses back against mine. "Listen to that code switch. Wow. It kills you that I'm Blacker than you, don't it?"

I step back. His grin is Cheshire. Frustration with him is normal. It is our new love language. But I am beyond frustration. Though I'm angry, it's not rage. I don't fear physical violence manifesting. I disdain him. I am disgusted. He is a stranger in this moment, and I do not like him, and I do not like myself because he is me, he is the filtered parts of me I placed into him, feathers from the wings of my better-natured angels, hoping he would be more like them than me, but he does not believe in angels, nor me. I don't know how to reconcile this estrangement, so I walk wordlessly to the door. He says to my back,

"Probably just want an excuse to drink the wine, anyway."

I squeeze the copy of *The Autobiography* into a cylinder, then I turn and launch it at him. The book unfurls in the air and the flat of it smacks him in the face. In truth, I do not mean to hit him with it, and I stifle a laugh at the ridiculousness of it all, and hope he will laugh, too, and we will come together in a sitcom moment where I am Carl Winslow and he is Eddie Winslow and after we've argued about him not talking to me like I'm one of his little friends, or about why drugs are bad, or about being pressured to have sex, we find our common ground and I go to shake his hand because I respect him as a man and he refuses and I am confused and then he pushes my hand out of the way and pulls me in for a hug and my arms hang in the air because I am unsure what to do because I want to hug him like a little boy but want to respect that he is becoming a man but then I hug him back and we exchange fierce slaps to each other's backs to reaffirm our heteronormative masculinity and the studio audience swoons at this display of manly yet tender affection and Harriette Winslow played by Vanessa enters the room from offstage worried we are still fighting and places her hands on her hips and gives us an approving nod she thinks we don't see but we do and we release our embrace and drape our arms over each other's shoulders and I wipe a tear clinging to the corner of my eye and Vanessa says something sweet like "my boys" and the studio audience applauds because there is a sign that tells them to do so but also because there are fathers and sons and mothers in those seats and some of them are genuinely moved by our coming together and they look at each other with the same look Vanessa gives us and they go home and try to remember the loving moment we just had when they snipe at each other about things that are truly petty because if the Winslows can make it work then damn it so can they and then the music comes on and my pre-recorded voice tells the audience watching at home that we taped in front of a live studio audience and then the show is over.

This is what I want. This is not what I get.

What I get is Malcolm blinking in disbelief that I have hit him in the face with a book. What I get is a vacuum into which all sound is sucked as we stand across from each other, gunslingers with hands at the ready, unsure who will move when and do what when they do. What I get is a twitch at the corner of his eye before he reaches for the lamp on the nightstand and hurls it sailing past my head, thumping against the wall before it shatters on the ground. I should be thankful that he hit the wall and not my head, but I know his aim suffers the same affliction as mine, one in which to hit the desired target, we must aim about a foot off center of said desired target. That means he was aiming for my head, and I am enraged, but also not a little sad. The next thumps I hear are footsteps down the hallway. Vanessa throws open the door. She sees Malcolm, shoulders hunched, fists balled, jaw clenched. She sees me mirroring his position, though I cannot tell how well my face hides my shellshock. She sees the book at his feet, the ruined lamp at mine.

"What did you do?" she asks. I turn to her to see to whom the question is directed, hoping it isn't me, but certain it is. And it is.

I press my hands to my chest. "Me? Who's got a broken lamp in front of them?"

Malcolm sneers. "Who *should* have a broken lamp upside his head?"

I hold my arms out to the sides. "Well come on with it then, Malcolm, you so hard."

Vanessa steps between us, her back to Malcolm. "Stop it! You're supposed to be the grown-up!"

"He threw a damned lamp at my head."

He peers around Van. "If I was aiming for your head, I would have hit it."

"Boy, you know you can't throw for shit, just like me."

"So you weren't trying to hit me in the face with a book?"

Van jerks her chin back. "Wait, you hit him in the face with a book?"

"Van, hold on."

"You threw a book at your son?"

"No. I mean, yes, I threw it, but I was not trying to hit him in the face. Come on. Why would I do that?"

"I don't know, why don't you tell me what would possess you to throw a book at our child in my house?"

"What would possess your son to say I go to church only for the sacramental wine? What have you been telling him?"

"You are an adult. He is a child who popped off. And you throw something at him?"

"I ain't no child," Malcolm mumbles.

Van speaks through her teeth. "Boy, not now."

Even as she admonishes him, she moves closer to him until they are standing side by side, settling into the space next to each other, ready to be photographed from below for the cover of their new album about to drop, titled Us Against You: The Way It Is, The Way It's Always Been. But all the tracks are retreads of the same songs they've been playing together for years. Remixes of the same themes, same rhythms, even repeating lyrics. And I'm tired. I'm not the one anymore. Time for my mixtape to hit the streets, called Straight Out of Fucks to Give.

"We argued about whether we should have you. You know that?" Vanessa's mouth drops and my vengeful inner child does a dance I'm not sure I can keep from taking shape on the outside. "Want to take a guess as to who wanted you and who didn't?"

There is no tremble or uncertainty in Vanessa's voice when she says, "Leave."

"Well, now you don't have to guess."

"Get the fuck out of my house."

"Yeah, all right. Malcolm, be ready to go when I come back next time. Don't have me waiting again." I step on the lamp shards on purpose and give my feet a twist as I push off, grinding the ceramic into powder, and leave the door open behind me as I exit. When I reach the door to the apartment, I open it. On this side of the doorway, I am a man who delights in the violent silence from Malcolm's room while I imagine they stand facing each other, or maybe they don't, maybe neither can make eye contact as they consider what and how and when they will speak to each other next, how different things will be from now until then, how they will reconcile this new computation, or if they can, and this man that I am here feels he has finally won a battle in a war in which he had felt outnumbered from the start, and that man walks from the apartment to the hallway with the purpose of the accomplished, though he lied to accomplish his purpose.

On the other side of the doorway, I am a man ashamed. I pulled the pin on a grenade and left it behind, the explosion evident by the slamming of Malcolm's door, Vanessa sure to be on the other side. The door would offer her no protection from the detonation. Both would be hit by shrapnel, the kind that embeds, that causes wounds that fester until the only options are amputations, a cutting off of connection, of emotion, of understanding. Fuses shorter. Patience less plentiful, if not nonexistent. Even the wounds that healed would leave scars, ones that would itch depending on the direction of the wind or the barometric pressure, or even when blood rushed to the area from embarrassment or anger, unwelcome and unanticipated reminders, no matter the cause, of the trauma that left their signature in their skin and on the muscles of their hearts.

No remedy exists in going back in there. There is no way to unexplode a bomb. I'd always warned Malcolm about the power of words, that they had both the potential to elevate and eviscerate, that they must be wielded as carefully as any weapon. And I had been so careless with mine. I tell myself that it was accidental, but I am no novice. I've fired this weapon before. I know better, and yet I know no such thing.

When I reach the church alone, I sit in the back row of pews, in a corner behind a column, out of view of the altar. I drone along to the homily when I bother to read along at all. I sit, I kneel, I stand, I kneel, out of memorization of the routine and not from an inner call to do so. Kneeling feels different. I do not appreciate the vantage. The call to serve rings loud and dissonant. The hymns are off-key. When we shake hands in a pronouncement of peace, I don't experience the usual warmth, I take note of calloused and clammy palms, of weak grips and false smiles and I feel anything but peaceful. When the service concludes, I avoid eye contact with the congregation and slip out before anyone has left their row. I cannot put enough distance between myself and that building, and I hope I will feel differently by next Sunday. I get the sense that I won't, and I am terrified by what that might mean.

Clicking awakened me. How long had I slept? My temples pulsed. Lactic acid pooled in my jaw muscles. My teeth chattered. My bathwater had gone from steaming to frigid. My head throbbed with the rhythm of a thousand hangovers, though I'd had little to drink. This haze hanging between reality and not reality was becoming tiresome to clear. I pushed off the sides of the tub to stand and fell back into the tub with a thump and a splash.

That's when I saw that my legs were not my legs. My hips were not my hips. From my navel down, my limbs had been spliced into threads, transparent and weightless, floating, tangling.

My legs were tentacles. My legs were not supposed to be tentacles. They were supposed to be legs.

I snapped. And I screamed. My voice unlike any version of my voice I'd ever heard, but still decidedly my own. I screamed until I had no air left, until the sides of my vision went brown, and then took a deep breath. It's the water, it must be, some weird refraction of lights, the bourbon, the Ativan, the possible concussion, the Lexapro preventing serotonin from finding the grooves in my gray matter.

Who gives a shit what it is? I've got to get out of this tub.

I hoisted myself again, but my legs wouldn't support my weight. Numb, that's why, too long on my posterior on the porcelain and they fell asleep. Certainly not because they're tentacles. I threw myself over the side, the lip of the tub pressing into my soft stomach, then walked my hands along the cold tile, dragging my legs/tentacles up and over the edge of the bath. Anticipating a thump when my thick thighs hit the floor, I instead heard a wet squish. Still tentacles. No change in lighting or medium made any difference. My legs had become goddamned danger noodles.

Then a knock at the apartment door. Because of course.

"Yes?"

Muffled from the other side of the door. "Hey, it's Freddy. Are you okay?"

"I'm just great. How are you?"

"Huh? I'm fine. I just . . . we thought we heard a scream downstairs. And a thump."

"You've really got to get more customers."

"Yeah, I know. So are you all right?"

"Fine. I slipped getting out of the tub is all."

"Oh, Jesus. Wait, why are you shouting? Are you still on the floor?"

"I'm fine, Freddy. Honestly."

"Don't be ridiculous. Let me help you."

"Not a great time, Freddy!"

"Why? I promise you—you've got nothing there I haven't seen before."

"I promise *you*, that's not the case," I said to myself.

"What?"

How had she heard that? "Nothing. Please go away, Freddy. I don't need any help."

"Okay, truthfully, you sound a little drunk and I'm not having you die on my bathroom floor from another concussion. So cover up or do whatever you got to do, because I'm coming in."

A towel hung on a rung attached to the wall within arms' reach and low enough for me to claw it down. I shimmied and shook until I was on my back and whipped the towel out in front of me ensuring it covered the snarl of tentacles splayed out on the floor. Equal parts terror and relief sent a river of adrenaline into my drug-drenched tributaries and the tidal wave washed away any indication of inebriation. Terror because how did I explain my current condition? Relief because I wouldn't be the only one to know what was happening to me now. Keys jangled, tumblers clicked, the bolt receded into its nest, and the front door creaked open. My elbows underneath me, I sat up, and I waited. Freddy pushed the door open.

"Oh, thank God," she said.

"What?"

"I seriously thought your head would be split open or that you'd broken a hip or something."

"Damn, Freddy, how old do you think I am?"

She grimaced. "Do I have to answer that?"

"No, thank you."

She mimed wiping sweat from her forehead. "All right, well, come on. Let's get you up. You've got to be freezing."

She stepped toward me, and I held my hands out. "Wait, wait."

"What? Is it your leg?"

"No. Yes. Not really. Sort of."

"You sure you didn't hit your head? Whatever, it's okay. We'll take it slow."

"Freddy, I can't stand up."

"Why?"

"There's . . . something underneath this towel."

Her eyes narrowed. "Okay." Then widened. "Oh." She thought she understood.

"No, no, no. That's not what I mean. What's under here . . . I don't think you're ready to see it."

"Oh, please. I told you I've seen one before. Relax, man."

"This is different."

She nodded toward the full tub. "Is this the shrinkage thing?"

"What? No. I just . . . there's no easy way to say this."

"Jesus Christ, say what?"

I took a deep breath. "I'll just have to show you." I closed my eyes and snatched the towel from atop my tentacles. Nothing from Freddy—at first. Then a deep breath.

"Oh. My. God. You weren't kidding."

I opened one eye a crack, then the other. Freddy had one arm across her stomach, the other held her hand to her mouth, though not a mouth agape in shock. Instead, she looked as if she might cry. Then I understood. Under the towel was not a surfeit of squiggly stingers, but instead my wrinkled feet, connected to my already ashy shins, connected to my flesh-covered femurs, all the way up to my too-wide hips. Altogether in my naked glory. Sweat bloomed on my forehead and needles filled the blood rushing to my ears and cheeks. I covered myself and Freddy's giggle burst through her barricade.

"That's what you thought I wasn't ready for? Although, I guess you're right. I wasn't quite ready for *that*."

"Very funny. You're a big help. Really."

I wrapped the towel around my waist. She offered her hand, but I moved it aside and stood unaided.

"Don't be like that. So you're a grower, not a shower. It's no big deal."

I brushed past her into the bedroom, sat on the edge of the bed. "You can go now," I said into my palms.

Freddy leaned against the bathroom doorjamb. "You really believed there was something else under that towel, didn't you?" She spied the empty mini bottles on the desk. "Bad drunk dream, huh? I've had those. Swore it was real, even after I was awake. Maybe time to stop mixing business with pleasure?" She picked up my pill bottle and rattled it.

"Put that down, please. It's not what you think. I'm not drunk."

"Okay."

"You don't believe me."

"Hey, you're an adult. But I mean it—you die up here, I'm charging you double."

I forced a grin, and she returned it, but her concern was apparent, and not unwelcomed.

Ask me. Please ask me.

She took a beat, then spoke. "I should probably get back downstairs. Clarence won't have anyone to talk to." She stepped away, then stopped. "I'm sorry, I just, I got to know. What did you think was under the towel?"

"You're not going to make fun of me?"

"I can't promise that."

"Then no."

"Come on. I promise to try not to make fun of you. How's that?"

I wanted to tell her, and I had run out of reasonable excuses not to. So I told her. Tentacles, Freddy. Tentacles. Despite my expectations, she didn't make fun. No eye rolls. No cautious steps backward until she knew she could make it to the door before this deranged, half-naked lunatic finally flipped and strangled her. She took a step forward, then another, until she stood at the edge of the bed. She patted my shoulder with the back of her hand.

"Scoot," she said, and I moved down while she sat. "Talk to me."

I did. I told her what they'd discovered about the bodies at the dig. How they'd found what they thought was a child. The tree branch and what I saw when I grabbed it. My threatening Mrs. Hunter. Officer Ryan kneeling on my back. Maintaining eye contact with her was hard, but every time I did, I saw she was fixated on my face, nodding as if sensing when I needed affirmation, listening with intent instead of thinking about what she'd say. When I was done, as when I had unburdened myself to her in the hospital, I found myself sitting up straighter, breathing easier, but still somewhat horrified to hear what she thought of all I'd just said.

"Well. You're definitely nuts."

I laughed, loud and hard, in a way I hadn't in some time, so hard my belly bounced against my towel and would have popped it loose had I not sensed my haphazard tuck's impending failure and grabbed it before another embarrassing reveal. She joined in, and our amusement filled the room and cleansed me the way a hot bath could not. Each round ended with a breath of relief, which only rolled into another giggle, until my eyes leaked, and my abdomen ached, and while it all felt so necessary, I also felt I might be perched on the ledge of hysteria. Freddy saw this and pulled me back.

"Okay, okay, reel it in. I'm funny, but I'm not that funny."

"That's true, you're not." I inhaled deeply and wiped my cheeks. "How are you not running out of here screaming?"

"Would that make you feel better?"

"Maybe. It's the normal response. The response I'd expect."

"Normal's never really been my thing, you know? Normal's never been great for folks like us. Normal doesn't pay attention, you know? Normal likes to dismiss, ignore. Maybe you seem like you've had enough normal."

"Maybe. Not sure I feel any less crazy."

"You work with words, my guy. You can't just toss 'crazy' around like most people do. You've had some serious shit crammed into that head of yours the last few days. Plus, the booze, the meds, a possible concussion. That's a lot for anyone, normal or not. And let's not forget this new giant spicy meatball just rolling around your already ridiculously full plate."

"I always hated spaghetti."

"Too much like tentacles?"

"Really?"

"Too soon?" I held my thumb and forefinger up, a small swatch of air pinched between them. "Fair enough. I have to say, I don't blame you wanting to take a tree branch to old girl. Matter of fact, I'm jealous."

"You and Mrs. Hunter acquainted?"

"She came around a few Februarys back wanting to do a 'special interest piece' on the bar, something about how I kept the place like Dad had instead of turning it into a beach-themed bar like the rest of the ones on the strip. Of course, I don't need to tell you what a 'special interest' piece in February is."

"No, you do not."

"Exactly. I said, 'Why February? Is that the only time people would be interested?' Well, she got all up in arms about that. Asked just what it was I was accusing her of. You know the type. She considered herself woke back during that millisecond when white folks thought it was a compliment to be called that, before they turned it into a slur. She ended up writing some piece none-too-subtly trashing the bar, talking about the outdated aesthetic. Blah dee blah dee blah. Ooh, I wish I had been there to see her face."

"Well, I can only imagine what she's going to write about me now."

"It won't be good, for certain."

"Freddy, that's not helping. At all."

"Yeah, well, lying to you won't, either."

Just a chuckle this time, no mania mounting. "You're a great listener."

"Part of the job, you know?"

"No, it's more than part of your job. You've got a gift. At least for the listening part. You're a little cheap on the pours."

"Maybe for you that's a good thing, yeah?" She patted my knee once and stood.

"What do I do about the property, Freddy?"

"What do you want to do with it?"

"Make it go away. Sell it and forget it ever existed. Can I still do that?"

"Honestly, I don't know yet. I've never dealt with something like this before. If the archaeological society is involved, there could be some complications. There are a lot more chefs in this kitchen now and they know recipes I don't. But I have to ask you something."

"Go ahead."

"Are you sure that's really what you want to do?"

I massaged my temples. "I don't know. Maybe? I'm sick of all this tragic mulatto nonsense, you know? Though I suppose that's an image I've cultivated, isn't it?"

She sat next to me again. "I know I've been loose with the jokes with you about the drinking and the pills and whatnot, not because I don't care, but because I know you were already going through some things before all this got dropped on your head. But this tragic mulatto thing—you were real with me, so can I be real with you? Like *real* real?" I nodded. "I feel you on this. You know I do, or you wouldn't have said what you said to me that first day we met up at the site. So listen to me when I tell you— you can't keep letting whiteness define your blackness or your mixedness or whatever you want to call it. I did that for a long time and all it did was lead to more questions, more asking myself what I was, when I already knew. That bullshit doesn't get to define you or your tragedy or get to decide how you react to your struggles or your trauma. All that belongs to you, and you get to experience all of it however you need to. You want to sell the land, sell it, if they'll let you. But I don't know, man, I don't think you should do it because you need to be free of someone else's notion of you, you know? If you did, would you really be free of it?"

I was stunned by her honesty.

She sounded like you, Malcolm.

Freddy nudged me with her elbow to bring me back. "But, hey, that's just me talking. Nobody said I know anything about anything. Take it or leave it. I'll make some calls, but let's talk tomorrow. You need some rest, and I got to get back downstairs."

I remained silent. She slapped her thighs, stood again, and made for the door.

"Freddy?" She stopped and pivoted. "Thank you."

She nodded, then tilted her head toward the bathroom. "Get that water up off the floor, huh? You already dented my wall. And see a doctor, will you? I'm not picking you up off the floor again."

"Lord, I should have just let you leave."

"Probably, yeah."

"See you later, Freddy."

She gave a sarcastic salute and closed the door behind her. Her footsteps faded down the stairwell. When I heard the lower door close, I inched the towel away from my knees. Still my knees. My brain commanded my toes to claw the hardwood, and they obeyed. I was me again, for whatever that was worth. While relief was present, it wasn't the dominant emotion. Worry wormed its way into my internal dialogue as all signs pointed to one hell of a hallucination, an additional indication I was in serious trouble. Despite that anxiety, yet another emotion ruled the roost.

Let's agree you'll not listen in for this part, shall we, Mal?

The night Van and I conceived Malcolm, we'd imbibed our fair share of liquor, and as we explored each other's bodies for the first time in ways I'd only imagined, we also experimented with some carnal communication. Van was a natural, each utterance more enticing than the next. Not to be undone, brain bathed in hormones, my vocabulary went from intimate to indelicate, though at the time, I thought it was the sexiest soliloquy ever uttered. Her face midway through suggested otherwise. When I'd given over my chromosomal contribution, I rolled to my back, hoping the mattress would open into a maw and pull me down into it, saving me from the embarrassment of what I'd said in the moment. Of course, it didn't.

Sitting on the edge of the mattress, that same sense of shame washed over me. I'd told Freddy too much, this woman I hardly knew. I should have kept my mouth shut, but I couldn't. I thought sure sharing would make me feel better. It didn't. Instead, the adrenaline of my bath time adventure blunted the competing chemicals in my bloodstream and my embarrassment vibrated with jackhammer intensity, and her comment about what defined me left me exposed, my insecurities laid as bare as I'd been on the floor of her bathroom.

I stood, wary whether my legs would hold me. The familiar throb returned to my calf, though not with the same intensity. The bathwater it seemed, as at the bay, had had some palliative properties. It tracked then that more fluid might be the answer, but bereft of my bourbon stores, I filled a glass from the tap and downed another Ativan, then sat at the writing desk and opened my laptop. The screen lit to life and revealed the browser I'd left open the last time I'd used it. I clicked on the search bar, then typed:

am i turning into a jellyfish?

Several suggested links appeared.

10 Facts You Didn't Know About Jellyfish.
Does the Jellyfish Hold the Key to Immortality?
Are You a Jellyfish Christian?

The second Ativan got good to me, washing away the ridicule and re-gret of my revelations. Numbed my lips. Deadened my limbs. Feeling no pain of any variety, I clicked on another rabbit hole, and went burrowing.

SEVENTEEN

Eyes opened. I couldn't lift my head. My legs wouldn't move. I tried speaking. Nothing doing.

Not again.

Except no pressure on my chest. None on my back, either.

Try talking again. Say your name.

One side of my mouth formed around the syllables, the other did not. A stroke, then. The tab for the drinking and meds come due. No more hallucinations. No more paralysis. Straight to brain bleed. Do not pass go. Except, no, not that, either. Something wet under my cheek, and under that, something flat and unforgiving.

The desk. I'd fallen asleep on the desk.

And drooled. Quite a bit.

My cheek had numbed from the pressure, as had my legs from too long seated in the chair. My neck and back had frozen in their slumped position. I pressed my palms on the desktop and lifted my heavy head. Several pops and cracks sounded as I straightened and faced the window. Though the bright sun peeked through the blinds, I shivered. Still clad in only my towel. A tin man without oil, I stood and stomped the needles from the bottoms of my feet, experiencing immediate regret when my jellyfish-stung leg screamed at me.

I woke the laptop and saw my email was open. A message from Emily waited in the in-box. The subject line read CALL ME. The body of the email contained no further text.

"Well, that can't be good."

I dressed, then called her.

"Hey, Emily, before you say anything, I'm sorry I was brusque with you on our last call. I'm in the middle of some frankly unbelievable stuff and, if I'm being honest, I'm having a difficult time telling left from right. That said, I shouldn't have taken that out on you."

"Apology accepted. Especially with what you sent me last night. All is forgiven and then some."

"Great, I'm glad you liked it." Wait, what? "I'm sorry, I sent you something last night?"

Her voice went coquettish. "'Did I send you something.' You don't need to be humble. How long have you been sitting on this pitch? Did you think it was too far out of your wheelhouse? Is that why we haven't talked about it yet? I mean, I won't lie, the first attachment freaked me out a little bit, out of context and all, but when you responded to my email with an explanation, I saw it as part of the larger project, and it made so much sense to me. You know I think you're incredibly talented, but, whew, I didn't know you had this in you. The meta-approach, the way you're writing about grief and family legacy and colonialism? Just a great, great concept. Perfect, really. Of course, I have several notes."

As she spoke, I opened my laptop and searched my "sent mail" folder. Two emails. One with only an attachment. No subject. The second with the subject RE: RE: WTF?! Both after three in the morning.

"Are you in town?" she said. "I have to see another client in Philly today and was going to call you to connect anyway. We should sit down and talk about just these tiny tweaks I think it needs." Her voice turned melodic. "We do this right, and I smell an auction!"

I opened the first email.

To: emily@randomnamehereagency.com
From: unnamednarrator@gmail.com
Subject: RE: RE: WTF?!

Devil Is Fine is the story of a biracial Black writing professor, grieving the loss of his son, who inherits a plantation from the white side of his family. In the process of selling the land, bodies of both the plantation owners and the enslaved individuals are discovered buried on the grounds. Questioning his notions of faith and family while exploring the impact of colonialism on his identity and beliefs, he becomes haunted by the ghosts of the dead while he writes a fictional account of the land's history.

To: unnamednarrator@gmail.com
From: emily@randomnamehereagency.com
Are you drinking again? What is this? What am I supposed to do with this? Call me when you get this. I'm worried.

Had all my openings not snapped shut as I read a pitch I hadn't recalled writing, I'd have been impressed at how I had turned lemons into lemonade. Things being what they were, what with my having become airtight, I clicked on the other email and opened the attachment. A force not unlike a shove propelled me against the back of my chair, said lemons hitting me square in the face, the impact knocking loose a gasp I masked with melodramatic hand over mouth, and all the air came rushing back in.

To: emily@randomnamehereagency.com
From: unnamednarrator@gmail.com
Subject: RE:

bettertoreignthanserverbettertoreignthanservebettertoreignthanservebetterreignthanservebetterreignth
anservebettertoreignthanservebettetoreignthanservebettertoreignthanservebettertoreignthanservebettertor
eignthanservebettertoreignthanservebettertoreignthanservebettertoreignthanservebettertoreignthanservebe
ttertoreignthanservebettertoreignthanservebettertoreignthanservebettertoreignthanservebettertoreignthans
ervebettertoreignthanservebettertoreignthanservebettertoreignthanservebettertoreignthanservebettertoreig
nthanservebettertoreignthanservebettertoreignthanservebettertoreignthanservebettertoreignthanservebette
rtoreignthanservebettertoreignthanservebettertoreignthanservebettertoreignthanservebettertoreignthanserv
ebettertoreignthanservebettertoreignthanservebettertoreignthanservebettertoreignthanservebettertoreignth
anservebettertoreignthanservebettertoreignthanservebettertoreignthanservebettertoreignthanservebettertor
reignthanservebettertoreignthanservebettertoreignthanservebettertoreignthanservebettertoreignthanserveb
ettertoreignthanservebettertoreignthanservebettertoreignthanservebettertoreignth   rvebettertoreignthan
servebettertoreignthanservebettertoreignthanservebettertoreignthanservebetter   servebettertorei
gnthanservebettert   hanservebettertoreignthanservebettertoreignthanserv   ignthanservebett
ertoreignthanser   eignthanservebettertoreignthanservebettertoreignth   ebettertoreignthanser
vebettertoreignt   ttertoreignthanservebettertoreignthanservebettertorei   rvebettertoreignt
hanservebettertor   nserv   ertoreignthanservebettertoreignthan   thanservebettert
oreignthanserve   i   rvebettertoreignthanservebettertore   toreignthanserv
ebettertoreignt a   reig   anservebettertoreignthanservebebe e   er   bettrtoreigntha
nservebettert ei   ttertor   nthanservebettertoreignthans veb   th   rvebettertor
eignthanserv e   servebet   toreignthanservebettertore   ans   terto   thanservebe
ttertoreignt s   nth   ebettertoreignthanservebette   n   rvebett   oreignthans
ervebetterto   th   ebetter   nthanservebettertoreignthanserve   nt s   ebettertoreig
nthanservebetter   ttertoreignthanservebettertoreigntha   hanservebette
rtoreignthanse   ervebettertoreignthanservebettertorei   oreignthanserv
ebettertoreigntha   ignthanservebettertoreignthanservebe   bettertoreignth
anservebettert   rtoreignthanservebettertoreignthanser   ettertoreig   anservebetterto
reignthanserveb toreigntha   rvebettertoreignthanservebettertoreignth   ervebetter   reignthanserveb
ettertoreignthan ebetterto   thanservebettertoreignthanservebettertor   thanserv   ttertoreignthan
servebettertoreig hserve   rtoreignthanservebettertoreignthanservebett   reignt   servebettertorei
gnthanservebetter ignth   rvebettertoreignthanservebettertoreignthan   ettert   ignthanservebett
ertoreignthanserv t   nthanservebettertoreignthanservebettertoreignt   rve   ertoreignthanser
vebettertoreignth   toreignthanservebettertoreignthanservebettertoreig   ha   bettertoreignt
hanservebettertorei   ebettertoreignthanservebettertoreignthanserveb   ore   nservebettert
orreignthanservebet r   thanservebettertoreignthanservebettertoreigntha   vebe   reignthanserv
ebettertoreignthans b   rtoreignthanservebettertoreignthanservebettertor   hans   ettertoreignth
anservebettertoreig n   ebettertoreignthanservebettertoreignthanservebe   reig   servebetterto
reignthanservebett rei   anservebettertoreignthanservebettertoreignthans   bette   ignthanserveb
ettertoreignthanse tt   reignthanservebettertoreignthanservebettertoreig   nser   tertoreignthan
servebettertoreig e   ttertoreignthanservebettertoreignthanservebett   ebettertorei
gnthanservebette   servebettertoreignthanservebettertoreignthanser   anservebett
ertoreignthanserv ert   gnthanservebettertoreignthanservebettertoreignth   ettertoreignthanser
vebetttertoreignthanservebettertoreignthanservebettertoreignthanservebettertore nthanservebettertoreign
thanservebettertoreignthanservebettertoreignthanservebettertoreignthanservebettertoreignthanservebette
rtoreignthanservebettertoreignthanservebettertoreignthanservebettertoreignthanservebettertoreignthanserv
ebettertoreignthanservebettertoreignthanservebettertoreignthanservebettertoreignthanservebettertoreignth
anservebettertoreignthanservebettertoreignthanservebettertoreignthanservebettertoreignthanservebetterto
reignthanservebettertoreignthanservebettertoreignthanservebettertoreignthanservebettertoreignthanserveb
ettertoereignthanservebettertoreignthanservebettertoreignthanservebettertoreignthanservebettertoreigntha
nservebettertoreignthanservebettertoreignthanservebettertoreignthanservebettertoreignthanservebettertor

"Are you still there? Hello?"

I said something unintelligible, even to me. The kid, in my vision? hallucination? time travel? at the bay, hiding behind his protector. That's what he'd said to me/Not me.

And there it was on the page. Over and over and over again.

Better to reign than serve.

Better to reign than serve.

All work and no play makes Jack a dull boy.

Jesus, Lord, help me. What is this?

Malcolm, is this you?

"So tomorrow is good?"

"One fucking second, Emily! Jesus."

A deep breath on her side. "That was uncalled for."

I inhaled too. "You're right. That wasn't about you."

A pause. "Is everything okay?"

"Not really."

"I have to ask . . . *are* you drinking?"

I checked my watch. "Let's talk later today, okay?"

"So you are in town?"

"No, but I will be this afternoon. I need to see my parents."

Bushes lining the retaining wall of my parents' front porch grew un-checked. Weeds weaved their way through the broken mortar connecting the pavers. The sweet gum tree in the front yard reached its branches over the roof, and the spiky balls it let loose left bruises on the aging shingles. Knowing Mom might well be sleeping, I rapped on the front door's small window. Through it, I watched my father shuffle round the corner from the hallway, hips and knees stiff, three of the four joints replaced with plastic and titanium. He pulled on the knob just enough to open the door, then turned away, doubling back on his original path, expecting I'd follow.

"Close that quietly. Your mother's napping."

"Glad to see you reached out to that landscaper I found for you."

With his back still turned, "Glad to see you dressed up again to come see your parents."

Though my father's household attire consisted of sweatpants pulled up just below his sternum with a T-shirt tucked into his tightly tied waist-band, thick white socks, and running shoes, he never left the house unless he was dressed to the nines—vest and bow tie, herringbone slacks, gator ankle boots—so fly couldn't nobody tell him nothing no ways, especially not why anyone, particularly his one and only son, found jeans, a T-shirt, and anything with exposed toes acceptable attire in public, especially when that one and only son was in his late forties and a working professional. To say I didn't see his logic would be somewhat dishonest. To say I didn't dress this way when I knew I'd see him as a means of childish antagonism would be just as deceitful. My smirk only graced my face when his back was to me. I knew he saw it anyway.

"Coffee?"

"I could definitely use one."

"I see that, too."

Sees all, knows all. I rubbed at my stubbled cheeks and chin, cleared the corners of my eyes, disappointed when I found bits of crust I thought I'd cleaned. The decorative mirror hanging adjacent the wall-mounted cordless phone reflected more red than white in my eyes. Stride unbroken, Dad pointed to a half-full carafe on the cluttered counter as he made his way to the living room. I poured a coffee for each of us. When I reached him, he was still in the process of lowering himself into the glider rocker, wincing all the way. I'd learned not to offer assistance because "what would I do if you weren't here," so I stood silent, save a sip from my steaming mug. After he'd settled in, I set his coffee on a tray table in front of him and took a seat in Mom's rocker next to his. He muted *SportsCenter*.

"How's that hip, old head? Still fighting the good fight?"

"Fought. Lost."

"You going to get it replaced? I think a fourth joint replacement gets you half off your next colonoscopy."

"No."

"No?"

"Who's going to take care of her while I'm in the hospital? You? You're too busy for all that."

"Well, if you'd check out an assisted living facility like I told you, you'd have help all the time and you could stop being in pain. What happens when your knee gives out on you while you're here? What if it's while you're going up and down the steps? Then what?"

"If all you wanted was to tell me how I was supposed to be doing things, you could have just called. You didn't have to stop by unannounced."

"You don't answer the phone."

He sipped his coffee. "That's correct."

I chuffed and took a sip of my own.

"What brings you by? You're not one for a drop-in. Do you need money?"

"When have I ever come here asking for money?"

"But you admit it's unusual, your being here?"

Just say it. Say why you're here.

"I'm meeting with my agent to talk about some things. I got into town early, so I thought I'd check in."

Coward.

"'Into town?' You were out of town?"

Never misses a beat. My leg itched and I scratched. The hem of my pant lifted and revealed my calf. He saw it. "I was at the beach."

"The beach?" His chair creaked as he leaned back and glided the rocker in small oscillations. "I thought you hated it there."

"I don't love it."

"I don't imagine you would."

"You remember?"

"You urinated all over me, son. That's not easy to forget."

"For the umpteenth time, Dad, it was the water."

"Sure it was."

"Yeah, well, even if I had peed on you—which I didn't—could you blame me? That was some scary stuff for a kid."

"For an adult, too."

"You were scared?"

"You were screaming. I didn't want you to get stung."

"But you waded out there like it was nothing."

"You don't stop being afraid of things when you become a parent. You stop showing your fear the way you used to is all." A flash of shame crossed his face, gone as quick as it came. He knew I knew what it was to be a parent. I let it slide, because I'd been unsure I knew anything of the sort. We drank.

"Why'd you disappear after, Dad?"

"I'd had enough for the day. I went back to the room."

"No. Come on. It wasn't just that."

"No?"

"I saw you. In your bed. When Mom brought us back to the room. Did you know that? I saw you shivering from all those stings. Mom tried to close the door, but she wasn't quick enough."

He sighed. "You'd been so afraid of things. Always so worried about what could happen at any given moment. Wouldn't climb on the jungle gym. Never too high on the swings. Something about that water, though. I'd never seen you like that. Unafraid. Curious. I thought if you saw me hurting, that would go away, and I didn't want that for you. It made me sad when you didn't want to go back. I didn't know why you wouldn't until now. Why didn't you say anything?"

"I didn't have the words for it then. What did I know about feelings? I knew I had them, but I didn't know what they meant. Something was wrong with you, and I thought it was my fault."

"It wasn't."

"Thanks."

He wrapped his hands around the mug and turned it in circles. His nails had grown to a point, skin thin over his finger bones. No pepper left in his Afro, only salt.

"Was that after you were crying that day?" He lifted his head. "I can't remember how old I was, so I don't remember if that was after the beach or before. You were crying so hard you went down to the floor. Mom held you. Do you know what I'm talking about?"

"I do."

"I never knew why."

"You never asked."

"I'd never seen you like that. I guess I was afraid to ask. To know."

"Are you still afraid?"

"A little, yeah. But I'd like to know."

He sat back in the rocker. "Do you remember the first time your mother took you to get a haircut?"

I did, like few days before or after.

Mom kept her hair long when I was a kid, and she took meticulous care of it. Her morning routine took at least an hour, and for whatever reason, I was fascinated by all the choreography. The shampoo, the conditioner, the blow-drying, the mousse, the hairspray. When she ran her comb through, it didn't get caught in tangles. She didn't wince when the teeth got stuck on a knot and pulled on her scalp. Not like mine. Dad's fingers caught in my curls when he tousled my hair. Every day before school Mom tried to comb out my curls and every day I went to school with a headache, only for them to spring back into a loose pile. Most of the kids at the Montessori were white. They'd point out my squirrel's nest, whisper about what must be living in there, accuse me of being dirty. On a day they'd been particularly cruel, Mom picked me up from school, and I broke down, told her all the things they'd said, told her how much I hated my hair, how much I wanted it to be like hers. When we returned home, I heard her talk with Dad about it, and though their tones were hushed, I remember sensing Dad was unhappy. I just didn't know with whom.

The next day, Mom told me she had a surprise. We were going on a trip. Dad didn't go, didn't say why, and neither did Mom, but my excitement boxed out my curiosity. I peppered Mom with possible destinations—McDonald's, Toys R Us, Kiddie City—all of which she said no to, sending me squirming. She pulled the car into her hair salon's parking lot. When I asked if she hadn't just gotten her hair done, she palmed my cheek and told me this visit was for me. I threw off my seat belt and hugged her tight, thanking her over and over. No more wetting my hair over the kitchen sink, no more of Dad nicking the top of my ear with his barber's scissors. No more knots. No more tangles. No more jokes at my expense.

The salon made me feel like a movie star. Wendy, Mom's regular hairdresser, squealed in delight when she saw me and took me by the hand, told Mom to get comfortable, that they'd treat me like the little prince I was. She led me to a cushioned chair with shiny chrome armrests that reclined when I pushed back while she guided my head backward into a padded neck cradle. I flinched when she turned on the high-pressure hose and tested the water temperature on her palm. The warmth worked its way from my scalp to my cheeks, my chest to my stomach, my hips to my toes. Her fingertips kneading my scalp sent a surge of static to my low back, a tingle I'd never felt. I closed my eyes as she massaged in the shampoo, the scent invoked images of flower fireworks and sliced citrus. She sat me up and rubbed my head with a towel made of clouds. If she hadn't held my hand as she guided me toward her styling chair, I'd have floated to the ceiling.

Who knew how intoxicating the smell of hair-dryer-fried follicles and chemically percolating perms could be? Certainly not me, but there I was, hypnotized by the scents of beauty being birthed. In the mirror-lined room, several white women occupied the other chairs. They stopped their conversations when they saw me. Their hairdressers leaned in and whispered to them, and my ears went hot, the magic muted, fearing their conversations composed of the same ill will that fueled my classmates' mockery. The temperature in my lobes cooled, however, when they smiled at me as Wendy had, seemingly so pleased I'd joined them for the day. I hopped into Wendy's chair, and it rose with a slow hiss as she stepped on the release bar beneath. She snapped out a satiny apron, deep purple, fit for the prince she'd said she'd treat me as, and fastened it around my neck.

She pulled a comb from a glass container filled with blue Barbicide and my scalp tensed in anticipation of the tugging and yanking that was sure to follow as she ran it through my tangles. But the comb passed through unmolested. No snags. No knots. Smooth and even. I watched in the mirror as she pinched inches of hair in her fingers and guillotined them away with a close-open of her shears. The wet clumps, though straight in her grasp, fell on my gown-covered lap and curled like cooked shrimp. Swatch after swatch fell, the hairs separating as they dried. Wendy covered my eyes as she sprayed from a bottle, remoistening my quickly dehydrating locks. She pulled a curtain of hair down in front of my eyes, the cold steel of her scissors gliding across the bridge of my nose as she cut the strands away. My vision unobstructed, I squinted at my reflection, imagining the style she was sculpting, but could not envision anything other than the collection of curls that typically sat atop my head. Pacing around the chair, she assessed her artistry, and decided it was time for the final flourish. She unholstered a hair dryer and blew through what was left of my hair. My scalp tingled as she ran the brush through, shaking the dryer so the air washed warm waves over me. When she finished, she sprayed a huge dollop of mousse into her hand and finger styled my coif into a firm but flexible masterpiece.

I couldn't believe what I saw when she stepped aside. No more nest. In its place, a length of hair, razor straight, swooped across my head in a side part. Not a curl in sight. My hair was the same as all the white children in my class. Wendy stood behind me with a handheld mirror to see she'd added the ducktail that had become the cool accessory all the kids with straight hair had been wearing. I hopped from my seat and wrapped my arms around Wendy's waist, and this time, I guided *her* by the hand, pulling her to the waiting room where Mom sat leafing through a worn issue of *People* magazine. When she saw me, she clapped her hands in front of her mouth in delight. She reached into her purse and offered Wendy a tip, but Wendy refused, instead asking that she bring this little gentleman back whenever my next wash and style was needed. I asked Mom if we could wash my hair there every day. She and Wendy embraced. As we left, I bounded across the blacktop to the car.

Mom had hardly stopped the car at the curb before I flung open the door and sprinted up the walkway to the house. I couldn't wait to show Dad my new do. Mom quick-walked to the porch to let me in, and I shouted for him, going room to room, Mom in tow, smiling all the way. We found him downstairs in the basement on his exercise bike watching *Wide World of Sports*. I did my best George Jefferson strut and stood in front of him, turning and pointing at my fresh new cut, my dope little ducktail. He didn't turn the television down. He didn't stop pedaling. He said he was glad I liked it. When Mom saw my face, she shifted her disappointment with Dad to shared jubilance with me. She said we should leave Dad to his workout while we went upstairs for snacks.

Dad's lack of enthusiasm hadn't surprised me all that much. He didn't cry during sad movies, he didn't dance to his favorite music, and his anger often only appeared in stern yet even-keeled admonishments that were more frightening than any shouting. The one and only time he'd spanked me was the one and only time I ever needed to be spanked as he was emotionless throughout in a way that scared me more than his corporal punishment ever did. Still, he'd known how saddened I'd been by my classmates' teasing, how each school morning began with a nervous stomach hampering my appetite for breakfast. I thought sure he'd see my happiness and join me in my excitement.

Sitting across from him now, he saw past me out the window onto the rear patio, saw past the present moment we sat in, lost in the same memory as me, but remembering it much differently. The rims of his eyes shimmered, the afternoon sunlight catching the cataracts clouding his lenses. He saw an alternate reality taking place in the same remembered timeline, one where his wife had brought his son home less than he had been when she took him to a place that processed out a perceived connection to his Blackness, that took another piece of his son away from him, in the same way that his almost entirely white school seemed to be doing by the day. Joining him in that reality, I experienced his pain when I came down those basement steps elated at the erasure I'd undergone, not mattering if I understood that erasure is exactly what it was, at least to him, and if his perception was his reality, then that reality roiled his guts and halted his heart. Understanding this, I wanted to tell him how the haircut hadn't helped, how the kids simply found something else to declare me different and therefore strange, how I held on to the hairstyle into the high school years as a delusion of defiance, and how recalling those days as an adult raised revelations sending me on a relentless pursuit of my Blackness ever since, a journey's end yet to be realized. But I was still that scared child in a sea of jellyfish, and all I could say in answer to his question was,

"Yeah, I remember."

He retrieved his reminiscence from that other time and faced me again. Lines creased his cheeks, a genuine, honest-to-God grin, and he reached his hand out and touched the tops of the curls I'd allowed to return.

"I like how you wear it now."

I cleared my throat around a sob that vaulted from my viscera and lodged in my larynx, forcing it back down to the depths. Dad sniffed, and the teardrops collecting at the bottoms of his lids receded like the tide. He set his coffee aside and pushed down on the arms of the rocking chair.

"Your mother is probably waking up."

I put my hand on his knee and he paused his ascent.

"Finish your coffee. I'll check."

He paused, sat, then nodded.

I walked the carpeted hall toward my mother's room, the room they'd once shared. On my way, I passed my childhood bedroom, now my father's, which it had been for many years, even before I left home for college. I didn't know enough, or perhaps never wanted to know why they had decided to sleep separately. As an only child, I never had a sibling serving as sounding board, coconspirator, or life coach. No one with whom I could share my thoughts, fears, and notions about why my parents spent less and less time together, why they seemed as roommates, romance absent from any aspect of our home. They were still together, and that had been enough for me.

Scratch that. It hadn't been. Not even close. But I'd become so fearful of divorce, of the idea of ever having to—and then subsequently always having to—choose between them should they go their separate ways. The anxious adult today blossomed from the seed of an anxious child, one who when he was old enough, recognized it might be necessary, on a daily, sometimes hourly basis, to remind his parents separately that he had no favorites, that he loved them equally, because if they ever detected that the balance had shifted, they would be compelled to leave, because what parent could handle the knowledge that they didn't occupy an equal space in a heart too big for their child's chest? It fell on me to keep them happy so I could keep me happy.

Time and distance lend perspective. In truth, I wish they'd never stayed together.

Mom's bedroom door stood slightly ajar, the bottom edge dragging along the plush pile as I pushed through. Perfume and medicated ointment shared the air, their cloying, astringent medley mapping every corner of the room. Awake, she attempted a forward sit from her propped pillow. I met her at the edge of the bed. She reached for my hand, her arm tremoring, rolling an imaginary pill between her thumb and fingers. Rice paper replaced the skin on her hands, thick blue veins traveling through, though her blood seemed absent of warmth as she gripped my fingers and pulled herself to sitting with deceptive strength.

"Hey, Mom."

Her mask remained motionless, but she took a deep breath and let out a contented sigh, a language I'd come to understand as a happy hello. Her wheelchair sat behind me, and I tilted my head toward it, but she slow-blinked and slow shook her head no. I removed the thick cushion meant to prevent pressure sores, pulled the chair until it was in front of her, and sat.

"I need to ask you something."

She watched me close, indicating she was listening. I took her shaking hands in mine.

"After Malcolm . . . after the funeral, I received a letter. From an attorney. Grandpa's attorney."

Her fingers rolled faster.

"He'd left something to Malcolm. It was supposed to go to him on his eighteenth birthday. Instead, it went to me."

Faster still. The tremors in her neck had increased. She avoided my eyes. I let go of her hands and retrieved my cell phone from my pocket. I tapped on the photo application and brought up the property pictures.

"This is what he left him."

She turned her head from the phone.

"Do you . . . you know this place, don't you? Is it ours? Did Grandpa buy this? Or did he inherit it?"

What remained of the muscles in her neck strained as if to turn her head further, as if my phone screen might burn her face.

"Is this in your family? Is this in *our* fucking family?" Fear gripped me, not because I was afraid of the answer, but because my control was slipping from me. "Don't you look away from this. It's ours, isn't it? Why?

Why would he give that to Malcolm? To me? Was he that sadistic? Did you know he was going to do this? Did you know?"

She watched me, her eyes as clear as I'd ever seen. Her cheeks quivered, flesh fidgeting at the corners of her mouth. Her porcelain Parkinson's mask split, fault lines forming where her skin pulled tight on her skull. I pushed away from her, horrified, as she opened her mouth, saliva stalactites sticking to her lips as she let out a wail that put me back in my room at Freddy's, and I wondered in that moment if she had been the haint hunched on my chest, telling me what lies in the dirt. With a speed I thought her incapable of, she swung at my hand, just missing the phone. She swung again, closer, and I pulled back beyond her reach. She leaned forward, her lamentations lubricated by a wet gurgle, and swung again, connecting this time, knocking the phone from my hand to the floor and losing her balance in the process. She slipped from the edge of the bed and hit the floor with a thud that almost brought bile to my mouth, fearing a fractured femur. She cried out, and I shouted for Dad, then crouched to help her back into bed. The phone had landed faceup, the picture not the panoramic I'd thought I'd shown her, but a photo of the remains of two bodies, positioned the same as the silhouettes I'd sent to Emily in the middle of the night. While helping Mom, I froze, staring at the image in front of me, a photo I'd not taken. Then something snapped me out of my trance.

Silence.

Mouth tight, eyes wide, shining despite the dull light filtering through her drawn curtains. Head still. Hands still. The only sound in the room her breathing, through her nose, slow and deliberate. No anger or fear. Pleading. I wanted to embrace her. I wanted to smother her. I wanted to love her to death.

Dad appeared in the doorway, out of breath and in obvious discomfort, though his expression became one of concern and not a little bit of aggravation at the sight of us on the floor. His presence snapped me out of my trance, and he came to my side and helped transfer Mom up and seated her on the edge of the bed. Though he hadn't yet asked, I babbled away about what had happened, how I'd tried helping her from her bed to her chair but pain in my leg had made it give way, the only part of that explanation that wasn't untrue, as the throbbing pressure in my calf had returned. Certain she was stable, I kneeled and pocketed my phone. When I stood, Mom's eyes followed, unblinking, still breathing that determined breath, demanding and desperate. Dad, despite what I had first interpreted as annoyance—and make no mistake, he was annoyed—tended to her with grace and calm. He pressed on her hip, her legs, scanning for telltale signs of trauma, finding none. While he showed her gentleness, my empathy for her ebbed from me in waves. And she knew it. Her eyes never left mine, nor the reverse. Dad said she should rest in case the accident's adrenaline dump masked pain she might not possess the ability to profess. He laid her down and she moved her head to the side.

Still, she stared.

Still, I stared.

Meticulous in his handling of her, Dad lowered her to the mattress. When I was a child and I'd done something wrong, egregious enough I'd evoked Dad's anger but only aggravation in Mom, she and I had developed a language only we spoke, one borne of that immense yet intangible link between an only child and his mother. While Dad tucked her in, Mom and I spoke through furrowed brows, facial tics, and tensed lips.

You can't tell him.

> *Like hell I can't. I can. I will.*

>> *Please don't.*

Why didn't you tell me?

How could I?

> *How could you not?*

>> *Some secrets should die with the people who carry them.*

Why Malcolm? Why me?

I don't know.

> *Yes, you do.*

>> *I know you love your father.*

Which is why I'm going to tell him.

Which is why you should never tell him.

> *Don't use him to protect yourself.*

>> *I'm protecting him.*

You were supposed to protect me.

I know.

> *This isn't fair.*

>> *I know.*

I will never forgive you.

I know.

A chorus of conflict swelled within me, an orchestra in its pit drawing bows across my nerves, playing pitifully out of tune. I squeezed my lids shut, signaling the end of our communication, and willed away the burning behind them. When I opened them, she had not averted her eyes. She implored me still, insistent. Finished tucking her in, Dad followed her sight line to my face, then back to hers.

"What are you two talking about?"

Shock shook us loose, turned our heads toward him. A smirk creased the corner of his mouth as he silently said, these things you think I don't know, I do, and I always have. With that, he pushed a wisp of hair from her forehead, and that fondness sent my resolve rolling off the precipice over which it peered, just out of my grasp.

My phone buzzed in my pocket. A notification. Then another. And another. They came in such rapid succession I thought it might be an incoming call, but the screen showed nothing but the time.

"I should probably go."

When he lifted his head, his smirk was gone, replaced by an understanding sadness.

"Five minutes early is on time," he said.

"And on time is late."

He gave my hand a quick squeeze. Elation and nausea swirled, and fireflies floated in the corners of my vision. I bit the inside of my lip hard. The pain sliced, sharpened my view.

"Walk me out?"

Dad planted his hands on the edge of the bed, but Mom gripped his wrist. On a second attempt, she squeezed again, then pulled. He sighed. When he turned back to me, she fixed her eyes on me, and somewhere in between the resting tremors in her neck, she shook her head no again, though the movement was more defined, more deliberate than before.

"You know the way, I guess," he said.

"I do. Good to see you, old head."

As I stepped away, this time it was he who held my wrist. "I know you're having a tough time."

My throat caught. "I am."

"Do something for me, then."

"All right."

"If your business takes you back to the beach, get out in the water again. Wade out deep. Maybe even swim. Find that place in yourself again where you were so brave you had to be rescued."

No amount of medication could mitigate the swell of emotion in my chest, filling until it had nowhere to go but up my throat and out my eyes.

I patted his hand and turned away before the tears spilled over. I was my father's son. I didn't want him to see me cry.

On the porch, I unlocked my phone and walked down the sidewalk toward my car. Before addressing the notifications, I opened my photos, searching for the pictures of the remains from the site. Feet from the car, I stopped. The pictures were gone. Only those of the site remained. Deleted when Mom knocked the phone from my hand, surely, except my deleted photos folder proved that untrue. My lower leg pulsed.

On the drive to my parents' home, I'd heard a public radio report interviewing scientists who speculated, based on their research, that the spinning of the earth's core, relative to the surface of the planet, had slowed to a stop and might even reverse. While the seismologists hazarded there'd be no perceivable repercussions to what sounded like a terrifying geographical phenomenon and thus appealed for calm as there was evidence of a cyclical nature to this slowing, there were also all sorts of possibilities these researchers seemed a little too eager to envision, despite the perilous prospects. A reversed core could change the surface spin and mean a single day could be hundreds of hours long. Perhaps changes in electromagnetic fields could lead to bizarre weather phenomena or even affect the function of insect and animal behavior, including humans. The earth, it seemed, was on a course for a hard reset. Unplug for thirty decades and plug back in.

Inspired by the thought, I turned my phone off. Shut it down, held it still in time while the earth reversed its direction around it, ley lines looping backward, restoring the missing photos and casting over the side the water filling the leaky, sinking boat that was my sanity the last few days. Thirty seconds and a press and hold of the power button later, my phone chimed back to life. The pictures of the remains had not returned. What did arrive however, were even more red notification bubbles. Dozens and dozens. On every social app. On my email icon. On my text balloon. A den of disquiet awaited unlocking with a tap from the tip of my finger on the key. After I'd opened it, I needed a hard reset of my own.

EIGHTEEN

David's surprise at seeing me surprised me, not because he was surprised—I expected that—but because the nature of his surprise was so exaggerated, the gulf between his open eyelids so wide, I was reminded of the cartoons you watched on my living room floor, half expected bright red veins streaking his sclera, his eyeballs bulging past their sockets, anchored by optical nerves, hearing the *ahwoogah* of a Model-T jalopy while his jaw elongated and dropped to his desk with a clang.

Imagining that, I missed you terribly.

"I didn't expect to see you today," he said.

"So I gathered."

"Shut the door, please."

"Well, that sounds serious."

"You're not wrong."

I closed the door behind me. He gestured to the chair in front of his desk, the legs so short, my knees nearly came up to my eyeline. "Did you intentionally buy chairs this low? So you can maintain an elevated position over anyone sitting across from you? If so, that's a gangster move, David. How did I not notice this until now?" If he detected the playfulness in my somewhat authentic question, his expression evinced the contrary.

"How are you doing?" he said.

"Kind of a complicated question right now."

"I can imagine. I am glad you decided to take the rest of your bereavement leave."

"I appreciate your letting me take it. Truly."

"Of course, of course." He folded his hands in front of him on the desk. He even went so far as to twiddle his thumbs.

"Why am I sensing something's coming that I won't appreciate? You're all . . . I don't know. Stiff."

He sighed. "This isn't going to be easy. But I do think, when all is said and done, you will appreciate the potential opportunity this presents for you."

"Can we not do this dance again? Just say it, man."

He cleared his throat and sat upright. "The university has asked me to invite you not to return from your leave."

"Uh-huh. Right. Wow. And the basis of this invitation?"

His posture went from austere to aggravated. "You're kidding, right? Jesus, man, take your pick. Our esteemed Black tenure-track professor comes into possession of a plantation?"

"Wait. How is that my fault?"

"And that same esteemed professor wields a club at a journalist?"

"Okay, I'll concede that seems bad, but to be fair, it was a tree branch, not a club."

He ignored the correction. "The same professor who can't sell his book?"

"By all means, David, don't hold back. How do you really feel about all this?"

"Don't do that. Don't make me the bad guy here, not again."

"Seems to me if you keep finding yourself in that role, then maybe I'm not the one responsible for putting you there, *you feel me?*"

"Right, right, because it's never your fault. Do you ever get tired of always being the victim?"

"I'm going to go ahead and give you the benefit of the doubt that the only 'you' you're referring to is me, and not some larger monolithic 'you,' because, *real talk*? It'd be in your best interest to disabuse me of the latter notion."

"You'd love that, wouldn't you? Something to say to the press, right? I don't mind telling you, man, I'm shocked. This isn't like you at all."

"Is there a camera in here? Is this a joke? Where the hell is this coming from, Dave? Seriously, how long have you been holding on to this hostility? I thought you were the guy who had my back no matter what."

"I could ask you the same question, pal. I've got to find out about all this nonsense from the news? From social media? Where was the phone call? The text to give me a heads-up? Do you have any idea how embarrassing it was talking to the tenure committee?"

"Please, allow me to apologize for your embarrassment, David, but you might have noticed that I have a thing or two on my plate at the moment."

We sat back, two boxers in repose from a slugfest in the center of the ring. I dragged my fingers down my cheeks.

"What about my classes? Registration is already filled for next semester."

"We've got someone coming in."

"What? Already? How?" Ah, of course. You're right, Malcolm. This had been in the works all along.

"New writer. His debut comes out in a few months. He wrote a retelling of *Native Son* from Mary Dalton's perspective. Called *Indigenous Daughter*."

"Indig—are you—David. You do know she's white."

"Uh, yes, I know. I teach Wright's text in my class. It's a clever play on the title."

"It's a stupid play on the title, David. Unbelievable."

"It's really quite subversive when you think about it. Not risk averse by any means. He's really saying something here, you know?"

"My God, you're not joking. Tell me this isn't a white guy that wrote this?" David shifted in his seat and avoided eye contact. "It's a white guy that wrote this. Come on, man."

"What? Give me a break. It's not like he's telling the story from Bessie's point of view. He's staying in his lane. He's an ally. Check his IG account, you'll see. Black square in 2020. He gets it, you know?"

"In his lane. David, the man is replacing the Black protagonist with a white . . . oh. Oh, now I see it. That's the point, isn't it? *This* is the new moment. That's what you're saying. This is what 'the people want'? To see themselves in our work instead of us?"

"I think that's a little dramatic."

"Of course you do." I ran my hands over my head. "Did you even read it?"

He squirmed. "I have the ARC."

"You didn't read it. Replaced me. Didn't read it."

More wriggling. "Hey, the critics are already eating it up. The kid's twenty-three, fresh out of Iowa's MFA. The buzz is unbelievable. All signs point to an instant *NYT* bestseller. He'll be the next DFW."

"So many shiny acronyms."

"Clever. Anyway, how do you not know all about this? He's repped by your agency if I'm not mistaken."

"Excuse me, what?"

"Oh, fuck me. I thought sure you at least knew *that*." I shook my head, dazed. "I tried to help you. Honest to God, I did. After the first read, remember? I said, maybe this theme is a little too heavy-handed, maybe you've done this already. I could have been firmer, sure, but you get touchy about that stuff, and then things were going badly with Malcolm, and I just . . ."

As he blathered on about how he could have been my savior if only I'd let him, I wanted so much for you to be there, Malcolm. You'd have known just what to say to him, known how to verbally eviscerate him, spilling his bullshit all over his lap. But you weren't there.

Or were you? Because what the hell was in my pocket?

Not my keys. Then what? I shoved my hand in and, to my surprise, my fingers closed on something small and rubbery. I extracted my hand, opened it, and saw a bright green toy horny toad, erection at full mast.

Back at the beach, after Mom had dragged me from the novelty store and just before going back to the hotel, I asked for money for a soft pretzel. Instead, I went back for the horny toad. Something about the frog's forbidden nature made me have to have it. Standing in the aisle, box back in my hand, ready for the checkout counter, I lost my nerve. How would I hide it from Mom? What would she do when she found it? She'd had no qualms about throwing a scene the first time I'd shown it to her. Who knew how she'd react this time? I placed the box back on the shelf and sulked back to her, told her they were out of pretzels, and went home empty-handed, so afraid I was of defying her.

And yet here the thing was, after all these years, in my pocket. Had you put it there, Mal? Somehow, that had seemed the most realistic answer amid all the surrealism of the past few days. Maybe you were right. Maybe Freddy was, too. Maybe exercising a little defiance was what I needed then. What I needed now.

I tossed the toad on David's desk. It landed on its back with a slight slap, its penis wiggling back and forth in all its tumescent splendor. David opened his mouth, paused, then spoke.

"What the hell is that?"

"I feel like the answer to that is kind of obvious, David."

"Does that . . ." he said, peering as he leaned over the desk. "Does that frog have a dick?"

"That, in point of fact, is a horny toad, and that horny toad, if we're going to get technical, not only has a dick, but appears quite happy to see you."

"Right. And you just carry this toad—"

I waved my finger. "Horny toad."

"—horny toad—in your pocket?"

"Nope. In fact, I didn't even have it a minute ago. But now I do."

"Uh-huh. And you threw this on my desk because . . . ?"

"I don't know."

"Right. Anything else you plan on throwing at me?"

I shoved my hands in both pockets. They remained empty, but I couldn't help envisioning that the other pocket had a horny toad, and yet another toad had replaced the one I'd thrown. In this fantasy, I threw those two on the desk as well. My pockets refilled. I threw those. Refill. Throw. Refill. Throw. David would watch, awestruck, a child at a magician's show in wide-eyed wonderment at a stream of scarves pulled from a breast pocket until my pockets were empty, the biblical rain of toads terminated, a towering pile of well-endowed water animals wobbling atop his desk. We'd watch each other over the mound of adult-themed amphibians while some somersaulted down the pile, pole-vaulting off their erect penises.

"No," I said. "Nothing else."

"Good," David said, an upturn at the end. "And what would you like me to do with this?"

"Consider it my resignation. This place doesn't get to fire me. You don't get to fire me, David." I walked for the door. "By the way, if you thought the press about me was bad before, wait until I tell them about your plans. My replacement? Whooo, boy."

David leaned back in his chair, barely able to contain his smug self-satisfaction. "Come on. What'd I tell you before? Times have changed. You know as well as I do it won't matter if you do talk. There'll be what, maybe a minor dustup? A little outrage in the news? Like anyone pays attention to that before the next catastrophe grabs the headlines. Even if it exceeds people's fifteen-second attention spans, then what? *Maybe* the university will respond by setting up a DEI committee. Maybe. Hell, they'll probably have me lead it, that is until interest wanes, which we both know won't take long. We'll dissolve the committee, but we'll get to say we did our part. Everyone agrees. Applauds our efforts. End of story. On to the next."

"Yeah. Yeah, you're probably right." I turned again for my exit, then snapped my fingers as I reached the doorway. "I did think of one other thing you can do with that toad, David."

"Go fuck myself?"

I winked at him and flashed him a finger gun. "*My man.*"

Emily sat shelling salted edamame at the table. She shot impatient glances about the room, her tightly pulled ponytail slicing the air. When she saw me, she waved big but made a show of checking her watch. She stood, tugged on the hem of her fitted blazer, and embraced me, kissing both cheeks before pulling out my chair and retaking hers as I sat.

"Sorry I'm late."

"That's okay." Her voice took on a flirty musical quality again, drawing out her okay. "For genius, I'll wait."

"You'll let me know when genius gets here, yeah?"

"Ever so humble. You know I've always thought you were one."

"Always?"

"Oh stop. Yes, I was a little worried about the other manuscript. But this pitch? I'm sorry, getting right into it, aren't I? Can we, though? Get into it? Because, my God, I cannot stop thinking about this idea. This is nothing like your first book, or the new draft. This concept is so self-referential and clever and full of commentary, but like, not in the way you'd put people off. Sad and funny and magical, all at the same time." She fanned herself. "Whew. It's heady stuff. I mean the first-person narrator, him losing his son, then his son haunting him—"

"What?"

"What? Did I misinterpret something? It's not your—sorry—the narrator's son?"

I'd not had the courage to read this pitch I'd apparently written and sent, worried that opening the document would somehow pull me back to the space that created it, a place where I wasn't in control. My mouth went dry. When my father rescued me from the water, I'd been hit by a wave surprising in size as I waded my way out. Knocked on my rear, I gulped a mouthful of salt water. The taste lingered for what felt like the rest of the day. Hearing her summarize the pitch with such unbridled enthusiasm, hearing that you were my ghost, that same taste filled my mouth, floated on my tongue, pressed against the insides of my cheeks. I dared not swallow or speak. Emily eyed me for a reaction I would not give.

"Anyhow, I just want to make sure that sort of autofiction style is the route you want to go. I know how uncomfortable you got with people comparing you to your protag on the first one. It's fine with me, though. I love it. Did I mention I have notes? Because if you're able to implement them, this thing will sing. Seriously, I haven't seen anything like this since—"

"*Indigenous Daughter?*"

"Wait, did I send you the ARC? Whatever, isn't it fabulous? I'm so excited. *Daughter* is going to be huge."

"I doubt in the ways you hope."

"Oh, please."

"Emily, what's wrong with you? It's awful and I haven't even read it. Nor will I."

"I mean, I get why you'd say that. Of course, I do. And honestly, you're right. Kind of. It's amazing and also awful."

"So why sign him? Why would you be a part of putting something like that out into the world?"

"That's not a serious question, is it? It is? Okay, here it is. Because controversy sells almost as much as voyeurism. And hell, is his book even that controversial nowadays? But if we're being honest, you know as well as I do that if readers aren't consuming your pain, they're generating outrage, justified or not, and the bad press and the good press all equal earned-out advances and options for films 'based on the controversial bestseller,'" she said, making unironic air quotes. She reached across the table and patted the top of my hand. "But all the same, I understand your worry. We've got a veritable army of sensitivity readers going over the ARC." She sat back and crinkled her chin as though a thought had occurred to her. "As a matter of fact—"

"No. Absolutely not. I'm not coming within fifty feet of it."

"That's fair, that's fair. I get it. You're going to be far too busy with this new project anyway. Okay, so, my notes on the pitch—"

"Yeah, Emily, about that—"

"Hold that thought." She clapped tiny applause in front of her eager face. Vest-and-bow-tie-clad waiters brought plates of food to the table. "I ordered for us. I hope you don't mind. I was starving and just took a guess at what you might like. I know you veer toward the healthy side, but I remembered you like delicacies, too, right? I think you'll love this."

The waiter placed a salad in front of me, adorned with a pile of shimmering pink strands. "Is that pickled ginger?"

"*So* much cooler," she said, slurping a slew of noodles. "Jellyfish."

"What?"

"You *have* to promise to save me some. I've heard and read such good things about it. It looks amazing."

"What made you think I'd want to try jellyfish?"

"I guess I thought I was being clever. You know, because of your synopsis."

"My synopsis?"

"Where the main character thinks he might be turning into a jellyfish?" She inhaled more noodles and they gave her lips a greasy whip when she reached the end of them. "I swear, it seems like I remember this thing more than you do. Did I imagine the jellyfish?"

"Am I imagining this?"

She either hadn't heard me or didn't care to acknowledge. "Anyway, leave me at least a bite. I've always wanted to try it."

I brought my fork close to the pink pile atop my plate. My leg thrummed. The closer the tines, the more violent the vibrations in my calf. I poked at the lettuce and fixings beneath, a kid eating the bottom of the cupcake, saving the top for last. My fork brushed up against the dehydrated heap and I let out a quick yelp as a hot knitting needle jabbed my calf. Emily lit up with the assumption I'd taken a bite.

"Is it *so* delicious? I totally should have ordered that."

"Emily, about this pitch—"

"Right, right. So here's the thing. I love the idea. I've said that, right?" She didn't wait for an answer. "Now, you're not going to like this part, so bear with me for a minute, yeah, because we're going to have to talk around some elephants sitting in the middle of this room. Your boss . . . he's not entirely wrong. And I think you know this. The industry has definitely . . . shifted . . . since your debut."

"Shifted? Reset. But that's no reason for me—" She held up her hand, and though it pissed me off, if she wanted to bury herself, who was I to knock the shovel out of her hand? I stopped.

"It's every reason. *Every* reason. I know how important it is to write about your experience. I *know*."

"You do?"

"Hello? Woman over here. Minority! Solidarity!" She thumped her sideways fist to her chest.

You at my shoulder again, Malcolm. In my ear. Then out of my mouth.

"White woman, Emily."

She registered a brief affront. "Well, yes, of course, but you know what I mean. Believe me when I tell you, if you stick with these themes, especially in today's climate, I don't care how smart and funny it is—which this pitch certainly is—it will not sell if you don't make it accessible."

"Accessible? As in white folks will read it?"

Is this what it felt like when you stood up to me, Malcolm? I get it. Man, what a rush.

"Well, not to put too fine a point on it, but since you did, yes. It's what the people want."

"Didn't you just get done telling me that's what they *don't* want?"

"Oh, no. They still want you to excavate your pain, and they'll pay to read about it if—*if* you give them a way to see themselves in it, and in a positive light. Take someone from your—oopsie, your *protagonist's*—I keep doing that, sorry! From your protagonist's mother's side of the family. Maybe this family member is a teensy bit racist, but through the main character's experience with his grief and his 'ghosts,' this relative sees the light of day. Maybe they're even the one to pull him out of his grief, and it brings them both to this improved level of understanding of each other."

"They sound like a white savior, Emily."

She shoved another forkful of noodles in her mouth. "Tomato, tomahto." She wiped her mouth with her cloth napkin. "But that's actually the smaller elephant. I saw the article about the plantation. And about you threatening the reporter." I opened my mouth, but again with her damn hand. "Nope. You don't need to explain."

"I don't?"

"Hell no. That's mine and your publicist's job." Her eyes flitted side to side, and she leaned in as if someone might be listening. "Truth is, this is gold. It's the same as *Indigenous Daughter*—"

"Excuse me?"

"Hang on, hang on. I'm just saying that being the bad guy is twice as good as being the hero. Especially now, especially for, you know . . . folks like yourself."

"Now hold on—"

"Come on, we're grown-ups. Let's talk like grown-ups. And as grown-ups, we know with this incident, you'll have people wanting to see you succeed and fail, and on both sides of the racial discourse. This will get the haters who've never even read it talking about the book, saying it sucks, which will of course increase curiosity and sales along with the fans you've already got and the people cheering you on. Plus, this meta-angle of you *actually* owning a plantation? With this and my notes? It's a win-win, my friend. You're back."

I sat back, dazed. First David, now Emily. I'd not seen these sides of them before, and I questioned whether that was intentional, because it most certainly was, but whose intent was at play—theirs or mine—was unclear. Had they not wanted to be seen or had they not wanted me to see them? And why could I see them now? Yes, there was a better-than-average chance I was in the middle of a chemical- and concussion-induced break, but that wasn't it. In seeing them, I was finally ready to see you, Malcolm. Really see you. And in seeing you, *you* let me see *them*, see all the things I thought I'd seen but hadn't.

Well, almost all the things. Because despite this fancy new pair of X-ray glasses you'd granted me, the person I couldn't yet (wasn't ready to) see was me. Luckily, there were few mirrors about.

"Hey, hello," Emily said. "Did I lose you?"

"Just about." Puzzled but unbothered, she spooled another bite of noodles around her fork. "Emily, you ever see that Roddy Piper movie where he puts on sunglasses and can see everyone around him is an alien, and they're all pretending to be human while they're hypnotizing the population into submission, bending them to their whims?"

She answered around another mouthful. "Who's Roddy Piper?"

"Forget it."

She swallowed and eyed my plate. "Okay, I can't wait anymore. What are you doing eating around it? Don't be a chicken. It's not going to sting you." She reached across the table and plunged her fork into the jellyfish. Pain shot through my leg, from the bottom of my foot through the front of my calf and up across my kneecap into my thigh, which contracted as though the doctor had hit me with a reflex hammer, sending the tip of my dress shoe deep into Emily's shin.

"Ow, Jesus Christ! What the fuck, man?"

A laugh left my lips before I could seal them. I held the next one at bay with a fist to my mouth. I swore I heard you laugh, too, Mal.

"You think that's funny? Goddamn it, that really fucking stings! What in the name of Christ did you kick me for?"

My phone buzzed in my pocket. While I fished for it, Emily pulled her pant leg up and examined her shin, where swelling the size of half a golf ball had already taken up residence. She gasped.

"Oh my God, dude, you broke the skin!"

The text was from Dr. Sattler. I held up one finger as I opened the message. "One sec, Em. This is important."

"'Important?' Are you fucking kidding me? I think you fractured my shinbone! What on earth is wrong with you?"

Come to the site ASAP.

Out of town. Can it wait?

A message bubble formed as soon as I'd sent mine.

Get IN town. Can't wait.

Emily, flabbergasted, waited for an explanation. I tapped a quick response to Dr. Sattler—

OMW

—then placed my cloth napkin on the table and pushed my chair away.

"Wait. What are you doing? You're— Are you leaving?"

"Yeah." As I stood, her fraught face stirred something, put me back in David's office. It occurred to me that while I fantasized emptying my pockets of a plethora of turgid toads, not only had I stood up for myself, but I'd drained myself of what at one time was an endless reservoir of suffering saved for fools. You'd freed me, Malcolm. "Emily, you're fired."

"I'm fired?"

"Yes. But thank you for lunch. It was perfect. Though I do have several notes." She shouted something at my back, but her voice had been muted by my inner monologue. Walking out of David's office, I'd left behind a job and benefits. Walking out on Emily now, I'd left behind any chances at a similar job or any other meaningful source of revenue and had certainly kicked any chances of another book out the window as hard as I had her shin. I should have been terrified. Rigidity had ruled my days, routine the remedy for my mind's raucous and often unrealistic ruminations. Any deviation from my schedule sent me spiraling, frantic to repair the fractures in my world order. More than that, I'd found false comfort in doing what I'd been told I was supposed to do. That I'd left behind two means of gainful employment in less than twenty-four hours should have left me fetal on the floor, sucking my thumb. But by the time I'd reached the restaurant's vestibule, I was surprised at the lack of desperation driving me back to Emily, hat in hand, the dearth of desire to crawl back to David's office, apologizing for my antics, and begging for my job. Instead, I walked out the door, whistling.

There was a time when the bumper-to-bumper bedlam of a beach trip down I-95 would elicit one of two, if not both, emotional manifestations.

1. Rage. Not the run-of-the-mill steering-wheel-slapping, expletive-shouting road rage given respite by deep breathing and continued driving, but the ire that impedes vision, the kind that makes you check your rearview, ensuring your eye and mouth aren't drooping from the kind of brain bleed moving a quarter mile in thirty minutes can produce.

2. A cat made of anxiety and claws, sitting on my chest, said claws piercing my pleura, whiskers brushing my lips while it steals my breath until I'm certain I'll need to pull off the road to recover, leaving me then to wait for some good Samaritan to let me back into the crawling line of traffic, thereby eliciting the effects of manifestation number one.

This drive back to the beach, however, was different. Due to Dr. Sattler's defiant desire for my posthaste return, I ended up in traffic at the peak of rush hour, but neither of the normal maladies made themselves known. Instead, I laughed, loudly and often, about the events of the last few hours. The meeting with David played on a loop in my mind's eye, and I rewound The Tossing of the Toad on his desk over and over, replaying the lines around his eye, the twitches at the corner of his mouth as his eyes darted from my face to the toad's rocking red-tipped penis, keeping time to some song neither of us could hear. The frog's googly eyes morphed into Emily's wide-open baby blues, her expression one as unsure as I was about whether I had punted her lower leg as if it were covered in pigskin, and I lost it all over again. While I'd felt your presence in both instances, I still wore some worries that my amusement might move into hysteria, given these bizarre, wholly unbelievable circumstances. Perhaps it really was the medication. Perhaps it really was my move back to the bottle. Or perhaps the collected convergence of reckoning with the immediacy of my connection to colonialism coupled with crippling grief and their subsequent aftershocks on the already unsteady tectonic plates of my psyche had transitioned me from a near psychotic break to a dissociative state. Whatever the case, I'd rarely been in such a pleasant mood.

My arrival at the plantation played thief to my good humor.

The denim-and-khaki-clad masses had increased in number as though they'd ignored a mystic man's warnings to stay away from water and not eat after midnight. Dr. Sattler's red neckerchief was a beacon amid all the blue and beige. I beelined down the gravel path toward the tent serving as her field office. She stiffened when she saw me and shot her eyes to the tall, tan-suited gentleman standing next to her. At the sound of the stones beneath my feet, he spun and flashed a mouthful of veneers, extended his class-ringed hand, and shook mine with a grip I'm certain he felt assured my awareness of his alpha status. I slid my hand back, squeezing his fingers in his palm's stead, and while the corners of his mouth dropped slightly, his lupine appearance never left. The direction he intended for this conversation was clear, so I flashed my teeth, too. He released his grip and wiggled his fingers.

"I understand you're the owner?"

I nodded. Dr. Sattler stood by, lips tight and tucked, rocking from heels to toes. I raised my eyebrows at her, and she glanced down and away to the excavated graves where we'd met the day prior. The two that had been fully excavated sat empty. A third smaller one was vacant as well. The one where Ellie's associate had discovered a child. The wolfman in a suit prattled on.

"We really appreciate your flexibility in allowing our team to work here."

"Yes, well, as of yet, no one has offered me any other options. Where are the remains?"

He exhaled with contrived compunction. "I will admit, the process is a bit of a whirlwind. Obviously when remains are discovered, the authorities have to be involved, and when the remains are determined to be nonforensic in nature, we then have to determine if the bodies are indigenous in origin."

"I understand. Where are the remains?"

His jaw muscles jumped, impatient with my impatience. "Since those remains were determined to be nonindigenous in nature, the decision as to what to do with those unfortunate souls then resides with both Dr. Sattler and our organization." To Dr. Sattler, he said, "We are so glad you reached out to us when you did, Ellie. We wouldn't have been able to move as quickly as we did to preserve this incredible piece of the historical record."

"Did you say your organization?"

"Did I not introduce myself? I'm sorry. Dr. Grant—"

"Of course you are—"

"—with the National Museum of Natural History."

"Right. So, Dr. Grant, where are the remains?"

"You have to understand, it's quite remarkable to find remains this well preserved so close to the water."

"So I've been told."

"Yes, well, in many cases, we'd see significant degradation of organic material. With the remains now exposed by the excavation, the humidity, and the increased contact with the salt in the air . . . well, we had to move as quickly as possible."

"Good, sure. Dr. Grant, one more time, where are the remains?"

He peered at Ellie, then back to me. Ellie toed the dirt.

"We've prepared them to be transported to the national museum."

"Transported? You're taking them?"

"I can't emphasize enough how incredible and important this discovery is. Our team is already hard at work crafting a display that will honor these men's contribution to the story of the North Atlantic slave trade."

"Excuse me, what? Contribution? Did you say 'contribution'?"

Dr. Grant coughed. "Maybe that wasn't the best word choice."

"Yeah, maybe. They were enslaved. They didn't 'contribute' anything. You understand contribution implies being given a choice. These men, that kid—they had no choice."

"I stand corrected. And I apologize."

"Yeah, terrific. Where are they?" He eyed Ellie again. "Don't keep looking at her. This is clearly your project now. You're in charge, right? So are they over there?" I asked, pointing in the direction of a larger tent.

"Yes, but I'm afraid you can't see them."

"And why is that?"

"Again, we're extremely fortunate that the skeletons were so well preserved. Since the bodies were exposed to the elements, we've sealed them away so as to protect them from further harm until the truck arrives to deliver them to the museum."

"Deliver them to the . . . I'm sorry, but how is this possible? How are you allowed to do this? When did you do this? Who told you this was okay?"

He lifted his chest and straightened his thin tie. "As soon as I arrived, I directed Dr. Sattler's team to do so." His upper lip twitched. "Frankly, it should have been done immediately. As I said, we needed to move quickly—"

"I heard you. Seems to me you could have at least waited to speak with the owner of the property before you absconded with my—"

I stopped. Dr. Grant thrust his head forward. "Your . . . ?"

My leg throbbed. The saltwater taste returned.

"Certainly, you don't mean to imply that because these remains were on your land that we somehow . . . that we're stealing them from you? With all due respect, sir, these men, this child, they are not your property."

"That's not what I—"

His face assumed a concoction of counterfeit concern and artificial austerity. "Though, tragically, given your relation to the land, I suppose technically they are. Or were."

Ellie snapped. "Dr. Grant."

I did not snap. Instead, I vomited. No rumbling in the stomach. No warning wave of nausea or cold sweats. Just open mouth, exit insides. This was not your routine regurgitation, either. Oh no. What flew forth from my maw did so with all the force of a high-pressure hose. With each heave, my back arched in one direction, then the other, and when I thought my stomach had sucked in far enough to touch my spine, when I thought all the air had left my lungs, and my guts had been relieved of the last of their gastrointestinal accoutrements, I took a breath and expelled more bottomless bile. My puke parted the dirt at Grant's feet, splashed sick on his Kenneth Coles, and dotted his slacks with digestive debris. When I'd finally finished, he surveyed what I'd wrought, arms outstretched. Dr. Sattler covered her mouth and turned away, desperate to hide either a snickering fit or a dry heave. Dr. Grant stammered as he scanned himself up and down.

"What . . . why . . . why would you do that?"

Some grist of a meal I hadn't recalled eating remained in my cheek. I tongued it free and spit it out, causing Grant to hop back, likely fearing another mouth monsoon. Ellie held back no longer and the laughing fit sprung loose. Grant reddened. I showed him my teeth again, though this time hoping another chunk of something had stayed lodged there. He walked off, hips stiff to keep his soaked slacks from touching his lower legs, grumbling something about finding a change of clothes and a warning for an impending dry-cleaning bill. I'd hardly noticed. With him gone, the graves sat before me, unobstructed and empty. I approached the edge of the smallest one. Dr. Sattler came up beside me.

"Are you okay? That was wild."

"Dr. Sattler—"

"Ellie."

"No, I think I'll stick with Dr. Sattler, thank you. What just happened?"

Her face highlighted her hurt at the retraction of our familiarity. "I'm sorry. I had no choice. I had to call the national museum. It's procedure, part of the archaeological society's policy. I didn't think they'd move so quickly."

"But you knew they'd take them."

"Not for certain, but . . . yes. I knew it was a possibility. A probability. He's right, though. At least partially. This is such an important find. People need to know what happened here. Taking the remains to the national museum is a great way to educate people about the slave trade. How enslavement isn't just a Southern narrative. They'll help continue an important conversation."

"All due respect, Dr. Sattler, but in case you haven't noticed, this particular conversation is one a lot of people aren't so interested in having anymore."

A low rumble sounded in the distance. On the return drive, the sky had darkened, the blue fading to slate, the sparse clouds merging into a quilted pattern, fat with rain, fit to split. At the bay, the breeze blew across the tops of the tall grass, and by the time the thunder proper rolled, the sky assumed the greenish gray of hard-boiled yolks gone rotten. As I stood at the lip of the smallest grave, the bottom appeared to pull away, deepening the dig, creating a sense of imbalance, as if on the ledge of a tall building.

"Dr. Grant said 'men.'"

"Yes. The pelvic width indicated they were all men."

I pointed at the grave. "Not this one, though. He was just a boy. Isn't that what your man said? He was a child?"

"It was an educated guess at the time, I'm sure, but judging by the bone length and growth plates, yes. He was just a boy."

"Just a boy." I stepped farther forward until only my heels touched ground. "This isn't right, Ellie."

"I don't know what to say."

"They were taken from their home, against their will. And now you're going to take them again? Even dead, they have no choice. That can't happen."

"But maybe this is a way to tell their story."

"By making them a sideshow? No."

"I think that's a mischaracterization. How would anyone know what happened to them if we don't take . . . if we don't show the world? Maybe it's a chance to set things right."

I stepped back, kneeled, and scooped a mound of soil from the edge of the grave, holding it in my palm. "What lies in the dirt?" I whispered, and squeezed the earth.

And I was lost.

I am back in the room without doors, no walls, no way out. Only eyes to the outside, where I hear that voice that is mine, but Not, watching again those pale hands that are mine, but Not, and I watch on in terror, screaming into my prison void, at what these hands hold.

She who is Not my daughter kneels by the side of the boy's protector, pleading to God for his life, as well as the life of the one whose neck my fingers wrap around, my hands squeezing his throat. He grips my wrists with both hands, pulling, prying, seeking reprieve from my grasp for just the slightest bit of air. Though I am furious, I am amused by his resistance. I admire his pluck. He has told me many times over how much he despises this life on this land, yet he fights for that life like the animal he is. But I am older, my palms thickened with skin layered by my many years, my hands a vise around his throat, the center of which has all the resistance of an eggshell. I've but to pinch my fingers together to crush it.

You will not kill him, I say, he is not an animal, and you will let him go, but the ether envelops any sound I make.

But the boy.

Though he is on death's door at my hands, when I scream inside my head, there is a glint of recognition in his face.

He hears me. In here. He hears me in here.

Off to the side, my walking stick lies broken on the ground, the pewter pommel with which I bludgeoned the boy's protector blotched by blood. So, too, is his protector's face ruined. The cavern of skull that held his eye now amorphous and swollen, his instrument of vision a victim of my violence. He, of course, has brought this on himself, and that he has not moved since I struck him incenses me further, as there is work to be done, and he the most capable of performing it. That he did not mind his place meant I had to put him in it with the only language he and his kind understand. The boy will pay the price for his folly.

No, I scream again. Again, the boy's face tells me he hears me.

And he who is me but Not me—he notices the boy's noticing.

Better to reign, boy? Is that what you said? Where did you learn this phrase? Surely you don't expect I'd believe you capable of reading Milton, let alone understanding him. Is that my daughter's doing? Is that what she's made you believe, child? That you'd do better to reign in hell than serve the Lord our God?

His answer is a gurgle. Saliva bubbles at the corners of his mouth. Still, I demand satisfaction, must have an answer, must know what feeds this boy's bravado, must know how he can glower at me with such rage and defiance when his life is well and truly in my hands, and so I grant him relief from my grip, an adjournment of my anger, just long enough to bless his lungs with delicious air, and he gasps, consuming oxygen as would a hungry man at a plentiful repast. If he fills his chest with penitence, if his ribs reverberate with his recalcitrance, then perhaps I will bestow upon him the tender mercies of the God he denies and bring him to the light rather than sending him to it. I gesture to his protector, broken and un-moving, to my daughter, weeping, wailing, slavering in her supplication.

Do you see what your obstinacy has wrought? Are you repentant? God does not want your companion's fate to be yours, but his punishment was for your foolishness. Ask God for forgiveness. He only asks in return that you serve Him, and He will open His kingdom to you. He will forgive you, and I, in His likeness, will do the same.

I want to scream again, not only for the child's life, but for the familiarity in those words. My mouth, then, and now, has taken shape around them before.

The child takes another breath, then narrows his eyes.

I already been made to serve. I ain't going to serve living and dead. If your devil is real, send me to him. If I got to choose between your God and the devil, then the devil is fine. Send me to him so I can haunt you and yours until all your dying days.

The child releases his grip on Not my wrists. I expect he will close his eyes as I grant him swift release, but instead, he trains them on me with an emotion I cannot fathom, given his predicament. He is calm in the face of his fate. It is as though he wishes it. And I am unnerved. Though we are in the midst of the hottest summer I can ever recall at this home, I stand in a column of frigid air. The child does not see past me, nor through me. He knows the eyes are the window to the soul and he has thrown mine wide open. He terrifies me. And I will be frightened no longer.

I feel my intention, and I scream once more. The boy squints again, and though his eyes bulge and veins vibrate across his temples, he smirks.

I see you, he says.

Not for much longer, this other me says.

I ain't talking to you, the boy replies.

His words stun me and Not me into stillness. My fear mounts, here and there. I feel my face smile, though I know his mirth hides his terror. The boy grins back and my guts go liquid.

I squeeze. The eggshell breaks.

Not my daughter is become a banshee. Her shriek sends birds in flight from the reeds. But her scream sends no shivers through me. It is as if I have hardly heard it. For us, there is no sound save the boy's breath, as it leaves him in his final exhale. Thinking of his threat, I seal my lips, stop inhaling through my nose until the boy is evacuated of air, lest I breathe him in, lest his soul take up residence in mine. Ours.

But those eyes. Those eyes lose none of their focus though the entirety of the boy's body goes slack. He sees Not me from wherever he has gone.

And he sees me.

When his rattles are silenced and he has shuffled loose the coil, I loosen my hold on him and the child drops to the ground in a heap. Still, he watches. Watches us both. I will our eyes away, but I cannot, will not. Not even when Not my daughter leaps to her feet and flails, winging openhanded slaps against my face and chest, asking what I have done in that way when the obvious answer is too painful to reconcile, asking because admitting it is too terrible, asking in the way she can blame me for her agony, not just from the act I have just committed, but by confirming the truth of her own eyes. She grabs me by the arms, digs her nails into the flesh of Not my limbs and screams, something about love, and father, and child, and I know she is not talking about me. The child she speaks of is not the one I've sired, but the one she carries.

And because I know it, he knows it. And I eye the egg in her throat.

Dr. Sattler shook me by the shoulders.

I was free from him again.

The sky leaked large drops, scattering the dirt at our feet. Heat lightning laced through the clouds, the thunder rolling without pause.

"It happened again," she said.

In my hand, I'd compacted the silt into a cylinder of mud. I dropped it. "I didn't . . . ?"

"Come at me? No."

"But something?"

"Your face. Your skin and hair." She shook her head. "Just like last time. No more than a few seconds, only as long as you were . . . gone, I guess?"

"A few seconds? What do you mean?"

"I mean, you picked up the dirt, there was, I don't know, this moment where you changed, and then you went sort of catatonic, so I shook you. I don't know if that's, like, the medically correct thing to do, but here we are."

A couple of seconds, she said, while the time there was glacial.

"Are you okay?"

"Are there other remains? . . . Are there children?"

Her face collapsed. "There are."

"Is there a baby?"

"How could you possibly know that?"

This time the nausea came as a warning shot, and I held back a heave. "I have to go."

Ellie remained silent as I walked away as fast as my lame leg would let me. Even if she'd protested, I couldn't stay on that ground another second. Each step sent sharp slivers up my shin and calf, above the knee. Under one of the tents, Dr. Grant spoke with a colleague, his dress slacks replaced by a pair of oversized cargo pants he held bunched at the waist. He eyed me as I walked past and something in his demeanor made my heart drop, said stay and deal with him, but my flight was stronger than my fight. I had to go to the one place that now, more than any other time I could recently remember, felt like home.

No. Not yet. Defy.

I hear you, Malcolm.

I walked with purpose and came face-to-face with Grant. "You can't do this."

"I'm sorry. But it's done."

"No, you're not sorry, and it's not done. I might not be able to stop you now, but I'm not going to keep quiet about this. You don't get to take them twice." I turned to leave.

"Twice? I don't—"

I spun on my heel and stood inches from him. "You don't get to take them twice."

He held his hands up in surrender. His team, tense, stood at the ready—for what, I'm not sure any of us knew. Grant avoided my eyes. I wagged a finger at him and walked out of the tent.

The wind picked up as I neared my car, and out past the bay, waves whispered. There is a hush just before a wave folds and crashes into itself, a silence that precedes the violence. But the quiet is more than an absence of noise, more as if the water draws sound to itself, a void barren of discord. It lasts only a moment in the smaller waves closest to the beach, this hush. One of the legions of in-betweens that are too much bother to mind. We are never seeking quiet. No noise machines designed for relaxation and slumber mimic the absence of sound. Instead they offer radio-station static, an inadequate imitation of water churning sand, hoping it drowns the talk in our heads, hoping for one noise to cancel the other, the result only more noise. Listening to the sea, I craved that quiet, not only from my voice, but those not my own. I was crazy or haunted and either way, I could not be free of them. Just then, the waves didn't only draw sound to them. They pulled at me, with a fisherman's line. I stopped my walk to the car, halted by the realization as to why you ran toward the ocean that day, and there was in me this compulsion to walk into the sea, where I would wait and wait for the water to rise, for its crest and rolls to wrap around me, for the waves to lift me from my feet. In this vision, I would float. I would feel nothing. And, if only for a moment, I would hear nothing. Then, when the wave broke upon the shore and pulled me under, I would not fight. I would not make for the surface. I would succumb to the hush. I craved this quiet because these ghosts would not let me go.

Delmarva Daily
OPINION
SILAS JOHNS OWNED SLAVES—BUT WAS HE ALSO
MISUNDERSTOOD?
Collin Aiser

August 4, 2023

(10-minute read)

An inheritance of undeveloped land on the bay has led to a shocking discovery, and an unearthing of a past long forgotten—and perhaps unfairly maligned.

After an author from the Delmarva region discovered he'd been left land by his maternal grandfather, he made the trip down the I-95 corridor to inspect property that had, unbeknownst to him, been in his family for generations. With its proximity to the country club and its idyllic setting on the bay, the value of the land was clear, and plans were set in motion to put the estate up for sale.

However, during a routine perc test (a soil test that measures water absorption), a gruesome discovery was made—a body had been buried on the site.

As per state law, the authorities were immediately involved. After the remains were determined to be neither forensic nor indigenous in origin, the state archaeological society intervened. Continued excavation of the land revealed eight bodies in total, five of European descent, including an infant, and three that DNA analysis revealed to be West African in origin, all males, two adults and one adolescent. At the time of this writing, a more in-depth study of the DNA continues in the hopes of determining parentage and region of origin of the bodies buried there.

Perhaps even more disturbing than the discovery of the remains themselves is that one of the adult West African males appears to have suffered a grievous injury premortem, suggesting he met a violent end at, one would assume, the hands of one Silas Johns.

But is that the entire story? To answer that question, we must first answer another: Who was Silas Johns?

The original owner of the Johns plantation, Silas was a colonist and self-made man, originally living in the Maryland region before moving to the bay, where he met his wife, who bore him three children, two sons and a daughter. Skeletal evidence shows that Johns and his sons were hard workers, demonstrated by significant wear on the spine and joints of the extremities. While such erosion was not nearly that of what was found in the bones of the two adult slaves, it is clear that Johns and his progeny did not shy away from the manual labor necessary to keep their plantation running. This is a far cry from the brutal overseer narrative most often associated with similar situations.

Further examination of historic public records shows Johns to have been a generous contributor to the community at large, donating portions of his considerable wealth to the building of the first county courthouse, as well as several taverns, where many legal proceedings had been held in absence of the venue Johns eventually made possible. While some might find it distressing that additional records speak to Johns's more volatile nature (he was known to, on more than one occasion, swing his walking stick at the heads of those who had displeased him, often in the very taverns he'd help build), it is important not to lose sight of his significant contributions and influence on the development of the community we all enjoy today. The county courthouse stands today as a beacon of the work ethic and ingenuity Johns brought to the region.

Once Johns and his family passed, the property fell into ruin and was eventually covered over with soil, his colorful history lost to the ravages of time. How fortunate then, to have that colorful—if checkered—history rediscovered by one of his own descendants. That said, in our current socially charged landscape, a great deal has been made of (and will continue to be made of, no doubt) Johns's treatment of his slaves, the method of their burial (the remains were placed in the Christian tradition), and his involvement in the possible murder of one of the adults.

*However, one cannot assume that a man's documented flamboyant na-
ture justifies tarnishing his legacy with accusations of murder, particularly when, as previously stated, the fossil record demonstrates that
Johns saw fit to share the load of managing his 250-acre plantation,
a behavior atypical of most slave owners, if not altogether progressive.*

*As the state archaeological society, now working hand-in-hand with
the National Museum of Natural History, continues their work on the
site, we are certain to learn more scintillating facts about this fascinating, if possibly polarizing, individual.*

NINETEEN

Comrade Clarence held the door for me, the mirth in his face magnetic, and for a brief second, I felt safe.

"Ayyyye, Snore-ah Neale Hurston! Welcome back! What it is?" His smile dropped as I reached the entrance. "Damn, what's wrong with you? You paler than usual, light-skin. Looking like you seen a . . . Ohhhh, that's it, huh? That haint still messing with you?" He put an arm around me. "Come on, youngblood. Let's see if we can't run them spirits off, yeah?"

"Yeah."

He kept his arm around me until we found our seats at the bar. Freddy brightened when she saw me.

"Well, there he is. Thought you were trying to stiff me on the rental." She winked before her face fell the same as Clarence's. "Jesus, are you all right?"

"No."

"Pour him the good stuff, Freddy. The stuff you don't sell."

She held up a finger, ducked under the bar, and disappeared behind a door to the back. She returned with an ornate bottle of brown beauty and peeled the wax seal. She poured two neat fingers and slid the glass my way. I retrieved my prescription bottle from my pocket and dropped two pills into my palm.

"Uh, is that such a good idea?"

"You want me to swallow them dry?"

"If it means not mixing pills and alcohol? Then yes."

"Right." I spun on my stool and spoke to an invisible studio audience in the empty bar. "Kids, today's hypocrisy lesson is brought to you by the letter *E*!"

She tilted her head. "The letter *E*, huh?"

"That's right, the letter *E*, as in 'evangelize,' or *E* as in 'enable.' As in I don't come here to be evangelized. I come here to have my bad habits enabled. If that's no longer how you do business, say the word, and I'll leave. I mean, it's standing room only as usual in here, so I'm sure someone will fill this empty stool right quick."

I dropped my eyes to my drink, ducking the well-deserved counter right hook to the sucker punch with which I'd just tattooed Freddy, one that sent her jaw to the side and put her fists on her hips.

"You sure that's not *E* as in ease your ass on out—?"

Clarence waved his hand under his chin, giving Freddy the let-it-be signal. While he did, I palmed the pills in my mouth with a pop, then took a swallow of bourbon while keeping my face down. Clarence wasn't kidding. The bourbon was indeed the good stuff. No burn, all smoke, as it slid down my throat and warmed my innards. I imagined the Lexapro bubbling and dissolving along the way, waiting for that sweet relief to work its way into my veins, cross my blood-brain barrier, and soak my synapses in serotonin-blocking beauty. While I waited, Freddy watched. She jutted her chin, then sighed. Her hands fell from her waist. She reached for my glass and refilled it, saying nothing. I sipped in silence.

"No more after this. Got it?"

"Yeah. Got it."

"Well, on the bright side, Richard Left," Clarence said, "you look like shit."

"You should have seen me yesterday."

He raised his glass, then drank. Tension bent but not broken, I mouthed Freddy an apology. She closed her eyes and nodded.

"Safe to say I can rule out a fat commission check on the sale, huh?"

"Seems so. Sorry about that. Hey, what would you do with the money?"

"Are you kidding? Buy another bar, of course. I mean, check this crowd. Doesn't this place just scream second location? Aren't I the picture of an accomplished businesswoman?"

"No complaints here, young miss," Clarence said, raising his draft glass. Freddy bowed. She leaned her elbows on the bar. "What would you do with it?"

"That's easy. Legal fees."

"For?"

"Well, let's see. Earlier today I threw a big-dicked frog at my now-former department chair right before I walked out on my only secure job, which honestly wasn't all that secure to begin with. From there, I drove right to a meeting with my now-former agent and in the process of discussing a book I didn't remember pitching to her, I kicked her so hard in the shin that I made her bleed. Oh, oh, oh, and let's not leave out that not thirty minutes ago, right before I drove to have a drink with you fine people, I threw up all over the shoes and dress slacks of a government-employed grave robber. So, like I said, easy. Legal fees to keep me out of jail."

Freddy tucked in her lips. She cut a look at Clarence, then back to me. Her cheeks bulged and her eyes glistened.

"What?"

Her cheeks puffed again.

"What, Dizzy Gillespie? What is it?"

Clarence spoke. "A big-dicked frog? Have you lost your natural-born mind?"

At that, Freddy fell out, laughing until she had no air, took a ragged breath, and then she laughed some more. Clarence tossed his head back in a scream and water leaked from his eyes.

"This is great. Thank you. I'm so glad you can enjoy my pain and misery."

My pout sent them into further hysterics, and any attempts at maintaining a mean mug crumbled as my chin crinkled, my lips loosened, trembled, then vibrated as I raspberried and joined in. And it felt so damned good. How freeing, the ridiculousness of it all. We hollered until my throat ached and my sides cramped. Just when I thought we'd finished, one of us let out a "wooo," and went into it all over again. A couple came in the door, saw us slapping the bar top, hooting and hollering, and decided they didn't want to be in on the joke. They turned and left, which left us all in momentary calm before cracking up again. Freddy took a cocktail napkin from a holder on the bar and dabbed at her lashes.

"You really kicked her?"

"Right in the shin."

Between giggles, she asked, "What did she do?"

"You mean before or after I fired her?"

"Wait—you fired her?"

"Yup."

Clarence chimed in. "So you just went and literally kicked her ass to the curb?"

Freddy squealed so hard she wheezed.

I pointed to my forehead, then Clarence's. "Great minds, comrade."

"Whew, that's cold-blooded, Jack."

He raised his glass. I clinked mine off it and we took a slug.

We went on for another two hours, talking about anything and everything, except for the nightmare of the last few days. I regaled them with the origin of the frog, which sent them into another bout of hysterics. Freddy poured herself a drink, and then another, and then another still, forgetting she'd allowed me only one, and I remiss in reminding her. Clarence talked sports, grilled me on the Philly teams about whom I maintained an internal database just adequate enough to get me through high-level conversations, filling in my knowledge gaps with daps, knit brows, and/or empathizing head nods when it seemed prudent to either celebrate or mourn a team's or a player's wins or losses, stats that I pretended I knew with the assuredness of an award-winning actor. We took good-hearted shots at each other, kids playing the dozens, searching for any bit of comedy in the lives we presented to the world.

Before long, the bourbon bottle had been drained an inch from the bottom. My teeth tingled and I licked my lips, ensuring they had not at some point slid from my face, and massaged my cheeks, sore from so much smiling. But the conversation dwindled, as conversations between cohorts who hardly know each other often do, descending into uncomfortable silences remedied only by drinking more and faster than you had when the negative space had been filled by camaraderie and mirth. Clarence had been around the block enough times for enough years such that he recognized when that moment had arrived.

"I knew another writer . . . don't look at me like that, nigga, you ain't the only one . . . anyway, he said something I won't ever forget, and maybe you shouldn't, either."

Freddy rolled her eyes. "Here we go. Clarence's sage advice. Get ready."

"What, I can't be his magical negro?"

Freddy wide-eyed him and gestured toward me. "Hello? He's Black! What does he need a magical negro for?"

"Don't we need magic, too, Freddy? Hell, don't we deserve it from ourselves? Don't we need someone in our lives to help us see the things the way only we can so we can get out of our own way to see them? Why we always got to give that away to some white boy who lost his golf swing or driving around some geriatric Southern belle to absolve her of her racism? Come on, now."

Freddy blinked. "Shit, I don't think I can argue with that." She flourished with her hands. "Proceed."

"As I was saying . . . this fellow said that white writers have messed up the ghost story for everyone else. That they're always made out to be these terrifying things here to do us harm, when in most cases, if you really sit back and think about it? They're here to tell us something. They're messengers. They got something to say that we weren't ready to hear without them. I liked that."

Freddy tilted her head. "The hell does that have to do with anything?"

"Are you even listening? My man here said he got a haint. I'm saying, maybe he's thinking about it all wrong. Maybe he doesn't need to be afraid of it."

Freddy waved him off. "Psssh, that's on you. You the one scared him with all that talk."

"Ah ah, now hang on. I never said his haint was out to do him wrong, did I? Did I?" He pointed at me. "See? He's thinking about it now, too."

Freddy's face was one I hadn't seen since the remains had first been uncovered, stunned in a way I was certain I'd mirrored, then and now. Clarence's off-the-cuff comment reverberated like an aftershock. Magical, indeed.

"Well, I'm a take my commie ass out of here before I get too drunk to drive."

"You are too drunk to drive," Freddy said. "Besides, what are you even talking about? You walked here."

"That's what I mean. If I get too drunk to drive, I won't be able to walk home."

Freddy shook her head. "Clarence, that makes no sense."

"Or does it make all the sense?" He patted her hand. "Good night, young miss. Thank you as always for your hospitality." She sandwiched his hand with hers. He squeezed my arm as he walked by. "You going to be all right, youngblood."

"I don't know."

"Wasn't a question. You going to be all right. Now, if you two will excuse me, I got to get up early in the morning to help a white boy get his golf swing back." He gave me one firm pat and then ambled toward the door, lifted his fedora, and winked. I don't know if it was the incessant lightning that had been flashing out the window for the last hour playing tricks on my eyes, or if the pills and the potables were pushing me closer to constant hallucinations, but when Clarence winked, he appeared not to walk out the door, but to simply fade away.

"Did you see . . . ?"

"What?"

I shook it off. "Nothing. I just . . . for a second there, I swore Clarence disappeared."

"Who?"

"Huh? What do you mean, who?"

"What do you mean, 'what do I mean?' Who just disappeared?"

"Are you drunk? Clarence? The man who's been drinking with us all this time?"

"We've been the only ones here." Freddy stepped back from the bar, pressed her back up against the counter behind her. "Maybe it's time for you to go."

Desperate for a denial of my delusion, I scanned her face for falsehood. My despair must have been quite clear, as within seconds she cackled.

"Come on. Are you kidding me right now? Don't do that!"

"I'm sorry, I'm sorry, I couldn't resist."

"That's just mean is what that is."

"Kind of funny, though." She held up the near-empty bourbon bottle and swished the remnants around in front of me. "Make it up to you?"

"You know you're breaking your own rule."

"Yeah, but you've had a day. I'll cut you off tomorrow. Deal?"

"I mean, I don't *not* want it."

She uncorked and poured, holding the bottle upside down until the final drop had fallen. She poured herself another drink from a well bottle. "Lord, I haven't laughed like that in a minute. I know Clarence hasn't."

"What do you mean?"

"His wife passed a few years ago. They used to come here together all the time. Barflies, the two of them. My first real regulars."

The bar, as usual, was empty. "You mean your *only* real regulars."

"Touché."

We sipped our drinks.

"So . . . do you want to talk about it?"

"'It' has become quite nebulous for me. So many things could be 'it.'"

"Pick one, then."

"Why?"

"What do you mean?"

I leaned my elbows on the bar. "Seriously, what do you care? I've not exactly been pleasant to deal with since I've arrived. I've put my foot in my mouth so many times I can still taste my socks." She screwed up her face and stuck out her tongue. "So what is it?"

She crossed her arms and sighed. "Maybe I want my moment like Clarence. Maybe I want to be the magician, the feisty gay bartender with whom you have no shot despite your wrongheaded ideas of some nonexistent sexual tension—and don't act like I'm not right about that, towel boy—who listens to all your problems with a knowing nod and tells you how to fix your issues, how to reconcile all these big feelings you're clearly having but won't talk about, not really anyway. Don't I get that opportunity, too? Can't I play that role in your story?"

"Number one, you made me tell you what I thought was under the towel. I'm still shocked you didn't have me dragged out of here by the white coats."

"The who?"

"That's not even a thing anymore, is it? God, I'm old."

"Oh, you can say it but I can't?"

"All right, all right. Number two, if you can actually do any of those things you said, bring it on. I will gladly rewrite your narrative and make you magical as hell."

She sighed. "No. I can't. Not really." She leaned on the bar again, her chin in her palms. "Here's the thing, though. Since the day you walked in here—and I'm guessing for even longer than that—something's been bending your back. You're carrying something heavy as hell. You can only do that for so long, until something in you breaks."

"Sounds like you know a thing or two about that."

"I'm a biracial lesbian. What do you think?" I raised my glass to her. "There's no one else here now. Just you and me. No one to hear or judge whatever it is you've been carrying. Maybe try putting that weight down."

"I don't think I can, Freddy."

"It's about your son, right? Malcolm?" I nodded. "You said you've been 'talking' to him, yeah? Maybe . . ." She took a deep breath. "I can't believe I'm saying this, but maybe Clarence is right. About the whole messenger thing. Maybe you talking to your son started as a way to cope with his loss. And I get it. But now, maybe with everything you said you've seen and heard . . . maybe he heard you. Maybe he's telling you he's ready to talk back. Instead of talking at each other, you can talk *to* each other." She shook her head. "I don't know. Maybe that sounds just as crazy as all this other stuff. But don't you think all of this is happening for a reason? Were there things you two left unsaid?"

I swirled my drink, watched until the whirlpool receded, the waves calming, the surface flattening. I finished it in a gulp.

And I put the weight down.

TWENTY

He is seventeen.

And he is the oldest he will ever be.

I can't do this, Malcolm. I'm not ready.
I'm here. You can. You are.
I'll try.

Though he has no doubt done so begrudgingly, he is dressed to the nines—with one exception. All the details that would make my father proud are there. A crease in his slacks fine enough to split hair. Shoes shined. Perfect knot in his tie. Shirt pressed, no curl in the collar. Finished with a faded zip-up sweatshirt, frayed at the cuffs, one he wears everywhere, no matter (or perhaps because of) the occasion or the volume of my admonishments. He steps out from under the awning and snaps the hood over his head, protecting him from the precipitation. I lean across the console and push open his door as far as I can. He sits, buckles up, and assumes the position he has in all of our rides together as of late, elbow on the door, chewing at his thumbnail, watching out the window. It is at this point that the game begins, a game I've yet to win. He who speaks first loses. Thus far, he is undefeated. After five minutes, I add another hash mark to his win column.

"How much did she pay you?"

His head half turns from the window, thumb still between teeth. "What do you mean?"

"The slacks, the tie. How much did she pay you to wear something other than jeans and boots?"

"It doesn't work like that with me and Mommy. She asked me to dress nice, so I did."

I crinkle my chin and nod. "Well, I appreciate it. Your outfit is sharp. Could do without the hoodie, though."

He whispers something more acknowledgment than appreciation and turns his attention out the window again. I leave the radio off, hoping the noiselessness will spur him to conversation. I need an opening. It's been months since our argument about church, and things have not improved. In the days since the incident, he has fulfilled his obligation to spend time with me, but only just. He comes to my apartment, beelines for his room, and stays there until dinner, where we share a table and food, but no words. He is polite, asks to be excused, rinses his plate and places it in the dishwasher before he walks wordlessly back to his room. When the morning arrives, he is showered, dressed, and packed before I awake. In my pettiness, I have told Vanessa that the visitations have become point-less, that we don't afford each other the pleasantries strangers would, and that I'll not have that in my house. I am playing at reverse psychology, theo-rizing that my absence will make his heart grow fonder, but the passage of time tells me he has disproven my hypothesis. I come up with reasons to call Vanessa, to ask how he is doing, to see if there is even a remote sign he misses me. Vanessa is savvy as ever and will not allow me to make her the bridge across our ravine. Which brings us back to the car. Another five minutes pass and he does not give me any openings. We approach the turnpike exit. He sits up from his lean.

"Where we going, anyway?"

"Your mom didn't tell you? I wanted to take you to dinner."

"Yeah, but where?"

Malcolm, no, I can't do this. Not again.

We need this. You need this.

"I thought the drive would give us some time to talk. Some of the best conversations I ever had with my father were in the car. He taught me a lot on those rides. Figured instead of going somewhere local, we'd get out for a bit. I made reservations at a terrific Brazilian steakhouse in the 'burbs. The university had a Christmas function there one year and I thought you might like it."

He shakes his head. "Unbelievable."

"Oh, come on. Now what'd I do?"

"I don't eat red meat, man."

"What? Since when?"

"Does it matter since when? I don't now."

"Okay, well how was I supposed to know that, Mal?"

"That's a trick question, right?"

His ingratitude incenses me and my goodwill drains. "No, Mal. It's not. Please, enlighten me in the ways of telepathy so for future reference I can read your mind and save us both some aggravation."

"Ask, Dad. All you had to do was ask."

"You don't talk to me, Mal."

"You could have asked Mommy. You could have said, hey, where's somewhere he likes to go?"

"Yeah, well she could have told me, too."

"Right, of course, because why would you do that yourself when you can shift the blame to someone else. Why ask when you're afraid someone might tell you something you don't want to hear?"

"You know, for someone who doesn't eat red meat, you sure do seem to want beef with me today."

He lowers his chin and peers up at me, then sucks his teeth and rolls his eyes. "You always trying to be funny when ain't nothing funny. But you got to be a Dad to tell Dad jokes."

"What did you say to me?"

He hisses. "Nothing. Never mind."

"No, no, we're not never minding that one. You want to talk like you a man with your chest all puffed out, then stand behind what you said. I can't tell Dad jokes because I'm not a Dad? Is that what you said? I just want to be sure I heard you correctly since you over there mumbling like you got no damn sense." He turns his head to me, wide-eyed. "Yeah, you heard me, because I said it loud and clear for you to hear."

He cocks his head. "What is wrong with you, man?"

"Me? I'm here trying to take you to dinner, to talk about what's been happening with you and me, and you jump down my throat for the gesture. So what's wrong with *you*?"

"You! You're what's wrong with me!" He covers his eyes with his hand and takes a deep, shuddering breath. "Why are we even doing this?"

"Fighting?"

"No, this." He waves his hand, pointing back and forth between us. "Pretending that this is something either of us want."

This is the moment when the studio audience falls into a hush, right before the commercial break. While the advertisements air, the crowd shifts in their seats, anticipating how I might respond, though they're feeling quite hopeful they know how it will end, that they'll finally see the twist they've been waiting for, the one we've all seen in this kind of father-son drama on other shows before. All it takes is a declarative statement, a vocalization of a hard truth unspoken, danced around with intricate choreography, flipped over with verbal gymnastics, to spur the other side to confess what they've known all along. Now that Malcolm has asked the difficult question, my blinders will be lifted, my curtains parted, and in the light of a new day, I'll see all the mistakes I've made along the way with a clarity reserved for months-clean addicts and religious born agains. His bravery in asking the question will inspire mine, and all the things I was supposed to feel upon learning of Vanessa's pregnancy, all the things I was supposed to feel when we decided to be parents, all the things I was supposed to feel watching him play with his toys and teaching him to fight, all the things I was supposed to feel when he hugged me, when I wiped away his tears or bandaged his cuts, all the things I was supposed to feel when I cradled him as he screamed and cried through the night, when I dropped him in a drunken slumber, all of those feelings, would come upon me in a rush, and I would throw myself at his feet, pleading for forgiveness for the father I was and make promises about the father I'd now be, and I would ask him where he'd like to go for dinner and I wouldn't ask him about church and we'd like each other as much as we loved each other, because after all, that's what's supposed to happen. That's what a father should feel for his son. The audience expects I will say this, and when we return from commercial break, they scoot to the edge of their seats, elbows on knees, chins in palms, and Malcolm asks again why we're pretending this is something either of us wants with hope in his eyes because though he's trying to convince me he doesn't want this, he wants me to want this, because he does, too, and so I say:

Nothing.

The audience gasps.

We now return you to our regularly scheduled programming.

And we drove the rest of the way in silence, until—

It doesn't have to be in silence now. You had something you wanted to say, right?

Of course, I did, Malcolm.

And I had things I needed to say. And hear. So now is the time. Say to me now what you couldn't then. I'm here. I'm listening. I'm here so we can talk like we always wanted to. Go ahead.

Okay.

Feet away, rain makes a curtain, coming toward us fast as we approach, and drops smack the windshield as our two directions converge. The wipers slide and pop across the glass, playing metronome to my confession. And then it stops. The car. Time. The rain hovers in midair. Malcolm watches me. I turn to face him.

"I don't know, Malcolm."

"You don't know? So, you are? You're pretending?"

"I don't think I knew for sure until you asked . . . but I think maybe I am. Maybe I always have been. It all happened so fast, Malcolm. *You* happened so fast. It's not like your mother and I were young. Just the opposite. We'd planned our trajectories, and neither of ours included a child. But we were careless, and we needed to live up to our responsibilities. It didn't take long for your mother to fall head over heels for you. Before you were even a bump in her belly, she was smitten. Seeing her love someone like that, seeing the way her face lit up when she talked about even the idea of you in a way it never did for me, I thought I'd feel that way, too. Eventually."

"But you didn't."

"I wanted to, Malcolm. So badly, in fact, that I tried convincing myself at times I had. But in those moments when I should have been overcome with paternal love, the ones everyone tells you you will be, I just wasn't. But I thought maybe it just took time. I'd never been the most emotionally available person, so I thought as with anything and everything else in my life, if I simply worked at it, I'd get there."

This is hard.

It's important. Keep going.

"I thought about leaving. Moving. Letting the two of you have your peace, letting you have the unconditional love from your mother you deserved."

"So why didn't you?"

"Because then I blinked, and suddenly, you're this little person with all these big feelings, with this big heart and an even bigger brain. And it wasn't . . . I still didn't feel all those things they say I'm supposed to feel as a father. But, man, I liked you. I liked you so much. I wanted to be around you, hang out with you. I mean, look at you. You're a cool kid, Mal. Damn sure cooler than I ever was. You know who you are, and you don't apologize for it."

"It damn sure doesn't feel like you like me."

"I know. Because you were kind of right about something, Mal. When you said what you said about being Blacker than me—there was something to that. I'm jealous of you, Mal. Yeah, I said it. Man, I've been fighting my entire life to figure out who I am. For a while there, I thought I had it, too. Wrote a book, got a job teaching, living the lifestyle of it all, too. You couldn't tell me nothing. Don't get me wrong, I still had those doubts. Was I Black enough to warrant the job I'd gotten. Was I too Black for the people I worked with. That doesn't ever go away. But after I'd settled in, I'd settled in. It felt like I had to worry about that stuff less. Then we get pregnant. Then I'm a father. With a social drinking habit that was increasingly more than social. Now I've got new identities to manage. Dad. Alcoholic. Recovering alcoholic. Now I'm balancing all these things, needing new crutches to stand on because I don't feel like I can carry all of this without help."

"The church."

"I had a hole, Malcolm. When I couldn't fill it with alcohol anymore, I thought maybe fatherhood would make me feel complete. When it didn't, that hole got wider and wider, and if I didn't close it, I honestly thought I might die. And when I committed myself to it and I didn't die, I thought if it could fix that hole, then maybe it could fix what was happening between you and me. When you rejected the church, after I'd given myself over to it with the hope I could be the person I was supposed to be . . . Malcolm, I've lived my whole life with people telling me I wasn't enough of this or too much of that. It's probably maybe definitely why I pursued your mother as much as I did. Because I thought being with her would validate me in some way. When we had you, I thought the same about you, that because your approximation to visible Blackness was stronger than mine, that I'd somehow absorb that by proxy. But I shouldn't have put that on you. All I did was push you away and you just ended up closer to your mother, and it drove me crazy."

"Why? If you didn't want to be my dad, then why do you care how close I am to her?"

"Have you met me, Mal? When does anything I do or say make even a little bit of sense? I'm not even sure what it is I'm saying right now. It's all improv, my man. I've been failing my way through all this since day one."

At this, his tough façade falters, and he lets out a laugh, one that I've heard before, but not with this lilt, and there is lightness in my chest, but the laugh is so short that I crave it like no drink I've ever had, want it more than anything I have ever wanted, and the wanting and the craving scare me more than anything has ever scared me before. Because I finally want more of that laugh and everything that comes with it.

I want it now.

I want it every day.

I want it forever.

And it is too late.

But it's not too late, Dad. You said it. And I heard you.

"Thanks."

"For what, Mal?"

"Telling me all this. It's not exactly what I want to hear, but it's weird. It kind of feels better knowing it? That probably doesn't make any sense."

"It makes all the sense."

"I meant what I said about church. People used that place to justify slavery. Forced their burial rites on our people. You shouldn't have made me go."

"I understand that now. I do. But what do I do about that now?

"Malcolm?"

It's time.

No. Please don't.

It's good we had this chance to talk.

But there's more to say. I need you to tell me what to do next.

Bye, Dad.

The rain falls again. The windshield wipers clear my view. The car moves, the GPS directing us away from traffic, avoiding an accident by taking us off the turnpike and down a winding two-lane back road surrounded by trees. The slick asphalt hisses around the tight turns. Though the heavier rain has ceased, drizzle dots the headlamp columns lighting the road ahead. The car is quiet. Malcolm chews his thumb knuckle. I watch him, then the road, and back again.

"What?" he asks.

"Huh?"

"I can feel you looking at me."

I turn my attention back to the road. "My bad. But let's talk about it."

Stop this. Pay attention to the road. I can't do this again.

I cannot bear the quiet any further. I reach across the console and knead his neck. To my surprise, he does not flinch or pull away. This is when I will say what needs to be said. "You know—"

"Dad!"

My hand flies from his neck to the wheel. In the headlights' glow, a flash of ruddy orange fur. A white-tipped tail. Swerve. Tire slips on the slick, catches the lip of a drainage ditch, jerks wheel hard to the right. Foot hard to brake. Pain shoots up my calf. Too late. Off road. Down hill. Malcolm screams. Tree. Arms locked. Legs straight. Metal clangs. Glass breaks. Black.

Burning. Cheek burns. Neck aches. Head away from opened airbag. Bright but blurry, eyes unfocused. Hazard lights tick and tock. Run hands over my chest, legs. Somehow unhurt, save my face.

Then breathing. Wet. Ragged.

Not mine.

Vision sharpens. Windshield webbed with cracks from a hole where a thick branch has gone through the passenger side. Turn my head and follow its path to, through, Malcolm's chest. The branch a string, his body a bead.

"Daddy."

My belt will not unbuckle. I cannot free myself. I cannot reach across the gap to hold my son.

"I can't sit up."

His eyes are open but vacant.

"I can't breathe."

I pull and rip and tear at my harness, but it holds me fast. I reach across and knead his neck again.

"We're going to be late."

"It's okay, it's okay. We'll get there."

The corners of his mouth twitch. His face falls slack.

The GPS tells us to go back the way we came. A fox screams in the woods.

TWENTY-ONE

Freddy wiped a tear from her chin with the back of her wrist.

"You heard all that?"

"I heard *you*."

"Just me?"

"Just you. But you weren't talking to me. It was like you went into a trance. But I heard every word you said. You went in and out, like there was another side of a conversation I couldn't hear. Was . . . was he there?"

"What is happening to me, Freddy?"

"I don't know."

We sat, hushed. I turned my highball glass in circles on the bar. "Must have been fifteen minutes at least that I sat next to him. Maybe longer. I kept massaging his neck, but the muscles, they got tighter and tighter, but I kept at it, thinking I could keep that tension away, keep him comfortable, even though I knew he couldn't feel a thing. I thought maybe it still mattered."

"I am so, so sorry."

"It was just wasted time. All of it. I threw away years over narcissistic nonsense. Even the God stuff. Spent all this time trying to get him to understand why God was so important to me when I wasn't even sure I believed in Him myself. Not really. And if He exists . . . I sent Malcolm straight to Him."

"It was an accident."

"No, it wasn't. Everything I'd done up until that point put us in that car. Every choice I'd made since he was born—hell, before then—put us on that road at that exact time. If I'd just been who he'd deserved all along, or better still, if I had just walked away when I realized I wasn't meant to be a father, he'd still be alive."

"You can't do that."

"Do what?"

"You can't 'what if' what happened. You could have made a dozen different choices and still ended up there."

"But I didn't. I've spent most of my life afraid, Freddy. When it came to stepping into fatherhood or running away from it altogether, I was too chickenshit to do either." I downed the last of the bourbon. "You want to know how big a coward I am? I gave him a Christian funeral."

"Why?"

"Because it's all about me, Freddy. How have you not picked up on that yet? Because despite killing my son, I'd convinced myself it had happened because I'd had doubts about my faith, and his death was my punishment. A sign I needed to get back in line. Return to His service with a show of faith." Freddy retrieved a bottle from the shelf behind her. As she brought it over my glass, I waved it away. "I told myself, told Vanessa, that it was the right thing to do." I pointed skyward. "That Malcolm would see all the people who'd turned out for him, all the lives he'd touched. Vanessa didn't buy it. Frankly, I'm not sure I did, either. And now, knowing what I know about that plantation, what happened to those men, that boy, I have to wonder . . . am I just my grandfather's grandchild? Did I do to Malcolm what that side of my family had done to them? Robbed them of their homegoing? I can't stop thinking about what Malcolm would think about all of this. If he'd be ashamed of me. If he'd even want a relationship with me knowing this place is in my history and that I made it a part of his. It's already made me question everything I thought I knew about who I was. Who I am. What would it have done to him? How would I fix that?"

Freddy crossed her arms over her stomach, drink in one hand, eyes narrowed, pondering. She took a sip. "Maybe . . ." She shook her head. "No."

"Don't do that. What?"

"No, it's dumb and I've had way more to drink than I should've and it's going to make me say something stupid, or worse yet, sound like Clarence."

"Please. Say what you were going to say."

She took another sip. "It's just the sleep paralysis, the presence in the room, these things you've been seeing, the things you think are happening to you. You said you wonder what Malcolm would think about all this, how he would feel, what he would do. I don't know, but maybe you know. Maybe he's been trying to tell you all along. Maybe there are no ghosts. Not like you think. In the car, you needed him to hear you, and it's like you need to hear him now. Hear them. Whoever is with him, showing you these things. It seems like now you *can* hear them."

The idea lent spark to kindling, a brush pile in my chest that once lit, sent flames licking at my rib cage, sending warmth through my limbs, up my neck, and into my cheeks, sensations I'd not known since we'd played with those action figures on the floor. And though I hadn't known then, I knew now, as with the sound of your laugh, I wanted that feeling always, infinitely, forever after. I finished my drink and fished in my pocket for my wallet. Freddy frowned.

"Drove you off, huh? Knew I should've kept my mouth shut."

"No, nothing like that. I just . . . I should get some sleep." She nodded, though her face made plain she was wounded. I stood from my stool. Fluid filled the spaces they'd been denied access while I sat. The booze beat a path to my brain while my lower leg swelled and throbbed, pain buckling my knee such that I steadied myself on the seat cushion. Freddy flashed a wary expression, but I stuck out my lower lip and shook my head, selling a reassurance she wasn't quite buying. I slid my credit card across the bar, but she held up her hand and waved it back toward me. I slid the card back into my wallet, and the wallet into my pocket.

"Freddy. Thank you. Again. Always."

She slow-blinked and nodded. I tapped the bar with my knuckles and headed for the door.

Back in the apartment, I sat on the edge of the bed. Though I was more than ready for sleep, anticipation crawled under and over my skin, pinpricked my scalp, dampened my palms. I took a deep breath. *This is so stupid.* I spoke in a raised voice. "I'm going to sleep now. If you or your . . . friends, I guess, have something more to tell me, I'm ready to hear it."

I closed my eyes, cringed, and waited. But the bed did not levitate. The pictures remained firmly affixed to the walls. The rain on the windows did not turn to blood. No whispers or unexplained shadows. Simply a drunk fool, acting foolish, as was his want. I laid back, pulled the covers up under my arms and, despite my nervous energy, fell asleep.

When I awoke, I'd gone fetal and couldn't move.

Went to speak. Couldn't.

But nothing held me down.

A pale light cast a pall in the room, and panic squeezed my chest. The Lexapro and liquor cocktail had finally done me in. Here was the tunnel and the light at the end of it. But I couldn't walk toward it. I searched the apartment until my eyes landed on the source of illumination, though the discovery brought me no sense of relief.

My laptop sat open on the desk, and someone sat in the chair, draped in darkness.

I opened my mouth to call out, same result as before. But the sound stirred the shadow. They sat up with an alarm unusual for a ghost. They turned their head and peered over their shoulder. Even in shadow, the profile was familiar. The body followed the head in its rotation, the chair creaking as they turned to face me.

As *I* turned to face me.

Despite the fear, I remembered Clarence's words, and instead of crying out, I breathed. And I watched. And while I watched me in my chair from my bed, I also watched me in my bed from my chair. Then I turned away from me, back to the laptop, and the sound of my breathing gave way to a louder one—keys clicking under my fingers.

To: unnamednarrator@gmail.com
From: Song of the South Wedding Solutions (uncleremus@ssws.com)
Subject: Business venture

Dear Sir—

First, allow us to express our deepest condolences on the loss of
your family member. Nothing, not even an inheritance, can hope to
replace the special feelings our loved ones give us. We hope you are
finding some solace in what must be trying times for you.

Along those lines, we hope to bring you some light in the darkness.
It has come to our attention that you have inherited a plantation in, of
all places, the northeastern coast. While we're certain we don't have
to tell you this, there is a certain belief that the history of plantations
somehow belongs only to the South, a fact that is wholly untrue.
However, we see an opportunity in this misgiving, and it is our sincere
hope you'll arrive at the same understanding.

While in certain circles, the plantation wedding has become quite
gauche, the truth is there is still an incredible demand for these
events. We cannot deny that there are certain moral and ethical
implications regarding holding a wedding on a plantation. Harder still to
ignore are the fiscal implications in doing so. Truth be told, I'm certain
I'd shock you with the number of couples wanting to get married on a
plantation and what they'll pay for the privilege. We have a number of
potential clients in the Northeast who would pay even more if it meant
not traveling or asking their families to do so. The dollar amounts
offered us are staggering. As such, we're prepared to make you two
separate offers.

The first and most obvious is a retainer fee for use of your property
for wedding events. Our client list is long and exclusive (including

major celebrities you'd have to be dead not to know), and we're confi-
dent we'd have an immediate waiting list, booking well over a year in
advance. This agreement would require zero work on your part. We'd
handle groundskeeping, setup, and breakdown—you name it. Your
only job would be to cash your checks.

The second offer is to buy the land outright. We understand how a
connection to a property with such a complicated history can be, at
the very least, uncomfortable. We're prepared to remove that source
of discomfort from your life entirely by taking the property off your
hands altogether—and we're prepared to do that with cash.

The details of both offers are outlined in the attachments. We can
either work together as partners or make a onetime deal and go our
separate ways. Either way, like the song says, plenty of sunshine
heading your way!

Thank you in advance for your time and consideration of what we
hope you will find to be generous offers. We can't wait to hear from
you.

Sincerely,
Jacob Remus
Co-founder, Song of the South Wedding Solutions
"Wonderful Feeling, Wonderful Day!"

TWENTY-TWO

Morning. My head heavy, my tongue thick. The remembrance of last night's visitation (hallucination?) cut through the waking fog. I sat on the edge of the bed and waited out the spins, stood, and dropped back as pain lanced up my leg. The purple streaks had darkened to near black and slithered their way up over my knee. They hadn't been that way last night. What had happened? My other foot itched and I reached to scratch it. When the itch was relieved, I saw similar purple streaks form on top of my foot, weaving their way through my metatarsals. I'd never heard of a sting spreading to the other limb, but then I'd never seen myself from my bed writing at a desk in the middle of the night, so it seemed all bets were off. I leaned and caught the seat back of the desk chair with my fingertips, rolled it back toward me, then shifted from the bed to the chair and scooted over to the desk. I opened my laptop—and saw nothing. No open document. No new folders on the desktop. Everything was as it had been the night before. If indeed you all were trying to tell me something or, in the case of last night's sighting, if *I* was trying to tell myself something, we were all poor communicators, and I was losing patience with us. Would a little transparency hurt? How about we have these conversations in daylight, yeah? No more mystery or supernatural overtones. This is all frightening enough.

At that, my phone shimmied across the surface of the desk, vibrating with a call.

Well that's a bit on the nose.

I answered. A woman asked if I was me, and for a moment I thought about just how complex that question had become, but an urgency in her tone told me to save that conversation for another time, another person, so I said, yes, this is in fact he, to which she replied—

"Please hold for the mayor."

"Excuse me, did you say 'the mayor'?"

My answer was hold music, an instrumental recording of "Zip-A-Dee-Doo-Dah." I hummed along, then asked out loud just what the hell I was doing. The music stopped and Urgent Voice asked if I was still there. I confirmed. She introduced me to the mayor.

"Good morning, sir," he said. "Thanks so much for taking my call. How are you today?"

"I'm—"

"Fantastic, fantastic. So I won't beat around the bush. I've spoken with Dr. Grant regarding your unfortunate, uh, encounter? At the property yesterday?"

"He told on me?"

The mayor groaned. "You know, I thought it might go this way, but I'd hoped otherwise. Nevertheless. Let's just speak plainly, shall we? There's no need for you to pretend as if you're not aware of the potential devastating effects this issue might have on our community."

"I'm pretending?"

A disgusted snort. "Fine. That's how it's going to be? I'll play along."

"I don't—"

"Want to help, yes, I hear you. I'm certain you feel justified in that. After all, you've been thrust into an uncomfortable set of circumstances.

But you have to understand, this is just as challenging for our quiet little beach town as it is for you, believe me."

"I'm sorry, what's just as challenging?"

"There's no need to raise your voice, sir."

"But I didn't—"

"Sir, are you going to let me get a word in edgewise here or not? I'm trying to work with you, not against you. I'm an ally."

"An ally in what? What are you—"

"Frankly, you're not from here. You don't know what can happen if news of this situation spreads."

"Again, I don't—"

"Please let me finish a sentence, sir. That's all I ask." I said nothing. "Well?"

"You said—"

"Fine, fine. You want me to say it? I'll say it. We have a reputation as a progressive community. Come one, come all, that sort of thing. Black, white, straight, gay, nonbinary, any and all of the alphabet soup designations. The state was solidly blue in the last election, has been every year. Yes, we've got some outliers, but the auto racing brings in a lot of money for the region, and besides, who are you to judge? I mean, for Christ's sake, man, the president has a vacation home here. Do you have any idea what happens if this . . . this kerfluffle goes national?"

"Isn't it 'kerfuffle'?"

"Do you know how much this town relies on tourism dollars? We simply can't have this turn into some incident that ends up gaining national attention."

"I'm sorry, Mr. Mayor. You've lost me. At what point does my vomiting on a museum employee constitute a national incident?"

"Dr. Grant is concerned. He's informed me his federal colleagues flagged some internet chatter since your . . . run-in . . . yesterday. Something about a possible protest. One he says you said you'd organize if he didn't leave the remains where they are."

"A protest? I didn't say anything about—"

"Didn't Dr. Grant tell you they'd be removing the remains from the land and transporting them to D.C. for display?"

"He did. And I'll tell you what I told him. He doesn't get to do that."

"Yes, sir, he does."

"How?"

"Pardon?"

"How does he get to do that? Explain it to me."

He harumphed. "Sir, I don't have the time to explain the intricacies of property law to you."

"The time? Or the capacity?"

"The last thing we need is to have protestors show up, because then the inevitable counterprotestors show up, and before you know it, we've got a huge mess on our hands. We are simply not that kind of community. There's a country club right down the road from your property. Do you think their members want to see any of this nonsense as they're pulling up to play eighteen?"

"No, no, of course not. By the way, when is tee time?"

"Noon today. Why do you ask?"

"Oh, no reason." I pulled the phone away and shook off his obliviousness lest it be contagious. "What exactly is it you think I can do about any of this, sir?"

"I'm simply asking you to perhaps go down to the site and if there is anyone there, do your best to defuse this situation. Talk to the people. Tell them you're fine with what's happening, that this is how the process works, that you understand that history is better served by having these bodies preserved in the national museum and that you're working in co-operation with us. Can you do that?"

"Why would I do that, sir? Honestly. If it stops them from taking them—"

"Whoa, whoa. Stops them? What do you mean *stops* them?"

"What do *you* mean?"

There was a rustling, a covering of the receiver with his hand, and his voice, while faint, said to someone in the room with him, "He doesn't know. Grant told me he'd been informed. Unbelievable. This is a god-damned mess." Back into the receiver. "So no one has contacted you?"

"What's a mess, Mr. Mayor?"

His voice went whispered again. "Why in the blue hell does this shit always gets dumped on my lap, huh? Now I have to be the one to tell him? I swear to Christ, Marcy, heads are going to goddamn roll, and not one of them is going to be mine, you hear me? You tell those federal assholes that."

"Mr. Mayor?"

He cleared his throat. "Yes, so . . . the remains have already been trans-ferred. Apparently, it happened last night. I was told you'd been told."

"I had not."

"Yes, I'm now painfully aware of that fact." I didn't respond, content to let him wallow. He sniffed, followed by another aggressive throat clear. "So, as I was saying, and I'm sure this all seems a bit callow now in light of what was not supposed to be new news to you, but if you could just go to the site, and if anyone is there, perhaps preemptively calm them down, we of the Wide Spaces community would be quite grateful."

"I'll go, sir."

He let out a long, relieved sigh. "Thank you. Thank you. I really appre-ciate your doing this."

"You won't."

"Wait, what do—"

"What I mean is I hadn't said anything about a protest to Dr. Grant. Nothing at all. But it's a fantastic idea and I appreciate the suggestion."

"Now wait a minute."

"I've got to go now, sir." I went to hang up, then stopped, brought the phone back to my face. "Thank you, by the way."

"For?"

"You gave me something I didn't know I needed."

"But I—"

"Okay now, bye-bye."

I disconnected the call and blocked the number. My leg and temples throbbed in time with each other. I'd never been a fighter. Never brave.

My father had told no lies on that front. I navigated life with my head on a swivel, forever fearful of what the world might mean for me, a condition that followed me into adulthood despite my many attempts to leave it behind. But after listening to the mayor equivocate, something happened. Despite weeks of medication-mediated emotions, fueled by my newfound defiance, unadulterated anger swelled, the kind of mad that made fear seem foolish.

And it felt so, so good.

You'd have been proud, Malcolm. I wish you could've seen me.

I dressed and hobbled down the steps to the street where I'd parked, started the car, and drove off a little faster than usual. Maybe David was wrong. Maybe people cared after all.

It was time to cause some good trouble.

Delmarva Daily Online

Rumors of a potential protest today at the Johns's Landing plantation excavation have begun circulating online. At issue is what is perceived as a unilateral decision by the National Museum of Natural History to transfer to their facility the remains discovered on the site, including those of three enslaved West Africans, reviving a debate about to whom history belongs and who has the right to educate us about the past.

BLMisaterroristorganization

Haha the snowflakes have been watching Black Panther again. Killmonger wanted to murder white people and they want to turn him into an anti-hero. GTFOH.

STILLSHEPERSISTED

Why is it when people speak up against the wrongs of white supremacy, there's a blizzard of snowflakes calling other people snowflakes? Weird. But not really.

DontCallMeKaren

Not saying I agree with the snowflakes LOL but how r we supposed to educate people about slavery if we don't let the museums show us what it was like?

Antifa-irySWATter

No one seems to be getting up in arms about returning the European bodies to their home country. Wonder why that is? I'll tell you. More woke nonsense.

ReclaimingMyTime

Do you really need it spelled out for you? No one stole those Europeans from their homeland. SMDH. Are yt people okay?

BREAKIN2

Counting down until antifa shows up pretending to be "bad actors"
causing violence in 3, 2, 1 . . .

AltRightSaidFred

Supposedly the protest is being organized by the owner, a writer who
wrote some SJW manifesto a few years back, all about denying his
white side. How's that working out for you, buddy? Think the black
delegation will claim you now?

MarcusGarveysHat

We have and we will. Did you even read his book? He didn't deny
anything. He also didn't ask to be colonized. Y'all put that on him.

After the world watched George Floyd lynched on national television,
I made the unusual move of calling my father. My classes had already gone
virtual and I'd been in the middle of another necessary round of silent
treatment from you and your mother after I'd again said something stupid. Though someone who prided himself on his ability to be alone, I was
quite lonely, and admittedly a bit afraid. There was this looming sensation
of being trapped in an endless cycle of violence, progress, regression, and
violence again, made no less ominous by my empty apartment, absent
your weekly visitations due to the lockdowns. When he finally answered
the phone, I asked my father if he felt the same about this cycle, did
this seem too familiar, given all he'd seen until now, asked this man who'd
walked into the bare and bloodied feet of a lynched man when he was
just a teenager, were we stuck in a sequence of Watts of L.A. of Ferguson
of Minnesota, and did he feel the same sense of helplessness I did. Despite our mutual recognition of the horror before us, he said something
surprising. He had been heartened by the depth of different faces taking
to the streets, particularly the number of white people putting themselves
in harm's way, breathing in the same tear gas, wiping the same pepper

spray from their eyes, and while I was quick to point out how readily those weapons were wielded against us while our white allies stood unharmed, he reminded me that we were having this conversation from the safety of our own homes, that we only knew what we saw on the television, and that the world was such that small favors were no longer so small. Even in light of all that had happened in the last few days, the thought brought me some measure of comfort—as I'm sure he intended—then and now, as I drove to the plantation.

As I drew closer to the site, I imagined the road littered with cars parked on the side and in the grass for a half mile, as if for an outdoor concert. Tiny smart cars, hybrids, full electrics, and e-scooters covered in bumper stickers urging coexistence, medallions of fish with feet, magnets asking who rescued who (them or their dog), decals declaring their love of the Salt Life, and instructions to not only live, but to laugh, and oh yes, love. Of course, there'd also be pickup trucks with testicles hanging from the trailer hitch, window stickers of black-and-white American flags with the solid blue line, Calvin pissing on a Chevrolet logo, or ones reading 2A, applied by fingers neither cold nor dead.

I rounded the corner to the road leading to the property, full of a different kind of nervousness than I'd ever experienced. My fingers drummed the steering wheel in rapid succession. Time was you couldn't have pitched a protest to me without my delivering a diatribe about the risks and liabilities latent in taking to the streets. Yet there I was, itching to experience a combination of confrontation and solidarity. I'd gotten your message. No longer would I be the man things happened to, Malcolm. Because of you, I would make things happen.

But the road was as empty as it had ever been. Not a single car parked along the sides. And while it was all in my head, David's laughter was damn near deafening.

I reached the plantation entrance where police had established a new and what I could only assume was a precautionary barrier, a set of blue-and-white sawhorses set up end to end. A topless Jeep with an amalgamation of all the bumper stickers I'd hoped I'd see sat parked in the grass. A man and woman in Baja shirts and board shorts, heads adorned with brownish blond dreads, paced back and forth, hoisting homemade poster board signs that read "Send Them Home." Officer Ryan stood on the other side of the barrier, bemused by the bohemians' presence. I parked next to their Jeep and approached them. The beach bro extended his hand.

"You here for the protest, brah?"

Officer Ryan called out. "You want me to have these trespassers removed from the property, sir?"

I answered through my teeth. "That won't be necessary, Officer Ryan."

Ryan smirked. Beach Bro retracted his hand in confusion.

"This land is your land, brother?"

"This land is my land, yes. Hey . . . is this . . . are you two . . . you know . . . it?" He tilted his head to the side. "I mean, do you know if anyone else is coming?"

"Oh, yeah, definitely. Well, I mean, maybe. No, probably not." He called over to his partner. "Babe! You know if anyone else is coming?"

"I mean, we put it up on the app," she said. "I did kind of think there'd be more people here by now, now that you say that."

"Yeah, me, too," Beach Bro said.

"Wait, did she say 'app'?"

He pulled out his phone and clicked on a fist icon. "It's kinda wonky but it works sometimes. You can see we dropped a pin here. Hmm."

"What?"

"Nothing. Just no likes or comments. But hey, we're here for you, man. And look!"

He pointed back down the road. A dot in the distance grew larger, a small car driving toward us. I brightened and went up on my toes in the hopes of seeing a caravan behind them, finding none. But still. It was a start. The driver parked and out stepped Mrs. Hunter and her photographer. She closed the door and came to a hard stop when she saw me. I held up my empty hands. She sneered. Her photographer waved from his side of the car. I waved back, and Hunter whipped her head around toward her colleague. A scolded child, he retracted his hand.

"I thought there was a protest here today," she said.

"That makes two of us." I gestured to Beach Bro and Co. "Four of us, I guess."

Hunter snorted. "Well, this was a waste of time. Let's go." She snapped at her cameraman. He reentered the car, and they were gone as quickly as they came. Beach Bro came up behind me and clapped my back.

"Don't sweat that, brah. We'll stay all day and night if that's what it takes." His partner ahemed and tapped her watch. "Oh shit, right. We'll stay for the next few hours if that's what it takes."

"Wonderful. Thanks." With a pat on his shoulder, I left them behind and walked toward the barricade. Officer Ryan slid one of the sawhorses aside and with a bow bid me welcome. Dr. Sattler's eyes went wide when she saw me approach her pavilion. Under the tent were several long tables, topped by pottery in pieces, ceramic plates, and tobacco pipes. Similar artifacts lay on several tarps on the ground.

"You've been busy," I said.

Her voice had a nervous pitch. "Yeah, how about it, huh? I still can't believe how well preserved so much of this is. What a story these pieces can tell."

"Uh-huh, great. When did you know?"

"Know what?"

"Really? That's how it's going down?"

She rocked heel to toe and back. "Last night."

"And you didn't think to call me? Text me?"

"Of course, I thought to."

"But you didn't. Well, thanks for everything, Dr. Sattler. Really."

Her remorse was replaced by resentment. "You know what? Fuck you, man."

"Fuck me?"

"Yeah, fuck you. Did it occur to you that I have a job to do here? What did you expect me to do? Throw myself across the containment units? Lie in front of the trucks? I have to eat, too."

"You could have told me, Ellie."

"Oh, now I'm Ellie?" She sneered. "And after I told you? Then what? What would you have done? If I'd contacted you and you showed up, they'd know how you knew, and I'd be in all kinds of trouble. For Christ's sake, you threw up on Dr. Grant. Do you know how much shit I had to eat after that? I want to help you, but I also have to do what my employers tell me to."

"Just following orders, huh, doc? I've heard that somewhere before."

"Following . . . ? I'm Jewish, you sanctimonious prick."

I took a beat. "I'm sorry. That was uncalled for."

"You're goddamned right it was." An associate on the dig came to the tent searching for Ellie, who held up a finger when she saw her. "I have work to do." She took a deep breath. "Despite what you just said to me, I'm sorry, I really am. I can't even begin to imagine what you must be feeling. But maybe try to see this in a positive light. The things we've uncovered—"

"People, Ellie. You've uncovered people."

"Yes, of course. These people can tell the world about a chapter of the transatlantic slave trade story we didn't know existed."

"The world? The *world*? Is that supposed to be funny? Look out there." I pointed to Beach Bro, who waved back. "See how much the world cares? Nobody wants to know any more about forced labor on plantations and enslaved people. They want to forget it. They want us to get over it. And you want me to care about your job? You're a thief, Dr. Sattler. A thief disguised as an educator. Good for you."

Dr. Sattler clenched her jaw, spun, and walked out of the tent. I stood in the center of the artifacts and turned in a slow circle. On one of the tarps sat a corroded key. I knelt and picked it up.

A return to the unwalled room.

My white hands shove the young boy into a box in the ground shorter than he is tall. He falls in fetal and screams. I slam the door shut, the only opening in the door a slit wide enough for me to see his eyes.

You will be let out when you renounce your paganism. Then and only then. If the rod cannot remove your heathenism, then I shall spare it, but there will be no spoils for you, child. You will remain in this box until broken, do you hear me? You will cook until you claim Christ your one and only lord and savior, and I will sit, and I will watch, and I will wait.

I lean on Not my walking stick and kneel. The uncorroded key is in my hand, and I scream into the dark again, say throw it away, but my plea goes unheard as the hand that is Not my hand drives the key home and turns it. The click's echo explodes in our ears. I sit on a stump and bring an unbroken porcelain cup full of tea to our lips and we sip. The child's eyes go wild, not with fear, but fury. He kicks, and claws, and scratches at his prison, and the sounds make me want to do the same. But I am powerless to do anything but what I do.

And what I do, while he twirls the key around our finger, is sit.
And watch.
And wait.
The child lets out a ferocious scream.

I shouted and fell back on my ass. I flung the key to the side and heard it hit something. Just outside the tent sat an open equipment chest filled with tools of the trade—trowels, sieves, brushes, and shovels. I stood over the trunk and retrieved a shovel, then walked back into the tent. To the table. I picked up a beer stein.

I stand above the open hot box. The boy is emaciated. His lips dry and cracked. His skin ashen. He asks for water. I extend an arm and tip the stein sideways, dribbling water on the boy's lips. The child laps languidly at the drops before I dump the contents of the cup all over his face.

I smashed the beer stein on the edge of the table, sending ceramic slivers scattering across the surface. Beach Bro shouted from beyond the barrier.

"Fuck yeah!"

An onion-shaped bottle sat farther down the table. I grabbed it by the neck.

Seated on the wraparound porch, I pour wine from the bottle into a crystalline glass. Not my daughter sits in the field with the boy, pointing to pages in a book. They grin at each other. They sit close. My teeth grind and Not I holler for her to return to the house. She flinches at my bellowing. The boy does not. He watches her leave with sadness. I command him return to his duties. He rises from his squatted position in the tall grass but does not move with haste. Instead, he watches me as he has before, as though he sees beyond me to me. My teeth whet against each other fit to crack. My hand fiddles with a key hanging from my neck.

The wine carafe fell from my hand to the dirt floor. I raised the shovel above my head and swung the flat edge down with everything I had, smashing the bottle to shards. Dr. Sattler and two members of her crew stood at the outside of the tent. Her associates yelled for me to stop, for her to stop me, but she put her arm across them as they moved to enter the tent. Officer Ryan yelled for her, and she held up a hand to him as well. Ellie and I met each other's eyes. Hers pleaded with me. Mine said no. Hers closed. The calm before the wave crashed into the shore.

I swung with abandon, though not reckless, each strike calculated to destroy, to erase. Particleboard flew from the tables. Dust filled the air. Porcelain pinged off the plastic tent windows. The effort tired me quickly, but not before the necessary work was done. Adrenaline drained, my legs weakened. Panting. I planted the shovel's point in the dirt and leaned on it. Dr. Sattler kept her team at bay and entered the tent with caution, then stopped short, alarm awash on her face. That's when I saw it. The khaki covering my lower leg had gone from beige to bloodred. The wetness reflected the light of the late-morning sun. Protruding from just below my kneecap was a porcelain shard, embedded deep. Blood ran over my shoe and seeped into the dirt. Now, the dirt knew me.

"Are you okay?"

My vision swirled. Me, the other me, Not me, stood next to her, staring at me, shaking his head.

"No, I'm very much not."

And the ground and I met again.

I opened my eyes to a harsh white light, not the soft welcoming glow I'd been led to believe would illuminate my path to the hereafter. A gentle buzz overhead clued me in to my location, back in another hospital bed. At the end of my bed, my toes, tucked tight under the sheet, pointed to the ceiling, though one leg occupied significantly more space beneath the blanket. I wiggled the toes attached to the smaller limb, while the opposing leg's digits defied my orders, no matter how many times my brain barked the command. I propped myself on my elbows, but a throb in my temples sent my head back to the pillow with a pugilist's power. The borders of my vision contracted. A warm palm covered the top of my hand and squeezed. Your mother sat bedside. It took effort to part my dry lips.

"Are you here?"

She took her hand from mine and placed it on my forehead, her palm gone from warm to cool in an instant. "You've still got a fever," she said softly. "Go back to sleep."

"Will you be here when I wake up?"

"I will be."

"Okay."

I closed my eyes.

Voices awakened me. Vanessa spoke to a physician, both unaware I was awake. I shimmied up in bed again, my head clearer. They stopped their conversation and turned toward me.

"There he is," the doctor said. "How are you feeling?"

"What's my basis for comparison?"

Vanessa huffed. "He's feeling better."

"I'll tell you what I'm not feeling. My lower leg."

Vanessa's and the doctor's mouths tightened.

"What?" I said.

"How long has your leg been in that condition?" the doctor asked.

"A few days. Why? What's the deal?" He sat on the edge of the bed.
"Well, that's not a good sign."

A cocktail of calamity was the way he described the condition of my
calf. The venom from the jellyfish sting led to swelling within the muscle and fascia, something he called compartment syndrome, leading to a
significant level of tissue death, faster than he'd ever seen. A bacterial infection had settled in as well, though it was difficult to discern whether it
had started with the sting or if it was a result of the piece of porcelain that
penetrated my leg, which, as luck would have it, also pierced my peroneal
nerve, explaining the lack of sensation and movement. They performed
emergency surgery to clear out the necrotic tissue and relieve the pressure.
He showed me the orthoses I'd need for the foot drop and told me I'd
need a cane. Reassured I'd not lose the leg, I breathed out. His expression
was not one of shared relief.

"I sense there's a but coming, doc."

"I'm more concerned about the bacterial infection. Your fever seems
to be down presently, but we're going to keep you here for observation, at
least for another night. Something like this can quickly turn to sepsis if
we're not careful."

"Then by all means, let's be careful."

He stood and excused himself. Vanessa thanked him and took his place
on the edge of the bed.

"I promise, I was going to remove you from the emergency contact list.
I just didn't have time. I swear, I—"

She shushed me. "It's okay. I'm glad you didn't take me off. I want to
be here. David called me. He said you quit?"

"That's all he told you?"

She dipped her chin. "Is there more?"

"Oh, you have no idea. Is that why you're here?"

"What do you mean?"

"Van. Come on. You don't need to be here. Not after everything I've done."

She took a deep inhale, then let it out. "You've fucked up, there's no two ways about it."

"Well damn, tell me how you really feel. I am in a hospital, in case you haven't noticed."

"Be fair now. You said, 'after everything I've done.' Was I supposed to disagree? Was that what you'd intended?"

I chewed the inside of my cheek. "I guess I did, yeah. Sorry."

"One of these days, maybe you'll finally understand that because I don't care about you in the way you want me to care about you doesn't mean I don't care about you. I'm here because I'm hoping, the way I hoped on many days before, that today will be the day that becomes clear."

"I think it might be."

We took a cleansing breath.

"Do you want to tell me about it?" Preferring she not run out of the room to chase the doctor down and demand a psych consult, I shook my head. She pressed her lips together and nodded. "Okay, that's fine." She drummed her fingers on the bedrail. "So, a jellyfish, huh?"

"What?" She tilted her head toward my heavily bandaged limb. "Right. Did you know I *am* a jellyfish?"

"Come again?"

"After the sting, I did some late-night googling. You know how that can go. I fell down hole after hole. One of them was this link that asked, 'Are you a jellyfish Christian?' Of course, I clicked on it. Turns out I am."

"And what is a jellyfish Christian?"

"The site said something about being without a spine. Soft. No real opinions about faith. No tenets to which I hold. At first, I thought, no way, that's not me. Who had been more steadfast in their faith than me? How many fights had Malcolm and I had about my seemingly unwavering devotion to God? But the minute I asked myself that question, I realized I'd been a jellyfish all along. If I'd truly believed in all this . . . this fucking bullshit . . . I wouldn't have worked so hard to convince everyone else around me—to convince him—that it was the way. I had no real faith. I kept telling myself the same lie because I thought it would make me a better father, bring me closer to you, to Malcolm, and when I'd fooled myself, I had to make you and him believe it to maintain the lie. The further I pushed you away, the harder I worked to convince you both, because if I was wrong, what did that mean for me? If I'd had a spine, if I'd really believed in this nonsense, I wouldn't have been so desperate to make everyone else believe it, too. Then the remains on the plantation, the way they'd been buried . . . all I saw was Malcolm in that casket, lying there in the same position, in a way they'd never asked for, had it forced on them, and I did the same fucking thing to him, when he outright told me he didn't want that. But I did it anyway. Because I'm spineless. And there's nothing I can do to fix it. I can't take it back."

Vanessa's tears welled, then spilled over. She wiped them away. Then she slid down the edge of the bed, closer.

"Malcolm used to watch this cartoon," she said. "Something with these talking animals who helped sea creatures from their base beneath the ocean. Anyway, every episode they featured a different animal. One of them was this jellyfish that when it was injured, or toward the end of its life, or it suffered some other kind of stress or trauma, would go back to its infant state, and grow all over again. They called it an immortal jellyfish. We found it fascinating. Malcolm asked me to find out more about them and I did. You know what else I learned?" I shook my head. "Jellyfish are some of the oldest living creatures on the planet. They were here before us and will probably be here long after us. And some of them live something like twenty thousand feet below the surface. Can you imagine? These soft, delicate things that can tear apart like tissue, more water than anything else, who can hurt you if you get too close, are able to survive, even thrive, under such immense pressure. That's what I think of when I think of a jellyfish, you know?"

She'd moved close enough for me to reach her hand. I turned mine palm up and she placed hers in mine, interlacing our fingers.

"I'm so sorry, Van."

She squeezed. "I know."

All the accumulated stress fractures in the walls and dams I'd built broke through. I was my father, fetal on the floor of our home. I cried. Vanessa moved closer still, took her hand away and pulled my head to her chest. I wept. The harder I sobbed, the closer she pulled me. My arms hung limp by my sides, terrified to hold her lest she pull away. She stroked my hair and rocked me, and while she did, I started talking and I couldn't stop. Though fearful of what it might mean to share all that had happened with her, her strength gave me courage. The sleep paralysis, the visitations, the images on my computer—all of it. Never did her embrace wane. When I'd no tears left, I pulled away. I searched her face for disappointment, for suspicion, for disbelief, for judgment, and found none. She touched my cheek with the back of her hand.

"You're still hot."

"That's it? After all of that?"

"With all we've been through, I've never known you to lie," she said. "Not that kind of lie. If you say these things happened, I believe you."

"Why?"

"I think because you need me to." She paused, unsure, then suddenly resolute. "And more than anything, I think Malcolm would—does—want me to."

My face crumbled again. One more palm to cheek, then moved the back of her hand to my forehead. "You need rest. I should go."

"I'll be okay." I snuffled, then let out a sharp exhale, exhausted by the emotional release. She did the same. We sat in a silence that, for once, was not uncomfortable. After a minute or so, she peered at me with a playful smirk. "What?"

"A horny toad? Really?"

I mimed shock. "You know more than you said you knew."

"His face must have been priceless."

"His eyes followed that thing wobbling back and forth like a hypnotist's watch." She threw her head back. We laughed and laughed. When we were done, we wiped away a better kind of tears. "I'd really like it if we could be friends again, Van."

Her shoulders dropped. She touched my good knee. "I don't know if that's possible."

I understood. "I understand."

She squeezed my knee. "But maybe we can try."

"We can try?"

"Yeah. Maybe."

"Thank you, Van."

She nodded, then stood. "You were wrong about one thing."

"Just the one?"

She walked to the other side of the bed and retrieved my travel bag from the floor. "The woman who owns the apartment you're renting dropped this off while you were sleeping." She rummaged inside and pulled out my laptop, then set it on the over-the-bed table and wheeled it over so it sat in front of me. "The bodies at the plantation. Malcolm. You said you can't set it right. You can." She tapped the top of the computer. "Tell the story. Their story. All of them."

"I don't know if I can. I don't know if I'm the right one to do it."

"If you don't, no one else will. Or worse. Someone else will."

"But no one cares, Van."

She opened the laptop and the screen lit to life. "So make them. I'll check on you tomorrow."

And she left the room. I kept the laptop open a good while longer. A nurse came in to record my vitals and check my surgical dressing. I fell in and out of sleep, waking either chilled to the bone or drenched in sweat. I had lunch, then dinner. An occupational therapist helped me stand and negotiate my walker to and from the bathroom. All the while, my laptop sat open on the table. As evening approached, I nodded off. Perhaps I'd had a sleep jerk, bumped the table somehow, but one way or another, the screen lit up again, the cursor winking, beckoning, bidding me enter my password and begin my work. I submitted. My desktop appeared and I slid my finger across the trackpad and opened the file folder named *Devil Is Fine*. I double clicked. Therein was the image of the remains. I dragged them to the desktop, closed the folder, and opened a new document. My fingers hovered above the keys, curled in on themselves. I closed my eyes and typed.

The morning we buried you, a road flagger danced in the street.

TWENTY-THREE

Surrounded by empty chairs, Freddy checked her watch, then scanned the bookstore. Jordan patted her knee, urging patience, but Freddy wasn't having it. She looked back to me, seated at the front on a high stool, wide-eyed and imploring. Clarence, fingers laced across his belly, had nodded off. I moved the microphone aside.

"It's early yet."

Clarence awoke with a splutter and he searched the empty store for the culprit.

"It starts in five minutes," Freddy said.

"It's fine. Thanks for coming, by the way. You, too, Jordan."

"Of course," Freddy said.

"Couldn't keep me away," said Jordan.

I nodded at Clarence. "You, too, Bagger Vance."

He wiped the corners of his mouth. "Wouldn't miss it, Henry Dumbass."

"It's Doo-muhs," I said.

"Nigga, I know."

I shook my head. A bell jingled as a customer entered the store. Freddy flashed her teeth and crossed her fingers. The woman took a seat in the back row. Freddy clapped her hands, grinning. I mouthed for her to stop, and she made a show of composing herself. Jordan gave her arm a playful pinch.

"So how long are you staying?" Freddy asked.

"Just tonight. This is the last tour stop, thankfully. I'm fucking exhausted."

Clarence elbowed Freddy. "Did you hear that language?"

"I know, it's like y'all hardly know me anymore, huh? I don't even have my original parts." I tapped my cane on my prosthetic leg. Freddy grimaced. "Oh, stop. I'm fine. Know what's strange? It's been almost two years and it still itches sometimes. Phantom sensations, they call it. Even my leg is haunted."

She rolled her eyes. "They couldn't surgically remove your corny jokes, though, could they?"

"No, never that." She checked her watch again. "Would you stop? It's fine. This is not unusual."

"Well, that sucks."

"Considering how busy your bar is, I figured you'd feel right at home."

"Touché, sir."

Clarence hooted. "Got your ass again."

"I can run him over with my bike if you want, hon," Jordan said.

The bookstore owner interrupted our witty repartee, asking should we give it five more minutes before starting. I agreed as another customer entered and took a seat in the middle row, down the aisle from Freddy and Clarence. After the five minutes had passed, no further seats had been filled. The bookstore owner made her way to me again, head hung.

"I am so sorry. I promise you, we advertised in advance and often. We had so many more registrations than there are people here. I'm honestly shocked. And embarrassed."

"Please. These things are just so hit-or-miss. It's fine. Really." She thanked me, apologized again, and took a seat in the front row. "So, thank you all for coming. Since we've got such an intimate audience, let's keep it loose, what do you say?" The man and woman nodded. Freddy applauded loudly and whooped, then stuck her tongue out at Clarence and Jordan for mocking her. "Right, so before I start talking you all to death, does anyone have any questions?" The woman in the back row raised her hand. "Yes, ma'am?"

"Well, this is really more of a comment than a question."

The bookstore owner and I exchanged smirks. "Please," I said, "comment away."

An uncomfortable hour later, Freddy, Clarence, Jordan, and I stood outside the bookshop. A warm breeze blew down the main drag, carrying with it the smell of funnel cake, French fries, and salt water. I breathed deep. I'd missed the scents more than I'd realized.

"Well, that was a thing that happened," Freddy said.

"Ah, that wasn't so bad. I've had worse signings."

"Seriously?" Jordan asked.

"Seriously. One time no one showed up. But the folks that ran the bookstore sat and talked with me for a while. It was actually one of my favorite events."

"Huh. I guess I can see that," Freddy said. "She had an interesting point though, about making this story a novel instead of nonfiction. Did it ever occur to you to tell the real story?"

"Didn't I?"

She winced. "I don't know. I didn't read it yet."

"Wow. Nice."

"I know, I'm terrible."

"You really are," Jordan said.

Clarence chimed in. "You should read it. It's damn good. Great characters at this bar, except he's a little charitable with how busy the place is. But these two folks. You might say they're magical. Help the narrator figure himself out."

"More than either of them knows," I said.

"Aww," Freddy said. "So is there a happy ending?"

"Let's just say everyone goes home, one way or another."

"Well, that's cryptic," she said. "And so on brand."

"I'm nothing—"

"—if not predictable. I get it. Do you want to stop by the Scholar before you go?"

"Eh, I don't know, Freddy."

"Come on, just one? To toast a successful signing?"

"Or mourn the absence of one," Clarence said.

Jordan shoved him, and he cried elder abuse. Freddy shushed him. I patted my trunk over my liver. "Sepsis did a number. Still trying to make a transplant list."

"Jesus," Freddy said. "I'm sorry. A club soda, then?"

"I don't know, you guys."

"Boy, if you don't help her walk my old ass across this street, I'm going to take out the other leg."

Freddy stomped her foot. "Clarence!"

I surrendered. "A club soda it is."

"You guys go on," Jordan said.

"Babe, really?"

"Won't be the same without you," I said.

"That's sweet, but you musketeers should have this moment. I'll be there for the next one."

She pulled her braids back with a band, hugged me and Clarence, kissed Freddy, and rode off on her bicycle. We scanned the road for traffic, and our trio crossed to the Scholar. Freddy removed the cardboard clock that read "Back Soon" from the window and pulled two stools away from the bar. Clarence and I took our usual seats, draft beer for him, seltzer with lime for me. We talked. And we laughed. And despite the fact I was physically less than whole, I felt more complete than I had in some time.

An hour or so later, my phone buzzed in my pocket. Vanessa's caller ID scrolled across the screen. I held up a finger and excused myself.

"Did you see?" Van asked.

"See what?"

"Hang on." My phone buzzed in my ear. "I just sent you the link." I pulled the phone away and saw her message.

"Oh my God."

"I know."

"I don't believe it."

"Believe it."

Freddy moved to the end of the bar, closer to where I stood. She bounced from foot to foot, eager to hear the news.

"This might not mean anything, though."

"It's a start. And you started it."

"That's a lot to put on a book."

"You're setting it right."

Freddy cleared her throat. "Van, I've got to run. Some friends came to the signing, and I don't want to be rude."

"Tell Freddy I said hello. Let's have dinner when you're back in town."

"Dinner? I thought we were strictly a lunch thing."

"Just call me when you get back."

"Bye, Van."

She hung up. The phone's wallpaper behind the app icons had a photo of Van, Malcolm, and me. Freddy tugged me from my trance. "Well? Don't keep me in suspense. Did you hit the bestseller list?"

"I'd have to sell some books in order to do that. So no. Something better." I pulled up the article Van sent and handed Freddy the phone. She scanned, reading parts to herself until she reached the payoff. "Holy shit."

"Yeah."

"What are you two redbones down there gossiping about?"

"They're going home, Clarence," I said. I limped to where he sat and showed him the article: "Senegalese Government Issues Statement Regarding Return of Enslaved Remains."

"Ain't that something," Clarence said. "Sarah Baartman is smiling down on you, son." He gripped my shoulder with all the warmth of an embrace, recalling the road flagger and his kindness. I returned his squeeze.

Freddy put her hands on her hips, blew out a whoosh of air, and fanned her face. "You two are going to make me cry. Damn, talk about art imitating life. Now we definitely got something to celebrate. Seltzer with lime for everyone!"

"No."

"No?"

"Still got that stash in the back room?"

She cocked her head. "You sure?"

"Just one. I've got someplace I need to be."

"Done."

She poured. We drank. We said good-bye.

"So where are you staying?" Freddy said.

"Nowhere."

"Nowhere?"

"I'm going home." I motioned for her to come around the bar. She did, and I pulled her into a hug. Her arms hung in the air for a moment, then she hugged me back. I let go of her and turned to Clarence.

"You better go on with all that."

"I'm coming in, so do what you got to do." He hugged me back like I knew he would.

"Thank you, you two. For everything."

And I walked back to my car.

The sky turned orange and purple as the sun set. Off to the right, a sign stood signaling one-lane traffic ahead. Cars slowed to a stop, and we waited as the opposite line of traffic passed through. I lifted my head and saw the stop sign at the end of a pole. It didn't move until whoever held it spun it to "Slow." Our line moved. We approached the flagger, clad in reflective sunglasses, his pale cheeks ruddy with the heat. I gave him a nod as I passed. He returned it. I drove on.

I parked my car at the entrance to the plantation and hobbled to the beach. My absent lower leg thrummed in time with my very real thigh, throbbing in protest against the extra work to which it still had not grown accustomed, the infection having done a number on my endurance. Sweat soaked my slacks, sticking them to me. Waves rolled, crested, and splashed on the beach.

And there you were.

No longer in shadows. Not whispering in my ear. You were a boy again, your swim trunks too long, the hem hanging past your knees. You danced at the edge of the ocean. You waved me in.

I walked toward the water and when I reached you, you took my hand. The water ran up over my shoes. I took them off and walked deeper, let you guide me, until the water went up above my knees. My phantom pain stopped. I walked out farther still, then turned on my back, my legs floating, my feet poking just above the surface. You floated, too, and our hands drifted apart. Water filled my prosthetic socket, breaking the vacuum seal around my stump. The waves lifted me, and my false limb, freed from my pant leg, floated away. Tentacles poked out from the cuff of my pants. When I turned my head to see if you saw what had happened, you were gone. And I smiled. My pants, now too big to contain me, slid off, revealing streams of long, iridescent tentacles swaying in rhythm with the rise and fall of the water. I took a deep breath and went under. When I could hold it no longer, I opened my mouth wide. Water rushed in, but I did not choke. I did not drown. I breathed it in as oxygen, as if I were as much the sea as the sea was me. I did not return to the surface. Instead, the waves took me, out past the bay and into the Atlantic. I went deeper and deeper, farther and farther. I was unafraid. Brave enough I'd need to be rescued.

ACKNOWLEDGMENTS

I would be remiss if I failed to highlight the incredible efforts being put forth by Black, Indigenous, and other POC archaeologists, specifically in regards to repatriation. Organizations such as the Society of Black Archaeologists, and professionals including Dr. Alicia Odewale and Dr. Ayana Omilade Flewellen, are doing the difficult but necessary work of ensuring our stories are not lost, forgotten, or silenced by people wielding power to change the nation's enslavement narrative. I am indebted to Sandra Moore for bringing these inspiring efforts to my attention.

I must also thank Dr. Raquel Fleskes for giving of her valuable time in providing me with critical information from her work with DNA research. The evolution of this story would have been far different without your help.

My most heartfelt gratitude to friend and superagent David Hale Smith and his assistant, Naomi Eisenbeiss. Your tireless patience and advocacy are life changing. I can't thank you enough for all you've done for me. I would not have this career without you.

Working with editor Ryan Doherty made me feel as if I'd done something right on this journey. Your honest feedback and attentive eye elevated my craft. If not for your encouragement and coaching, I'd have never taken the swings I did in this novel. Thank you.

This book would not have been possible without the faculty and students at the Randolph College MFA program. Teaching there has been nothing short of a blessing, though I've learned far more than I've imparted. The radical creativity of the community inspired (and continues to inspire) me in a manner I thought impossible. My writing approach changed in beautiful ways as I immersed myself in the warmth and inventiveness that is the DNA of that special place. Whether reading from their completed works or guiding workshops of new pieces, the artists at Randolph took risks with their work, motivating me more than ever to write the novel I wanted to read. This is my Randolph book.

Shout-out as always to my badass friends and beta readers Ted Flanagan and Brannan Sirratt, as well as new addition Evan Mallon, a trio that never hesitates to give me the straight dope. Hearty thanks also to early readers Maurice Carlos Ruffin, Chet'la Sebree, and Ben Fountain for your invaluable feedback.

I've said it before, but it bears repeating. To the readers, bookstagrammers, and reviewers: I do not get to do this thing I love without you. Whether you love or hate my work, your input makes me work harder. Thank you so much.

My Peanut, Michelle, you are mythological in the way you hold me up when my anxiety and self-doubt drive me down. After twenty years, your capacity for love still astonishes. JJ and Miles, I hope I'll always make you proud, even when you're old enough to read what I've written. Thank you. I love you musketeers with all my heart.

ABOUT THE AUTHOR

John Vercher lives in the Philadelphia area with his wife and two sons. He has a bachelor's in English from the University of Pittsburgh and an MFA in creative writing from the Mountainview Master of Fine Arts program. He is an assistant teaching professor in the Department of English and Philosophy at Drexel University and was the inaugural Wilma Dykeman writer-in-residence at the University of North Carolina, Asheville. His debut novel, *Three-Fifths*, was named one of the best books of the year by the *Chicago Tribune* and *Booklist*. It was nominated for the Edgar Award for Best First Novel and the Strand Critics Award for Best Debut Novel. His second novel, *After the Lights Go Out*, called "shrewd and explosive" by the *New York Times*, was named a Best Book of Summer 2022 by *Book Riot* and *Publishers Weekly* and a *Booklist* Editors' Choice book of 2022.

CELADON
BOOKS

Founded in 2017, Celadon Books, a division of
Macmillan Publishers, publishes a highly curated list
of twenty to twenty-five new titles a year. The list of
both fiction and nonfiction is eclectic and focuses
on publishing commercial and literary books and
discovering and nurturing talent.